The Sandcastles of Irakkistan

Ken Coffman

Other books by Ken Coffman

Steel Waters
Alligator Alley (with Mark Bothum)
Twisted Shadow (with Mark Bothum)
Glen Wilson's Bad Medicine
Toxic Shock Syndrome
Immortality, LLC
Hartz String Theory
Endangered Species
Fairhaven
Mesh (with Adina Pelle)
Buffoon: One Man's Cheerful Interaction with the Harbingers of Global Warming
Doom
Fiona and the Black Faerie Prince (with Kristen Lolatte)
Real World FPGA Design with Verilog
Fianchetto

Print ISBN 978-1-941071-05-2
eBook ISBN 978-1-941071-06-9

Cover Design by Guy Corp, www.grafixCORP.com

STAIRWAY≡PRESS

SEATTLE

www.stairwaypress.com
848 North Rainbow Blvd #5015
Las Vegas, NV 89107
(360) 336-3366

Code of Conduct for the U.S. Fighting Forces

Article I
I am an American fighting in the forces which guard my country and our way of life. I am prepared to give my life in their defense.

Article II
I will never surrender of my own free will. If in command, I will never surrender the members of my command while they still have the means to resist.

Article III
If I am captured I will continue to resist by all means available. I will make every effort to escape and aid others to escape. I will accept neither parole nor special favors from the enemy.

Article IV
If I become a prisoner of war, I will keep faith with my fellow prisoners. I will give no information nor take part in any action which might be harmful to my comrades. If I am senior, I will take command. If not, I will obey the lawful orders of those appointed over me and will back them up in every way.

Article V
When questioned, should I become a prisoner of war, I am required to give name, rank, service number and date of birth. I will evade answering further questions to the utmost of my ability. I will make no oral or written statements disloyal to my country and its allies or harmful to their cause.

Article VI
I will never forget that I am an American, fighting for freedom, responsible for my actions and dedicated to the principles which made my country free. I will trust in my God and in the United States of America.

Well, I'd go fucking non-linear, that's what I'd do.
—Glen Wilson

Sura 2, Verse 30. "Behold", the Lord said to the angels. "I will create a vice-regent on earth."

They said, "Will thou place one who will make mischief and shed our blood while we celebrate thy praises and glorify thy holy name?"

He said, "I know what you know not."

Introduction—A Long Time Ago

THE UNDERGROUND NOOK was connected to a long, dark corridor terminating in an abandoned boiler room. A spooky, rat-infested spider's den, the boiler room had been unused for many years before Harlan and Shimon cleaned it out and filled it with third-hand scrounged and scavenged furniture. Inside on this day, Curtis and Shimon lounged on threadbare over-stuffed chairs under bare light bulbs hanging from wires suspended from the ceiling—paging through old *Penthouse* magazines and sharing pictures they thought the other would appreciate. At fourteen, they pretended to be sexually experienced experts on women, but there were many things on display in the magazines they'd never seen live and in person.

"Sister M-C probably shaves it like this one," Shimon said while pointing at the November fold-out. "I'd like to push my nose in and take a deep breath. I'll bet, down there, she smells like sweet ambrosia."

"Smoke another doobie, dreamer," Curtis said. "Come to think on it though, your schnozzle is big-enough, I'm sure she'd like it a lot better than the bitty 'lil Tootsie Roll hiding in your Fruity Looms. You been down here by yourself again? These pages are all stuck together. It's disgusting."

"Fuck you. I don't jerk off, I save all my cum for Mary-Kate. You're the one who pulls pud down here—that's why we call you Mr. Palmer."

"If Mary-Catherine ever lifted her habit for you, you'd have a heart attack and kick-bucket on the spot, loser."

Harlan would be there, but he was locked up securely in the trouble room. The charges were unproven, but the Monsignor was sure Harlan was responsible for stealing his Lincoln Towncar and crashing it into a tree in a scruffy patch of woods near Waterview Avenue in Cherry Hill; a questionable neighborhood by the Patapsco River. In reality, Shimon was the guilty party, but outwardly, he was a quiet, studious, polite and sweet-faced boy who melted into the wallpaper—no one ever suspected him of wrong doing.

There came a loud, confident knock at the door.

It wasn't the secret knock.

Curtis jumped up and grabbed the aluminum baseball bat they kept at hand in case of trouble. Hurriedly, Shimon shoved the magazines under a chair cushion.

"Put your peckers away and zip up your pants, queers. It's me. Jimmy."

Jimmy was much smaller than the other boys his age, so he seemed far younger. He wasn't in their classes—he was around because his Dad was the school janitor. Instead, Jimmy went to the mainly-black public school several blocks away, but he was ever-present in the hallways and lurked with the boys out back in their secret corner under their smoking tree. He carried a seemingly endless supply of his dad's Swisher Sweets cigars, so the boys tolerated him.

"How'd he find us?" Curtis whispered.

Shimon shrugged. "Beats me."

"Let me in," Jimmy said. "I have something you fuckbirds want."

"Go away, Irish turd-tard," Curtis said. "What you got?"

From outside, Jimmy rattled a bundle of something clinky

and metallic.

"It's something my dad helped me collect, asshounds," he said. "Keys. Master keys to everything; the kitchen, the freezer room where they keep the ice cream, the staff dorm, the sister's john, the headmaster s office. Even the trouble room. Also, I have a mayonnaise jar of sacramental wine from the priest's barrel."

Curtis and Shimon looked at each other.

"What should we do?" Shimon whispered.

"I think that should be obvious even to a brain-damaged halfwit like you," Curtis said. "We let him in—and show him the secret knock."

Sura 1, Verses 6-7. Show us the straight path—the path of those whom earn your favor; not the path of those who earn thy wrath or of those who go astray.

Book One—Chapter One

Khostarak

THE DIESEL ENGINE of the Balkancar forklift sputtered and spat clotted knots of acrid black smoke.

By the grace of Allah, please, not now, Talib al Razzek thought.

His mind was flooded with a growing sense of panic. The vehicle shuddered, but then the engine smoothed. Catching the attention of the nearest Irakki Republican Guard, he gestured at his sideboard tank.

"I need fuel," he yelled.

The guard, gesturing with his ancient AK-47, waved him toward the convoy of trucks they were loading.

Unload first, was the message.

"It must be done now," Talib shouted over the din while waving his hands.

"Go," the guard said, conceding.

The fuel truck was parked in a corner of the huge warehouse. Scattered on greasy concrete, broken glass glittered. The corner was dark under metal screen-shrouds protecting shattered sodium lamps. Behind the tanker, a massive Russian stake-bed truck was hidden. With lift engine screaming, Talib quickly dropped the heavy pallet on the bed of this truck. Swarthy men in sweat-soaked t-shirts threw blankets over the load and tied it down with hemp ropes. Talib worked the forklift around and picked up a new pallet. It was covered with the same gray canvas and stenciled Arabic characters; under the dim lighting it looked identical to the stolen load. Spewing sooty smoke, he returned his forklift to the line-up and settled his load on a semi-truck's trailer.

Sweating, he lighted a cigarette and watched as the last pallet was secured. In all, there were seven trucks in the convoy—a motley mix of Mercedes and Renault cargo trucks painted a flat, olive-drab green. In minutes, the Republican Guard climbed into the truck cabs and roared off into bright afternoon sunlight.

Talib stubbed out his cigarette and ran toward his truck. He jumped on the step beside the driver and shouted.

"Go!"

After leaving the Transportation Ministry warehouse, they cut off a taxi, navigated a traffic circle and roared across the River and onto Arbatuush Tamaaz Avenue. Traffic clogged the main street, but the driver cursed and honked as they inched forward.

Salaam, a neighborhood in the ancient round city of Khostarak, was a community of brick-and-adobe-wattle houses. After unlocking a gate, they backed the truck into a low-roofed garage. Men, grunting and heaving, pulled the heavy pallet off the truck—it slammed to the concrete floor with a crash. The wooden pallet was crushed. Talib stayed with the bundle while the truck raced away. He placed his hands on it and breathed great gasps of air. They had succeeded; the packet was now hidden and secure.

After pulling a heavy gate across the garage entrance he waved to the men watching from a window in the house and settled on his haunches. Lighting a cigarette, he rubbed his tired eyes.

He heard a hissing sound and glimpsed a flicker from the southeast before a TLAM-7—a Tomahawk Land Attack cruise missile—exploded. A mushroom cloud of smoke and dust climbed into the air. The concrete blocks of the garage collapsed. With his ears ringing and blood pouring from a puncture wound on the side of his head, Talib took a few steps before collapsing in the gravel of the street.

Allah will forgive my sins on the final Day of Judgment, he thought before dying.

Inside the collapsed garage, dust settled. The palleted bundle was crushed. From a gash torn in canvas, the edge of a dense packet of American five-thousand new-dollar bills peeked.

Steve Stephens

Steve walked to the coffee station for his third cup of the day; he didn't really want it, but he was bored. Generally there was someone by the coffeemaker and it was possible, though unlikely, that this person might have something new and interesting to say—something he had not heard a hundred times before.

Charles Livingston was there—talking to a new kid.

There was a lot of competition in this branch office of the DEA, but it was possible Charles was the most singularly boring man to ever set foot on the earth.

And now he had fresh meat—a new-hire victim who had not heard his stories a thousand times before—someone who didn't have the sense to run away screaming at the sight of the lurking Charles Livingston.

Why was Charles a fixture at the coffee station? He didn't even drink coffee.

Steve tried to think of the kid's name. She was a black female in her mid-twenties—with a name like Katisha or Kamoosha or Kalashnikova, or something. Regardless, it was a

'K' name—Steve was sure of that.

Charles, a Mormon elder with nine beautiful children, had a huge belly and always wore a set of patriotic suspenders—red and blue—with white stars.

Internally, Steve groaned. Charles would be talking about his best story—the most interesting thing he'd ever done—chasing a dangerous cocaine dealer and single-handedly taking the young man down with an athletic martial arts maneuver. Once curious, Steve looked up this case. Charles had hid in an alley and tripped a teen-aged cash-runner as he ran by—he immobilized the kid with flex-cuffs while the stunned and bleeding thirteen-year-old lay on the ground.

Sometimes field work like this was the DEA's job, and they did it, but mainly the job consisted of moving legal papers and police reports to different piles on their desks.

"Is there any coffee?" Steve said.

"Yeah," Charles said, "help yourself. I was telling Keshia about my big-league cocaine bust in the tenements."

Yes, Keshia, that was it.

Why didn't black people give their kids normal names like Rebecca or Jennifer or Betsy, or even Stephanie?

What's wrong with Stephanie?

"How many days you got left?" Charles said.

Steve doctored his coffee with Cremora and two packets of sugar, and then stirred it up. "One-hundred and eighty-three," he said.

He looked at the russet mixture in his mug. It looked terrible—not even vaguely drinkable. He poured it out and rinsed his cup, and then walked back to his office. As he walked away, he heard Charles' comment.

"Steve's a bit burned out," he said with sympathy in his voice.

You know you're in bad shape when a loser like Charles Livingston feels sorry for you.

Sura 2, Verses 2-4. Those who believe in the unseen ones, are steadfast in prayer, use what has been provided for them and who believe in that which has been revealed—they shall be sure of the hereafter.

Book Two—Chapter One

Khostarak–The Red Zone

THEY PLAYED WITH Irakkistani dinars—colorful notes picturing the deceased, black-mustached, dear-leader-president-for-life wearing a striped necktie and gazing confidently into the future. His confidence was despoiled by history because a year after the manly, cheer-infused photograph was printed on the dinars; his battered body was suspended from a rope from the ancient arch at the entrance of the old city.

Each poker hand required a twenty-five dinar ante, but the final pot generally contained a heaping pile of up to ten-thousand in dinar notes. Until 1990, each of these ten-thousand notes were worth USD $30,000, but now they could be purchased in hundred-count bricks for five new dollars from sidewalk cigarette vendors on al-Raasheid street.

The four players were a study in coincidental diversity—Shimon Goldfarb, Harlan Farris, Jimmy O'Connelly and Curtis Aaron Washington. Sweating, they handed around a tepid, half-full plastic bottle of diet Coke spiked with an illicit bottle of Captain Morgan rum. Their card game was convened in a cavernous room in a Tomahawk building—called thus because of the Tomahawk VII cruise missile that tore a ragged hole in the wall and blew up the place during the hot cycle of the Irakki war. The room was cooled—barely—by an old, tired Chinese air conditioner fed by a hundred-foot length of orange electrical cable they snaked between buildings and covered with gravel when their superior officers were not looking.

The hot wind blew dust through the ragged hole in the masonry walls. Army structural engineers had painted a red X on the front entry indicating its hazardous, keep-out status—which the card-players were happy to ignore.

When an Apache helicopter roared by, a clump of ceiling rubble fell into the pot in the center of their makeshift table. Harlan idly flicked it out with an index finger.

"Can anyone beat my three queens?" he asked while tossing two more ten-thousand dinar notes into the pile.

"Poodle doo. If you got three queens, I got an eighteen-inch dick," Curtis said, matching the raise.

"Eighteen-millimeter is more like it," Jimmy said, tossing in his cards. "Regardless, you big-spending assholes bought the pot as far as I'm concerned. I could make some money if you'd deal me good hole cards once in a while—I'm sick to death of twos and sevens."

Bright sunlight streamed through gaping window openings—the ornate window glass was missing. To prepare their private clubhouse—just like when they were kids so many years before—they'd spent many sweaty hours sweeping up shards and rubble. Looters had stripped the rooms of anything removable including the chandeliers that had once adorned the domed ceiling. The plaster walls were discolored where huge paintings and tapestries had hung.

After finding a bundle of Polaroid photographs behind a loose brick in a backroom wall, they'd convinced themselves this was one of Uday Khomenai's love nests. The photographs included those of a leather-clad group of men riding Husqvarna dirt bikes. One of the blurry snapshots showed a middle-aged man wearing a neatly trimmed beard and drinking from a bottle of Cutty Sark.

Uday, Harlan claimed. They gave up on arguing with him. Harlan was a stubborn young man; once an idea was locked into his head, it could never be dislodged.

If it was truly Uday, it was before he was shot eight times in a failed assassination attempt earlier in the twenty-first century—the man in the picture appeared hale and strong and full of life.

Shimon, slight and thin, was tanned dark by the sun. He wore a thin strip of mustache and could pass for an Irakkistani under casual inspection if he didn't speak. Round-faced Harlan motioned for the bottle. Husky and muscular, his fists were calloused from battering a punching bag in the Morale, Welfare and Recreation tent. Jimmy, the smallest of the group, was fair-skinned; he kept his reddish hair trimmed short and his eyes hidden behind impenetrable wrap-around sunglasses. Curtis had black spots on his light-chocolate skin and was bedeviled by ingrown hairs; his face was decorated with a constellation of weeping acne sores.

While they played, they batted sand flies and breathed dusty, oily air. A mangy cat poked its head in the cavernous room and sniffed. Like a sandy ghost, it quickly disappeared.

Harlan had taped Hustler magazine pictures on the wall and Shimon had covered the bare bodies with carefully-crafted black paper—improvised head-to-feet Muslim chadors. To admire airbrushed, gravity-defying breasts, the construction paper chadors needed to be lifted.

"So," Harlan said idly, "I'm walking with my squad on Chadiiri Street and I look up. On the second floor balcony standing between potted palm trees, this hottie waves for me to come upstairs."

"Christ on a go-cart, not this lame-ass, bullshit story again," Curtis grumbled.

"No, let him go on," Jimmy said. "Remember the first time he told it? We were supposed to believe he got out of fifty pounds of field gear to get nekkid with some Imam's granddaughter while his home boys were getting shot up by AK-47s and mortar rounds two streets over."

"This is serious; she had posters of David Bowie on her walls. No one else was home and she couldn't wait to unbutton my fatigues. Bare-assed naked under the burka, her tits tasted like ice cream."

"Dumb ass, I've been on the street a hundred times and I ain't seen a burka yet. This isn't Afghanistan or Detroit, cracker."

"Shut up, I'm talkin'. She couldn't wait to get her lips around my eight-inch Arkansas hickory stick."

"Anyone else notice? He always starts this shit when he's got nothing in his hand. I'm raising," Shimon said, while throwing a bundle of dinars onto the pot.

"Ah, I give up on you ignorant, Yankee-dipshit-assholes," Harlan said, tossing in his cards. "I fold."

"Told ya," Shimon said.

Curtis matched Shimon's bet and called.

Jimmy flipped over the river card. Shimon scratched his chin and studied Curtis's face.

"You got lucky on the last card, didn't you?" he said.

Curtis tossed in more bills. "It'll cost you thirty grand to find out," he said.

Shimon scowled. "A wise man knows when to cut and run. Live to fight another day, y'know?"

"Nice work, John Murtha[1]," Curtis said, grinning while

---

[1] "...since they're attacking our troops, and we have destabilized the area, I've changed my mind and I've come to the conclusion that now

hauling in his winnings.

"Screw you, Curt," Shimon muttered. "Did you get your card on the last flip?"

"You didn't buy the right to find out," Curtis said.

Jimmy gathered the cards and shuffled.

"She had a David Bowie poster on the wall…" Curtis sang in a high, sweet falsetto.

"Screw the flea-bitten camel you rode in on," Harlan complained. "I'm telling you a swear-to-God true story and you mock me. Stop yer yapping—cut the shit and deal the fragging cards. I feel lucky."

---

is the time to start to redeploy our troops to the periphery and let the Iraqis take over."

—John Murtha, former Marine Corps Colonel and clueless, long-deceased former Congressman from rural Pennsylvania.

Sura 3, Verses 131-133. Guard yourselves against the fire prepared for the unbelievers. Obey Allah and the Messenger, so you may be shown mercy. Hasten to get forgiveness from your Lord.

A garden—the length and width of the earth and heavens—is prepared for those who guard against evil.

Book Two—Chapter Two

Khostarak—The Red Zone

HARLAN CHECKED HIS Magellan GPS. It was not Government Issue; he'd bought it at the Ozark Wal-Mart on his last leave. Near that store, his family, including his mom, dad, two brothers, four sisters and elderly Aunt Opal lived in a double-wide with tar-papered plywood bedroom additions off the Arkansas Pig Trail Highway that led toward Cass. He hated the drafty winter cold of the old trailer, but loved riding the twisted scenic byways on his old Kawasaki motorcycle. In Irakkistan, he daydreamed of cool air in his hair and the crisp taste of a cold Lone Star beer. He'd give anything to be back home instead of bouncing around in a Humvee with intermittent air conditioning.

Jimmy, driving, peered myopically through the dirty windshield. CRACK. They were being fired on. His guys ducked so less of their bodies were exposed to the windows.

The windshield bore a long gash.

"Where's it coming from?" Harlan said.

"Muzzle flashes—two o'clock," Curtis said. "Second floor window. Should we uncap the M-2 and go get them, Sarge?"

"*I* think we should slide in next to this wall," Jimmy said, while flooring the accelerator.

"Roger that," Harlan said. "Let's hide out and sit tight. I'll call this in."

He thumbed the switch on the Mercury digital radio mike.

"This is Echo-Three, we're under kinetic fire." He read numbers off the GPS. "They're two hundred meters to the northeast—vector forty." They exchanged additional information. "Okay, guys, an Apache is in-flight. They want us to light it up for them."

A burst of automatic fire flew over their heads like angry wasps.

"I'll do it," Shimon said.

"Okay, but don't show them anything important to shoot."

Shimon popped the latches on a transit case and pulled out a ground laser designator. It looked like a lumpy toy rifle with a spotting scope. He jumped onto the street and ran along the wall to the corner. He used a hand mirror to look around the corner. They could hear the Apache coming; it was so loud the air seemed to rend. Crouching, Shimon pointed the designator. The Apache fired a Hellfire missile and the building exploded. Raining casings, the Apache fired a volley from its 30mm chain gun—then angled off.

Harlan waved for Shimon to return.

"We're supposed to wait for reinforcements. What's left out there?"

"Rubble and hamburger."

"Okay, I say we take a look. You guys in?"

The team nodded and piled back into the Humvee. They slowly and cautiously rounded the corner. A crowd of children had gathered around a body in the street. Fire guttered in the crushed house. After jumping out of the Humvee, Curtis craned his head back and forth like an owl and walked cautiously toward the body.

"I need some room," he called out over his shoulder.

Harlan gestured to Shimon. "What do we have?"

Shimon fished around in a pants pocket. "We have a few soccer balls in the Humvee and I'm carrying a pocketful of salt water taffy."

"Let's try the candy." Harlan took the bag and waved it to get the children's attention, then scattered the contents onto the sidewalk. The kids, shouting raucously, ran over and began filling their pockets.

"Has that Hajji been fully disciplined?" he called out to Curtis.

"Stone cold," Curtis shouted. "His head's caved in like a food bank melon."

"Sarge, the old man is having an embolism. He wants us to clear out. The I-Ps[2] are sending a cleanup crew."

Harlan scanned the area. The largest of the kids, grinning through a mouthful of sticky candy, gave a thumbs up sign.

"We have incoming Wasabis[3]," Curtis shouted.

A group of young men wearing black t-shirts, black trousers and thin beards assembled several blocks away. They seemed to be gathering their courage.

"Alright, they look like ferals[4]." Harlan waved for Curtis to come back. "Let's high-tail it and get the fuck out of here. The I-P's can clean up this mess."

---

[2] Irakki Police

[3] Wasabi is slang for Irakkistani insurgents, rabble rousers and trouble-makers—Saudi Arabian Islamic fundamentalists, Wahhabis. The name derives from the 17th century Islamic scholar and religious leader, Abdu l-Wahhab. Curtis coined the name Wasabi based on the tangy horseradish condiment he often enjoyed with his sushi.

[4] From FRLs or Former Regime Loyalists. Party members who believe their deceased dear leader will somehow return to power.

Sura 2, Verse 35-36. And we said, "Oh, Adam! Dwell with thy wife in the garden—and eat freely of the fruits as you will; but stay away from *this* tree lest you become wrong-doers."

But Satan made them disobey and caused them to depart from their holy state in the garden. We said, "Get away from each other, enemies, for there is an abode and bounty for all in your time on this earth."

Book Two—Chapter Three

Khostarak–The Red Zone

CAMP VICTORY WAS monstrous. Flickering fluorescent lamps bathed the huge room with harsh sterility. Overhead, lurid professional football league banners fluttered in the stale air. The mess hall was busy with jumbled masses of military and contractor personnel, but not overcrowded. While shoveling food into his mouth—a massive pile of corned beef hash topped with a poached egg and liberally soaked with Tabasco sauce— Harlan watched the plump ass of a female Marine as she inched through the buffet line.

The old man's nervous factotum stood beside Harlan's seat.

"Sergeant Farris?" he said.

"I'm off duty. Eating," Harlan said redundantly.

"Popcorn wants to see you."

Groaning, Harlan dropped his fork and looked up at the

orderly. The thin kid had to be at least eighteen for his Army enlistment, but appeared much younger.

"What's the light-col want with me?"

Looking nervous, the orderly said, "I don't know, but he's pissed."

"He's always pissed. Can I finish my breakfast?"

The kid shifted his weight from foot to foot as if experiencing a gastronomical crisis.

"He said right away."

Harlan pushed his dish away.

"Shit. You buss the dishes."

Outside the Lieutenant Colonel's office, a sorry-looking potted jade plant drenched in chewing tobacco spit wilted beside a bucket of sand. Harlan twisted his cigarette in the sand and blew a stream of smoke into the air.

Inside, a battalion of oscillating fans stirred the overheated air. Between the clerks typing reports on portable PCs and the Lieutenant Colonel's wooden door, seated on a broke-back leather couch with khaki shorts hiked up her thighs, a woman sat picking at a large scab on her leg. Despite a trickle of blood trailing down her calf, her legs were shapely and attractive. She looked up and eyed Harlan curiously as he walked by.

Harlan nodded. "What's up, ma-am?" he asked casually.

She snorted in reply and blotted the blood with a tissue. He knocked at the door and waited to be summoned.

"Enter," came the X-O's husky voice.

Harlan stood at attention while Lieutenant Colonel Cody Thompson read through a sheaf of reports. A horsefly battered its brain against a dusty window. The L-C dropped the papers on the desk.

"This TOC[5] paperwork will pile up and bury me. What does CANE stand for, soldier?"

---

[5] Tactical Operations Center

"Sir, Combined Arms in a Nuclear-Chemical Environment."

"What is JTCG ME-8710?"

"Sir, Joint Test Command Group, Handbook for Operational Testing of Electro-Optical Systems in Battlefield Obscurants."

"How'd you know that one?"

"Sir, it was on Sergeant's exam."

"If a tree falls down in the forest, how far away can it be heard?"

"Sir, if it's otherwise quiet, seven-hundred to eight-hundred meters."

"What does VMJT stand for?"

Harlan thought about it for a moment. "Sir, I am sorry." He said. "I do not know that one."

"Good, because I just pulled it out of my ass. For God's sake, Sergeant, stand at ease."

"Thank you, sir."

Harlan spread his legs and grasped his hands behind his back. The Lieutenant Colonel studied him.

"I suppose it's true what they say—you don't look like much, but you're a clever one. Are you perhaps too clever for your own good? We're working on the prosecution paperwork; we have you cold selling hootch. Ingenious plan, Sergeant, plastic Coke bottles topped off with Everclear from medical stores. I hate this fucking job. You have FEBA[6] experience. What about your FIST[7]? Are you as smart as Shimon?"

"No, sir."

"Tell me about Curtis?"

"He's a good man, sir."

"Where you from, boy?"

"Arkansas, sir."

---

[6] Forward Edge of the Battle Area
[7] Fire Support Team

"They approve of you hanging around with Jews and Niggers back in Arkansas, soldier? Let me guess, you judge a man on the content of his character? Instead of locking you in the hoosegow, they should promote your ass and make a diversity poster of your team, what do you think of that, boy?"

"I'm not sure I follow your point, sir."

The Lieutenant Colonel waved his hand as if fanning the air for gnats.

"I'm sorry, Sergeant. I don't sleep well in this heat and it makes me cranky. The air conditioner only works when the tech comes around to look at it. There's another one on order and it will be here a few years after I rotate home, that's the Army way of it. What have you boys been doing out in your crib? The Tomahawk building?"

"Sir, writing letters home and studying for our promotion exams."

"Right, studying, not brewing hooch and gambling. I'll get to the point. Your little multicultural cadre is getting a Developmental Assignment—an opportunity to increase your KSA[8] rating if you don't get your asses shot off first."

Harlan chewed his lower lip.

"Sir, if I might ask, why us?"

"I don't know and I don't care. I've been discouraged from asking too many questions if you catch my drift, Sergeant. Advice which I now pass onto you. Did you see that skirt outside?"

Harlan nodded.

"Army Intelligence. Major Karne. That's your new boss. You're dismissed."

Harlan saluted. The Lieutenant Colonel waved his hand dismissively. "Good hunting out there, soldier, and watch your hindquarters."

---

[8] Knowledge, Skills and Abilities

Outside, Major Karne stood as Harlan came out of the L-C's office. She was a tall woman and thick around the waist. Her short hair was feathered back and her eyes were slightly bloodshot. She tapped her sunglasses off her forehead to cover her eyes, then gestured.

"Walk with me, Sergeant," she said.

They walked out and traversed a gravel path winding in and out of sandbag piles and maze-like mounds of sculpted dirt. The smell of sewage was overpowering as they passed a line of portable toilets. Away from the busy camp section, a noisy family of ducks scampered out of their way.

"Here."

The Major pointed down a path that followed a concrete wall. Beside the building wall, a rusty chain blocked a stairway. A sign said: *Unstable, Do Not Enter.*

The Major nimbly stepped over the chain and they climbed marble stairs. After ascending three stories, they stood before a ledge. Over the Sincaacu River, the tops of the tallest buildings in Khostarak could be seen. Faintly, explosions could be heard. Hazy brown clouds of greasy smoke hovered over Saador City.

"I hate this fucking sandbox," she muttered.

Below, a skinny dog wandered along the wall sniffing at weeds. Unconsciously, Harlan shook out an American Spirit cigarette and lighted it with a plastic lighter.

"Mind if I smoke?" he asked as he blew a stream over the ledge.

"Mind if I violate General Order Number One?"[9]

She pulled a plastic water bottle from her knapsack. Pungent fumes filled the room. She took a tiny sip and Harlan gestured for her to hand over the bottle.

"Go easy on it, my connection rotated back home and I don't know how I'll get more." She watched him sip. "Are we

---

[9] General Order Number One prohibits alcohol in the Irakki theater of war.

going to get along?" the Major asked while looking him over carefully.

"We either will or won't."

"Are you often so philosophical?"

"Not so much. I assume, when you finally get to your point, the result will be me and my men in the cross hairs of some dune-coon's Kalashnikov."

Karne laughed.

"How'd you get the L-C to let us go?"

"I work for General Charden. When I speak, the General speaks."

"Are we going to dance for a while? What's the mission?"

Karne looked at the remaining few ounces in her bottle, then screwed the cap on with a sad sigh.

"We're looking for something."

"Something big?"

"On a pallet. That's all I can disclose for now."

"Two hundred thousand square meters of dust and dirt and we're looking for a pallet?"

"Yeah," Karne replied.

"I've seen you skulking around. What happened to your other team?"

"They got their asses shot off and rotated out. I'm not going to kid you, Sergeant. I move light and fast and I leave the slow and wounded behind to fend for themselves. All I care about is finding the prize and getting home. Got a problem with that?"

"I'd rather be home dicking a bar girl and sleeping off a bender. But I'm here now. Shall we get after it?" He grabbed her arm and pulled her close. She was so tall that they were eye-to-eye. "How about starting this mission off with a kiss?"

"I don't mix business with pleasure or fraternize with enlisted men, Sergeant. If you want to keep your hand connected to your body, you'll take it off me right now."

"Tough guy, huh?"

The Major sighed. She lifted his hand off her breast and bent his little finger sharply backwards. "How smart are you, Sergeant? Do I have to break this innocent little pinky to make my point?"

"Go ahead, but don't bitch to me if you need it later. You can play cute, but you and I know where this is going."

Karne tried not to, but laughed anyway.

"You're a cheeky cracker son-of-a-bitch. *That* I may have use for later. Your dick you'll keep to yourself."

She released his hand; Harlan rubbed the sore joint of his finger.

"It's good to identify the outlying parameters of our engagement," he said.

"The parameters of our engagement mean I'll kill you painful if you lay a hand on me again..."

Harlan walked to the window and looked out over the river. He flicked a cigarette butt into the hot wind and lighted another.

"Yada-blah-whatever," he said.

Sura 2, Verse 85. You slay your fellow man and turn them away from their homes, backing each other against the law and breaking the rules; and if they return to you as captives you ransom them—while their turning out was against the law?

Do you believe in parts of the Book and disbelieve in the others? What is the reward of such among you—those who disgrace the life of this world? On the day of resurrection they shall be sent back for the most grievous punishment. Allah heeds what you do.

Book Two—Chapter Four

Khostarak–The Red Zone

JIMMY APPLIED LIGHT machine oil to the disassembled pieces of his .37 caliber Mark VII semiautomatic. Curtis stood by the window and watched the approach pathway. Harlan sat with his head on his hands, deep in thought while Shimon read through the interdepartmental transfer paperwork.

"How are we going to play this, Sarge?" Jimmy asked.

"We don't know what the McGuffin is," Harlan said. "I think the epilogue of this story is us getting our asses shot off for playing a part in some bureaucrat's wet dream. I can't decide whether to play along or pull the ripcord."

"Pardon me, Sarge, but I don't know what you're talking about half the time. Do you know any English? What's a

McGuffin?"

"Shut up and put that blunderbuss back together—we might need it."

"Here she comes, boss. She's kind of cute, but..."

"What?"

"I don't like the look of the knuckle-dragging brute she's dragging along with her."

"For Christ's sake, this is intolerable. She didn't say anything about a passenger. Lock and load."

Jimmy engaged the bolt of his rifle and slammed in a magazine.

"*That* I can understand," he said.

Major Karne entered the building with a large man wearing wrap-around sunglasses. The man wore a tank top which emphasized the pumped up muscle of his huge arms. His head was shaved, but he wore a massive bushy mustache. Harlan cocked his .45 and placed it against the man's head.

"Put the pea-shooter away." Major Karne protested. "He's alright, that's my Lyle."

Harlan ground his pistol into the man's temple.

"Lyle, I want you face down on the floor."

"Are you sure you want to play it this way?" Lyle said.

"My patience is at an end. I'm going to put a large hole in the meat between your ears. Get on the ground."

Lyle looked at Major Karne. She shrugged. Lyle eased himself onto his knees.

"I just washed this shirt, jerk."

"Yeah, whatever, just get on down there."

Lyle lowered himself onto the dirty floor. Harlan put a boot on his back. For a few moments everyone just looked at one another.

"Tell me what this fucked-up mission is all about," Harlan said.

The Major hauled over a folding chair and flopped on it.

"Go ahead and shoot him, what do I care? When the time is

right, I'll tell you everything you need to know *when* you need to know it. That's the end of the story."

"Ah, shit," Harlan complained. He uncocked the .45 and clicked the safety. "Go ahead and get your ass up."

Lyle brushed dirt off his shirt. "Hick dumbshit," he said. "Someone told me you're smart, but that remains a questionable theory at this point."

"Can we do a more normal introduction?" Major Karne said. "This is my associate, Lyle. He speaks a little Arabic."

Jimmy pointed his rifle at the ground and reached out a hand for a limp handshake.

"Jimmy," he said.

Shimon and Curtis shook Lyle's hand too. Lyle pointed a fat finger at Harlan's chest.

"You and I aren't finished," he said.

"I'll save you one last sweet kiss before reaping your virginity," Harlan replied.

"Okay, now that we're all friends, let's get down to business. We're going to be rolling around Khostarak starting tomorrow morning."

"Did you get us an armored Hummer?" Jimmy asked.

"We'll be in a piece of shit Nissan Pathfinder to blend in— we're keeping a low profile. Front gate, eight-hundred hours. Civilian clothes, don't shave. If anyone asks, we're an NGO AIDS awareness group out of Canada. I think that's it." She stood up and brushed dust off the seat of her pants. To Harlan, she said: "The rumor mill says you speak a little Arabic too."

"The rumor mill is full of shit. I can order a cup of coffee, that's about it," Harlan said flatly.

Major Karne shrugged. "Okay then. We'll see you boys in the A-M."

Outside, once out of earshot, Lyle commented, "That Harlan Farris is a lying sack of shit. Are you sure you trust him to watch your back?"

25

"I don't trust anyone to watch my back, even you. I'll watch my own back."

"I'll enjoy snapping him like a Popsicle stick."

Major Karne sighed. "Thank God I'm not paying for your literary skill. Just to be clear, you'll do nothing until I'm done with him."

"Of course," Lyle said defensively, "I'm not stupid."

"That's another theory that remains to be proven," Major Karne said.

Sura 2, Verse 91. And when it is said to them, believe in what Allah reveals, they say, "We believe in that which was revealed to us; and deny everything else. *We* know the verified truth."

We say, "Why then did you kill Allah's Prophets if you were true believers?"

Book Two—Chapter Five

Khostarak—The Red Zone

WISPY CLOUDS SCATTERED light from the rising sun. It was too early to be hot, but the air was stifling. Far away, a rifle repeatedly firing single rounds echoed across the city. Between the Humvee and a brick wall, Jimmy patted a stray dog—feeding him pieces of pemmican cut with a clasp knife.

"Don't feed that mutt—we'll never get rid of him," Harlan complained.

"If he's hungry enough to eat this shoe leather," Jimmy said, "then he deserves our generosity."

A dirty Nissan Pathfinder with the left front headlight smashed out pulled up and idled at the curb. While Lyle, driving, watched, Harlan's men gathered their gear and stacked it in the back compartment of the SUV.

"Where're we headed and what are our rules of engagement?" Harlan said.

"You ask a lot of questions," Major Karne commented.

"You should take a cue from Curtis. He rarely speaks."

Harlan glanced at Curtis with a raised eyebrow. When Curtis had something to say, he could not be shut up.

Curtis smiled at Harlan. "Where are we going, ma-am?" he asked politely.

Major Karne laughed. "We have a hot tip from an informant. We're heading toward Saadir City to rough up some hajjis."

"That's a nasty neighborhood," Harlan said.

"Aren't they all?" Lyle commented.

They turned off the main street and the road turned rough and unpaved. Garbage was piled high against fractured buildings. In a shell-pocked doorway, two young men messed with a bundle of clothing. They looked up as the SUV approached, then started running. One of them stopped and aimed a small revolver. It snapped and a bullet creased the front of the Pathfinder.

"What are you waiting for?" Major Karne said. "Nail that Hajji punk."

Jimmy was the first one out. He cleared the truck door and slipped down onto one knee. In seconds he'd unleashed a burst from his Mark VII and the kid flopped backward like a rag doll. The other glanced backwards and then disappeared around a corner. Cautiously, with weapons at the ready, the team approached the crumpled body. The boy, younger than he first appeared, tried to raise the pistol. Harlan stepped on his wrist and pried the little gun from his fingers. Lyle gathered rags and pressed them onto the kid's stomach; they were quickly soaked through. Lyle chattered tersely in Arabic. The kid spat a bloody wad onto Lyle's camo trousers.

"Just your generic, ignorant, Islamic militant-punk," Lyle said.

"Let's see what they were doing," Major Karne said.

Dragging the kid, they walked back to the bundle. Shimon, with the barrel of his M16, carefully lifted an old t-shirt out of the way. The bundle hid a roadside bomb—an artillery shell with a blasting cap shoved through a hole drilled in the bottom of the casing with wiring attached to a dismantled cell phone. Curtis clipped the wires from the cell phone a few seconds before it started clicking with an incoming call.

"Lyle? I think this call is for you," Harlan said.

"Very damned funny," Lyle responded.

"Can I borrow your sidearm, Sergeant?" Major Karne asked.

Harlan hesitated, then undid the Velcro flap of his holster and handed it over. Major Karne walked the few paces to the kid and fired a round into his head.

She walked back and handed back the weapon.

"Any other questions about our rules of engagement, Sergeant?" she asked.

"No, that about covers it," Harlan said.

Before they climbed back into the SUV, Curtis and Harlan huddled.

"Lyle speaks fast," Harlan said, "so I'm not sure I caught all the Arabic. They're asking about a heavy bundle on a pallet?"

"That seems to be it. Not very helpful."

"Uranium, perhaps? What else could be heavy?"

"A lot of shit. Gold is fucking heavy."

Lyle tooted the horn.

"There's time for tea and a chat later, ladies," he shouted.

Harlan flashed Lyle a middle finger.

"Gold from the dear-leader's stash," he said. "Wouldn't that be something?"

"Yeah, wouldn't it."

Major Karne poked her head out of the SUV window.

"Uncle Sugar ain't paying you lollygaggers to wag your gums. Get your fucking asses over here," she yelled.

"Coming, mother," Harlan mumbled.

Sura 10, Verse 78-81. They said, "Have you come to turn us away from the ways of our fathers—so you and your brother might enjoy the bounty of our land? We shall not believe in you."

In response, the Pharaoh said, "Bring me every skillful magician."

When the sorcerers came, Moses said to them, "Throw what ye wish to throw."

When they had their throw, Moses said, "What you brought is evil sorcery. Allah will not fulfill your predictions—He will not reward the mischief-makers."

Book Two—Chapter Six

Khostarak–The Red Zone

THEY LEANED AGAINST a broken expanse of brick wall. Lyle was between Harlan and Major Karne—checking the clip of his rotor-gun and thumbing through the self-test menus and diagnostic displays of the smart weapon. They were several blocks from the Pathfinder—except for Jimmy left with the pickup. The team was scattered around a row of apartment buildings.

"You know we have eyes on us, right?" Harlan said.

There were kids on the dusty street playing with a soccer ball. Young men popped their heads up from the rooftops, looked at them and chattered on their cell phones.

"Fucking genius you found," Lyle said, "an expert on the blatantly obvious."

"If either of you had the sense of two gnats," Major Karne said, "you'd be in charge of this detail, not me. Shut the hell up."

"We're on site and in position, Major," Harlan said. "Is there any possible way to delay telling us what we're doing?"

Major Karne pressed a button on her satcom headset and leaned her head back against the bricks.

"I suppose not," she said. "Let's tie your team in." She pressed buttons on her personal communicator. "Everyone check in and let me know you're linked."

"Yo, Curtis online," Curtis said.

"I hear you five-by," Jimmy said.

"Shimon here, I have my big ears on."

"First of all—Shimon, you've been trying to hack my secure link with HQ. I'm not going to tell you to stop it, but the link protocol is encrypted with an organic, evolutionary lattice-matrix code. Enough said?"

"What does that mean?' Curtis said.

Shimon's voice was tinny over the secure link. "It means it doesn't matter how much Bangalorean CPU bandwidth I throw at it—I won't get there from here."

"Right," the Major said. "Okay, listen-up. There are missions so important that the UN-negotiated rules of engagement are thrown out the window. Missions too important for the coalition forces, too sensitive for the military and too complex for the KBR contractors. That's when they call me. There's a man in the third apartment from the left—on the second floor. His name is Mohammed Iain Puurem. *He's* our mission. Collateral damage is permitted—it doesn't matter as long as we get him."

"You *know* he's in there?" Jimmy said.

"He's RF-linked and sat-tagged. He's in there. I'll send his playing card so you'll know who to watch for."

She tapped the touchscreen of her communicator.

"Why are we here?" Harlan said. "Light him up and fly a T-Nine up his ass."

"We want him alive," Major Karne said.

She waited a few moments for the information to sink in.

"What's our play?" Curtis said. "Blast our way in? We're not going to sneak up on him—the element of surprise was out of play when Talibi Bob made his heads-up phone call when we crossed First and Main."

"We're the beaters driving the prey," Major Karne said. "Any time now, Puurem should drop through his *secret* exit in the back of the building and take a stroll down the street behind the apartment complex. He'll try to blend in—just another sandal-flopper on his way to the hookah joint for a cup of sheep-dung tea. Jimmy will drive by, shoot this fuck in the leg with the silenced-pistol in the Nissan's glove box, toss him in the back and we roll out, smooth like French-silk pie. Then we drop him off at HQ and the tequila shots are on me. Got it?"

"Wow," Jimmy commented on the link, "a subsonic Glock-75. Look what's following me home after this gig, mom."

Major Karne with a sour look on her face, sighed, but did not speak.

The controller's voice from the satellite link was metallic and emotionless.

"Target still stationary," it said.

Major Karne pressed buttons on her communicator. An infrared image was displayed on the team's heads-up display units.

"See the unit by the front door?" she asked Lyle.

"Yeah."

"When you're done masturbating your rotorgun, take him out."

"Okay, boss," Lyle said. "It looks like—if I aim about two feet off the center of the door—right about—here...."

In automatic mode, he loosed a brief blast which stitched a tight pattern on the door.

"Did I get him?" Lyle said.

"He's already cooling," Harlan commented.

"Target moving," the satellite system said.

Jimmy pressed the window control and the passenger-side window slid down. With the truck still moving a few miles per hour, he leaned over and shot Puurem in the upper thigh with the massive, bulky Glock. The gun made a sound like a finger's snapping. Jimmy stopped the SUV and jumped out. There were others nearby on the sidewalk, but they kept their distance. After hauling the mewling hajji into the SUV, he clicked a handcuff welded to the roll bar onto the man's wrist, and then handed the man a sterile compress and pantomimed to show him what to do.

"If you keep pressure on it, you probably won't bleed to death," Jimmy said.

It sounded like the man was cursing, but Jimmy understood none of the Arabic language.

Jimmy drove backwards, and then turned into an alley. Something loud clanged off the roof. He flinched and looked up to the roof of the SUV, but didn't see any problem. He kept driving and came out into sunlight. Guided by the GPS, he made two turns and pulled up to the team.

"We took a hit in the alley," Jimmy said, pointing at a ragged puncture in the roof. "Something big like heavy round from a deer rifle, but it didn't make it through."

"This truck looks like a POS," Major Karne said, "but it's selectively-hardened with kevplate."

"Ah," Jimmy said. "That explains it."

She glanced at Puurem, and then leaned over to take his pulse.

"Good," she said. "We're in business. Drive."

After dinner in the mess hall, the team, after traveling by circuitous routes, assembled at their Tomahawk Building. Jimmy flipped cards into a hat—Curtis leaned back against the wall and pulled his hat over his eyes and pretended to sleep— and Shimon played with his vPad. Harlan picked up a torn-up copy of Bill Buckley's *God and Man at Yale*.

"It would be more convincing if you pretended to read that rightwing trash right-side-up," Curtis commented.

"Fuck off," Harlan said. "Ever read a book without pictures, black man? They teach the darkies to read on the plantation?"

Curtis tipped his hat back.

"You want another go, honky—after all the times I mopped the floor with your ass?"

"Bring it."

"Okay, it's my turn, right? What year did Buckley's brother run for congress in New York?"

"1965. You'd have a chance if you could think of some hard questions. How many years after the first black Republican was elected was it before a black Democrat was elected?"

"Will you stop it, already? I get tired of you guys competing to see who the dimmest dimwit is."

Curtis and Harlan said it together. "Fuck you."

They sat in silence for a few minutes while Harlan flipped the pages of his book. He claimed to read three-hundred words a minute, but no one believed him.

Harlan creased a page and dropped his book on a bucket he used as a table.

"I like it," he said.

"What?"

"We've been bitching since we got over here about how the UN, the politicians, the mass media and the military brass tie our hands. We can't win a war if we're bogged down in bureaucracy and red tape—and sweating bullets every time some camel-skinned civilian accidentally gets lit up in the crosshairs."

"Yeah," Jimmy said. "We're soldiers—trained for warfare—breaking things and killing people. If it ain't worth the sidestream damage, then it ain't a war and we damned well should be back home tinkering with our hotrods and working on our beer bellies."

"You think Karne is going to cover our asses when she's done with us?" Curtis said. "It's more likely she'll pretend she never saw us before and let us twist in the wind with a hangman's noose around our necks."

"No," Harlan said. "We've been over this before. I think we can win this war."

"Oh, my Lord," Shimon said. "Not this again. It's the Arkansas caped crusader—gonna win a war that's been going on for thousands of years—all by himself."

"Not by myself," Harlan said. He bumped fists with Curtis. "My black brother Curtis will help me."

"How we going to know when we've won, anyway? There's always going to be Wasabi dickwads running around this godforsaken shithole—blowing up schoolgirls."

"When I can get a three-dollar cup Starbucks coffee on the corner of Khafir Avenue and Dhimmi Street with my Amex card, there might still be cleanup battles to fight, but we'll know we won the war."

"Before you take your victory lap," Shimon said, "check this out."

"What?" Curtis asked.

"Remember Chili Pappar and Blake Zee?"

Curtis made the sign of the cross on his chest. "Yeah," he said, "poor bastards."

"I think they were Karne's previous team."

"Nooo," Harlan said, stretching out the word as he thought about the implications. "Shit "

"Fuck me," Jimmy said, 'is that what happened to them?"

"Hard to say you won a war if you go home in a box," Curtis said.

"I wish I could rebut that point," Harlan said.

A voice came from outside.

"Don't shoot me—I'm coming in."

"Crap on a silver spoon," Jimmy said. "It's Karne. How'd she find us? What's she doing here?"

She walked into the room.

"You should be nice to me," she said. "I brought tequila and not the shit the civies distill from rotten potatoes and avocados in the utility room out by the swamp coolers—real Two-Pistols Reposado—blue agave stuff from Jalisco."

"Where's your dancing bear?" Shimon said.

"Lyle? I gave him the night off. Can I sit?"

Harlan waved at their collection of overturned five-gallon plastic buckets.

"Sure, pull up a chair," he said.

Curtis wiped the mouth of the 750ml bottle and took a small sip. He passed it to Shimon.

"You didn't need us for the mission today," Harlan said.

Major Karne shrugged. "True enough," she said. "I wanted to get a feel for how you guys operate in the field. I've read your files and talked to your superior officers, but that never gives a complete-enough picture. Speaking of things we didn't need to do," she pointed at Jimmy, "you could have popped Puurem on the head and tossed him in the truck. You didn't need to shoot him."

Jimmy looked at the bottle and scowled. "You told me to." He took a drink and passed the bottle along.

"So you did—and I like the sound of compliance," Major Karne said. "I like a man who follows orders." She gestured for the bottle.

"Let's talk about something interesting—like Pappar and Zee," Harlan said.

"Ah, you figured that out. That was a major cluster-fuck—a situation that spiraled out of control."

Curtis leaned forward. "A major fuck up by whom, Major? You?"

"Whom. I like that, Curtis. Most people would incorrectly say *who*."

"Most people would say you're evading his question," Harlan said.

Karne held the bottle up to the sunlight and swirled the gold-tinted fluid, then took a sip and passed the bottle along.

"Fair enough," she said. "Our information was fucked up, because it came from a fucked up source. Then Pappar and Zee fucked up and then I fucked up. It was a FUBAR situation the whole way."

"They died and you lived," Shimon said.

"If it makes you feel any better," she held her index finger and thumb a quarter-inch apart, "I almost bought the farm too. I think the sniper hesitated for an instant, perhaps because I was a woman, but it was enough time for Lyle to get him with a high-velocity, full-metal jacket."

"What are you leaving out of this story?" Curtis said.

Major Karne looked at him with a blank expression.

"I was in the open and in his sights. I couldn't think of anything else to do, so I opened my shirt and showed the sniper my tits."

The four men could not avoid the instinctual reaction; they all tilted their heads to stare at her chest. Curtis was the first to break off his critical examination and look into her eyes. Harlan was the last.

"And that worked?" Jimmy said.

"Apparently," Karne replied.

She took the bottle from Harlan's limp hand and finished the last fraction of an ounce. She threw the bottle over her shoulder and it smashed against the wall.

"Hey, it took a long time to clean up this place," Shimon complained.

"Doesn't matter, you guys are moving into the city," she

said.

"What? Off base?" Jimmy said.

"Don't let her distract us from the point," Curtis said. "I'm not satisfied—we're not done talking about Pappar and Zee."

Karne took a deep breath. "We're always looking for the bomb-makers," she said. "Our job was to get Avril Molitkaatkta into a car—a car marked with UV-active paint. His car was in a garage with a roll-up door and he could get to it by going through a secret panel in the back corner of his mosque, then down a passage, through a couple of connecting doors in an apartment building, and into an electronics junk shop—where his vehicle was stored. He had a safe house in Sepil Kavl and an Apache would take him out on the highway. Like today, we were supposed to press him, flush him out—make him run. But, he didn't run. Instead, he hunkered down and wouldn't let the school kids go home. We could hear them inside—singing and praying. The area was supposed to be secure, but they had a sniper with a .55 caliber Russian Endikov—on the top of a hotel—a half-mile away. He used some kind of explosive round—when he hit Zee dead center in the chest, there was nothing left but pieces. Lyle was roving, but the shooter was outside of our perimeter."

"What happened to Pappar?" Jimmy said.

The Major bit her lip. "He and Zee were tight. When Zee bought it, Pappar went mad. He stormed the mosque—going after Avril on his own."

"So the sniper got him on the run?" Curtis said.

"No," Karne said. "Lyle found the shooter with his scope. He didn't have a clean shot, but he hit the rifle and that messed up the shooter—broke his arm and blinded him. A few minutes later, a back ops team went to the apartment building and finished him off."

"If the sniper didn't get Pappar…" Harlan said.

"The backup plan was a thousand-pound Guided Bomb Unit dropped from a Stealth Bomber way the hell up in the no-airisphere. I called it in."

"Wait," Jimmy said. "I thought that Silver Dome mosque was blown up by Iranian agents—a bomb set off by Sunni militants."

Major Karne picked at a front tooth with a fingernail. "It wasn't a great cover story, but there are some who bought it," she said.

"You blew up a mosque full of kids to get one guy?" Shimon said.

"For twenty years, we tried fighting this war like a police situation and it didn't work. As stupid and self-destructive as we Americans are, after ten years, there were people in the chain of command who became—impatient—and wanted a small team who would play outside the rules and get things done. Effectively. Efficiently. Avril was a bad guy and, like a coward, he surrounded himself with involuntary hostages— assuming our gutless fear of seeing pictures of dead school kids on network news would make him safe. In this case, that was a bad assumption. Now he makes bombs no more."

She stood up and kicked her plastic bucket against the wall. "Any more probing questions?" she said.

Jimmy raised his hand. "Yeah," he said. "Can we see your tits? I hear they're worth dying for."

Harlan slugged Jimmy s shoulder.

"Hey," Jimmy said.

"Moron," Harlan responded. "I have a question. What's the deal with you and Lyle?"

"You're asking if he's fucking me? If we're lovers? That's a fair-enough question, so I'll answer it. Yes. Sometimes we are intimate. He has the equipment and a certain amount of skill— when the time and situation is right, I let him fill me. Does anyone have a problem with that?"

One-by-one, she looked into their eyes—saving Harlan for last—but no one spoke.

"Fine. You guys can live in The Red Zone if you like

bunking with the unwashed and eating powdered eggs and shit-on-a-shingle in the canteen, but our budget includes rooms for you at the Maakti Hilton, covers the restaurant and bar bill, room service and full access to the room's minibar. Also, there is no restriction against guests, even overnight ones, if you follow me."

"I'm in," Jimmy said.

"Day-by-day, what's our assignment?" Curtis said.

"You'll get a satcom implant. When I call, you come running. Otherwise, do what you want. Stay sober during the day and you'll live longer, but that's your call. Unless your bad habits interfere with the mission, I don't give a runny shit."

"I want a car," Harlan said.

"Not a problem," Karne replied. "What else?"

"What else should we know?" Curtis said.

Major Karne considered the question. "Don't spend a lot of time standing by your hotel window. The glass is not bullet-proof and the hajjis take a shot now and then. What else?"

"I'd still like a peep under your shirt," Jimmy said.

She scratched her upper lip with her index finger and looked at Harlan, only Harlan, with a blank, inscrutable expression.

"Sorry, Jimmy, but I think that's highly unlikely," she said.

Sura 2, Verse 49-50. And remember, we delivered you from the people of Pharaoh where you were beset with hard tasks and punishments—they slaughtered your sons while your women watched. It was a tremendous trial from your Lord. Remember that we divided the sea to save you—and drowned the Pharaoh's people as you watched.

Book Two—Chapter Seven

Khostarak

NEARLY ALL OF the visiting UN diplomats, NGO activists and TV network correspondents stayed at the Maakti Hilton—a seven-story, glass-faced building in the center of Khostarak's business district, such as it was. There was oil and natural gas in the plains of Irakkistan and uranium and rare earths were buried in the country's mountainous fringes, so, regardless of the war, there was business to be done.

Seven tall buildings decorated the downtown area. The largest, owned by British Petroleum, was fourteen stories tall and was the most prominent landmark in the ancient city as it spread out on the flat terrain. The lazy Sincaacu River wound through the city and there were parks and even nearly a mile of running track on the riverbank dike.

People lived in the city, almost a million of them. The crime rate was high and the people in general were poor and

there was too much sectarian violence between competing
Moslem religious sects and the West, but, like everywhere else
on Earth, the regular people lived their regular lives.

In room 608 of the Maakti Hotel, Curtis covered the lower
half of his windows with aluminum foil so a sniper could not see
him walking around, but he left the upper part of the windows
uncovered so sunlight could flood the room. He wasn't paying
the bill, so he did not care if this made the air conditioner work
harder.

Harlan asked him to be ready to leave at ten o'clock. Curtis
finished tying his bootlace and glanced at the clock.

9:55.

There was a tap on the door. Harlan was five minutes
early—he was always five minutes early.

Curtis opened the door and Harlan slipped in.

"How's my uppity-nigger?" Harlan said.

"Isn't it a little early for your KKK meeting to be over?"
Curtis replied.

"Let me look at you," Harlan said. He stared at Curtis's
face. "I wish I could grow a 'fro like that."

"Your cracker-ass redneck Arkansas homeboys would lynch
you in two seconds. Why can't I shave my beard? The damned
thing itches."

"It's coming in good, but you need to trim the sides a little
and let the chin part grow out more."

"Are you trying to turn me into Richard Prior or
something? I wish you'd just tell me what you're doing instead
of acting all secret agent and shit."

"You'll see," Harlan said. "Let's move out."

Curtis flopped on his couch and put his boots on the glass-
topped coffee table.

"I'm not going anywhere until you give me a hint."

Harlan laughed. "Remember the girl I told you about? The
pretty one with the David Bowie poster on her wall?"

"The one that doesn't exist except in your overheated

imagination? The one we're all tired of hearing you bullshit about? Yeah, I remember, you won't let us forget."

"Her name is Telleh and I think it's time for you to meet her," Harlan said.

Harlan's car was a dirty Toyota Yaris. Under thick dust and oily grime, it was blue, except for the crushed driver's door which had been replaced with a white one. Harlan waved at Ali, the underground parking lot attendant, and forced a place in the bumper-to-bumper traffic. Hooting horns were ever-present— Harlan ignored them and drove north to cross the river.

After a few miles, the apartment buildings thinned out and there were more single-family homes—and more goats and chickens in the street. They parked in front of a two-story duplex. Harlan, after getting out and stretching his back, tossed a coin to a ten-year-old boy wearing an Oakland Raiders t-shirt.

"Car wash this time?" Harlan said.

The boy laughed. "Next time," he said.

There used to be a brick arch across the entry, but it was smashed in the center—the broken ends reached toward each other, but did not meet. Harlan pushed open a wrought-iron gate. The small yard was filled with red gravel and weeds. Curtis was impressed. It wasn't much of a front yard, but he had not seen *any* front yards in Khostarak. Generally these people built their house fronts on the street and if they had an outdoor area, it was a private terrace in the middle of the property enclosed by concrete block walls.

The front door was huge—hardwood and covered with engraved images. Hand-painted tiles framed the door jamb. As they approached, the front door opened. The girl wore a pale-blue head scarf which wrapped around and covered the lower part of her face. Her hair was dark brown—nearly black. Bangs, cut at an angle, hung across her forehead.

One aspect of being veiled—it emphasized a woman's eyes. This girl's eyes were very pretty—blue to match the scarf and accented by manicured eyebrows. There was no helping it, Curtis was captivated by her.

Harlan spoke in Arabic.

"Curtis, I would like to introduce you to Telleh," he said.

She bowed her head and closed her eyes for a moment. Curtis aped the motion.

"Before we do anything else," Harlan said, "please show Curtis your room." To Curtis, he said, "Don't go in, that's not allowed, but you can look inside."

Telleh laughed and motioned for Curtis to follow her up a carpeted staircase. At the top of the stairs, they traveled along a hallway—so narrow, Curtis's shoulders nearly touched each wall. They stopped at a door and Telleh opened it.

Her English was not very good, but Curtis understood her. He was not allowed to step over the threshold of her room.

Curtis leaned over and looked inside.

There was a large poster on the wall.

The white duke—David Bowie.

Downstairs, men sat on a wide, low couch covered with light cotton fabric. Telleh served them hot, black, bitter tea in tiny china cups. The men had an audience—from the kitchen, at least three girls between five- and twelve-years old peeked and whispered between themselves.

Telleh taught Harlan new words by pointing at items around the room and slowly saying the words. Harlan reciprocated by telling her the English words. To Curtis, the language sounded similar to Arabic, but with a mix of Indian and Turkish flavors. Mostly, it was odd and alien to his ear.

"What language?" Curtis said.

"I don't know if you ever noticed, but most people around here don't speak Arabic—particularly the weird amalgamation the military teaches."

"That wasn't my question, asshole."

Telleh giggled.

Curtis looked at her. "I apologize for cursing."

She chattered a long sentence.

"What was that?" he asked.

"I didn't follow all of it," Harlan said, "but something like *Allah blesses man with a tongue for poetry and a mind for swill. It does not please Allah that all of a man's thoughts be spoken.* Well, something like that, anyway. The most common tribal language in Irakkistan is a mixture of Pashtun, Cercu and Blyyn. One of the problems around here is people who live twenty miles from each other can't talk to one another. Except for a few enlightened souls, the elders discourage learning other languages and they claim translation ruins the purity of the tribal language."

Telleh took the teapot back into the kitchen. Curtis leaned over to speak privately with Harlan.

"You lied about making out with this girl, Harlan, you prick. You were right about Bowie poster, but you've only seen it like I have, from outside."

"Look at her, Curtis. She's really something special. You have to help me win her."

Irrationally, this made Curtis angry.

"What are you talking about? I can't do anything. Besides, maybe she'll like me better She's cute."

"I found her. You go find your own. And you *will* help me."

"No, I won't. Why would I?"

"Because you're my friend and this is important to me."

From the kitchen, Telleh giggled and a chorus of schoolgirl giggles followed her lead. Curtis realized he thought he was whispering, but he wasn't. He leaned closer to Harlan.

"How much of this does she understand?"

Harlan shrugged. "Not half, but not zero either. When the old man comes in, I don't want you to freak out."

"What old man?"

"Her grandfather. I mentioned some elders who are enlightened? He's one."

Curtis sat back and sipped his tea.

"I don't get any of this," he said.

The old man did not move very fast—but with Tellah's help he eventually found the couch and sat down.

"He can see, but only if he gets really close," Harlan said.

"No shit," Curtis replied.

The old man's face was six inches away from Curtis's. His breath smelled like old melons and sewage. He ruffled Curtis's kinky hair and pulled—while tut-tut-tutting in a disapproving tone—on the beard on Curtis's chin.

"He wants you to grow that part out," Harlan said. "Just on the chin—leave the part on the sides short."

"The only reason I'm growing a beard at all is because you told me Karne wanted me to—for an undercover mission."

"I didn't exactly tell the truth about that part of things," Harlan said.

Sura 11, Verse 40. When our command came and water sprang forth from the valley, we said, "Carry in the arc two of all things, in pairs, and your family and those who believe—except those against whom the word has already been given. And there were few non-believers.

Book Two—Chapter Eight

Khostarak

SOME OF THE cheese and olives served for lunch tasted good, but some of it tasted, to Curtis, like something scraped from a camel's hoof. To be polite, he really tried, but some of the ripe, pungent, moldy cheeses were nauseating and he had to wave them away. This made the old man grumble like a cantankerous old mule, but it was something he did constantly, so, after a while, his grousing and snarling became part of the background noise.

Dates in yoghurt tasted good—Curtis asked for a second helping of that.

Telleh was in and out—serving and cleaning up dishes, so Curtis had plenty of time to study her figure. She wore cotton pants with a swirly design embroidered on the outside seam—and fabric ties at the ankles above black, no-heel slippers. Her silky blouse flowed loosely over at least three other layers, so Curtis could not tell if she wore a bra or if she even needed one.

She was slim, but had womanly bulk in her hips, buttocks and chest. Worst case, on a scale of one to ten, she was an eight— she might have been a perfect ten, but the clothing made it impossible to tell. Regardless, she was lovely and moved around the room with a dancer's smooth grace.

The overall effect was irresistible. She was charming.

Harlan alternated between watching her himself and shooting evil, warning looks at Curtis.

Harlan was willing to leave after lunch, but they were recruited for storytime. The scene was surreal—Harlan read a children's picture book in English, and helped Telleh understand the words which she translated for two small boys who were prone to jumping up and mimicking the exciting adventures of BarBar, the cheeky monkey.

After an hour and a half of this, they got up and prepared to leave. While Curtis watched, Harlan tried to kiss Telleh on the cheek, but she deflected his face with a soft, slender hand and evaded him. The two men walked out the front door.

There was no way to explain it, but the street did not feel friendly. The boy who was paid to watch the car was nowhere to be seen—in fact, no one could be seen. The street appeared deserted.

On the driver's side door, someone had scrawled a rude word in broken English.

FUK.

Harlan, with his boot, worked at the mud and dust until the word was illegible.

"This smell right to you, Harlan?"

"Nope," Harlan replied. "Let's go coop for a half hour, then make a drive-by and see if anything is brewing."

"Okay," Curtis said.

Harlan started the Toyota and they drove a half-mile to a gutted, bombed-out house. Harlan pulled over and turned off the engine. Curtis rolled down the window to see if a breeze could be captured. The air was still and hot.

No breeze.

"I've had enough of being led around like a bull with a ring through its nose. Start talking, jerkwad."

"You saw her. She's not just beautiful, she's radiant—like a Middle Eastern angel."

"I'm not talking about the girl, dipshit. You're a horny, Arkansas hick-billy with great expectations and no fucking common sense. I totally get the girl thing. Stop taunting my patience and tell me what's up with the old man, you ass-licking, hickory-headed, redneck, dick-nosed, puissant-peckerwood, scum-slurping son-of-a-mangy-bitch."

"I love the way you talk when you're riled."

Curtis reached over and rammed a knuckle into Harlan's bicep.

Hard.

"Damn it, I'm talking already. Is that your answer to everything, you Yankee-Baltimore fuck? Violence? That hurts."

Curtis wound up to hit him again.

Harlan spoke quickly.

"The old man is a tribal elder, you know that. He used to be more influential, but he's mostly retired now. However, the other tribal leaders, most of them, will listen to him. And, he has an idea."

Thinking about what to say, Harlan rubbed his shoulder and looked out through the windshield at something that was a long ways away.

"I'm waiting patiently for you to get to something I don't already know," Curtis said. "What's with the beard you want me to grow?"

"The old man is a scholar of the Qu'ran—an Islamic intellectual. He's written a bunch of books and is very influential in interpreting—and creating Hadithas. There's a story—vaguely-written—about a strong-horse prophet who unites the tribes and prepares the way for the Twelfth Imam."

"I'm afraid of what you're going to say next..."

"This strong-horse is a foreigner—a moor. A black man."

Curtis pounded the heels of his hands on the dusty dashboard.

"No. No, no, no."

"With my brains and your black skin…"

"We're through talking. I'm used to you coming up with stupid ideas—insane ideas no one with an ounce of sense would entertain for a second. No more talk—in fact, I'm never going to speak to you again. We're done. That's it."

They sat for a minute. Harlan took a breath as if preparing to speak.

"No. Not a single word," Curtis warned.

Their communicators crackled.

Major Karne.

"I remember that house you guys are sitting by. That was one of ours; Lyle tossed a knapsack into the entry—with about a pound of C-4 in it. Six hajjis turned into mincemeat and the smart one that ran out the backdoor? Turns out he was a talker. All in all, it was a good day."

"We enjoy your love stories, Karne, but we're a little busy at the moment. What's on your mind?"

"I like to give a new team a week of rest and relaxation to take off the pressure and see what they'll do when left to themselves. Usually, the teams settle in with whisky and rent-wives, but I must say—you guys are really fucking boring."

"Would you please get to your point, Major?" Harlan said.

"Down time is over. I need you guys. Go to the target location we beamed to your GPS—right away and directly with no fucking around. Don't even stop to take a piss. Out."

"I think her charm, over time, will wear a little thin," Harlan said.

"We're still not talking," Curtis said. "Drive."

Contrary to her order and increasingly excited instructions to *turn around and go back* from the dashboard GPS unit, Harlan retraced their path to Telleh's house. The neighborhood was quiet—Harlan drove by slowly and stopped at the end of the block by a produce shop. After loosening his .45 under his shirt, he stopped the car, but left it running, and then walked causally to the bins to pull out a worse-for-the-wear pear.

He flipped a coin to a man sitting on an overturned bushel basket and tearing the husks off emaciated ears of corn, then stood by the rear of the car watching the street and eating his pear. He could feel eyes on him, but there was no movement on the street until the boy who watched their car came out with his skateboard. The boy gave Harlan a thumbs-up—Harlan pitched the remaining hunk of his pear into the trashy gutter and returned to the driver's seat.

"That's as good as it's going to get," Harlan said.

"We're still not talking," Curtis replied.

Over the communicator, Major Karne spoke. "Didn't I mention that time is of the essence, gentlemen? The girl's house is *not* between point A and point B, no matter how I draw that straight line, but maybe I'm mistaken. I was never much good at geometry—or perhaps I was unclear. How about this? Get your useless asses over here. Now would be soon enough. Okay?"

"Don't get your Maxipad in a bunch, Major," Harlan said. "We're en route."

He engaged the clutch and rolled onto the dusty road.

"Ahead, turn left," the GPS unit said.

"I'm not sure I'll ever get used to big bird knowing where we are at all times," Harlan said.

Curtis said nothing.

They pulled up beside Major Karne's Pathfinder. Lyle had a smirk pasted on his face—he looked at them for a second then returned to looking at the status display on his rotorgun.

"Nice of you guys to find time for us in your busy

schedules," Major Karne said.

"What have we got?" Harlan said.

"This is something you want to see—we're trying something new."

Karne spoke a command into her communicator and a Huey-2 heavy-lift chopper with rotors pounding the hot air rumbled in from the east. Under it was a massive, rusty-iron box. It appeared heavy—it swayed on steel cables underneath the chopper.

"This is going to be sweet," the Major said.

Harlan nodded to Shimon and Jimmy.

"Hey, guys," he said.

Jimmy, through a set of giant Bushnell field glasses, watched the approaching chopper.

"I don't like the look of this," he said.

He passed the binoculars to Shimon, who immediately worked the electronic focus.

"What am I looking at?" Shimon said.

The box got closer and the chopper hovered, and then slowly settled the giant box over a house. From inside the house came signs of panic.

"What's going on?" Harlan said.

"We get complaints about civilian casualties when we take out a house with a guided bomb or missile. There are shaped charges in the box. We'll destroy the house and everything in it without even waking the neighbors."

Shimon tapped Harlan on the shoulder.

"They were smart enough to put vents in the box, but I don't think this will work out like they think. I suggest we get behind something heavy before they light that thing off."

Lyle, eyeing the box through the scope of his rifle, laughed.

"Chickenshits," he said.

Shimon tapped Curtis on the arm. "Get behind the truck," he said. The four moved to the opposite side of the Pathfinder. "Not there," Shimon said, while gesturing to Harlan. "Stand behind a wheel."

Harlan looked down, shrugged, and then moved.

The bomb detonated with a loud snap and a cloud of dust jetted out of the iron box. A piece of spinning metal, twisted beyond recognition, slammed into the Pathfinder between Lyle and Major Karne. Another piece slammed into the front tire, which immediately went flat.

Karne and Lyle looked at the metal. It missed Lyle by six inches, but a small fragment of something bounced off and slid across his thigh. A trickle of blood dampened his trousers.

Shimon peeked at the box from around the back of the Pathfinder.

"We should be okay now," he said.

The helicopter lifted the box and flew back to the east. From under the box, there was nothing but rubble. The house was gone. The adjoining houses still stood, but were heavily damaged from high-speed debris that flew out through the vents.

Harlan walked around the vehicle. Lyle had leaned his rotorgun against the truck and wrapped a handkerchief around his thigh. Major Karne was talking on her communicator—calling for a new vehicle and a towtruck to pick up the Pathfinder.

"What was the rank of the genius that thought this up?" Harlan said.

With an acerbic expression, Major Karne replied tersely. "General," she said.

Two hajji civilians leaned over a rusty, trodden-down chain link fence and complained loudly.

"I thought it would be something like that," Harlan commented. To Shimon, he said, "Thanks, good call, that."

"Physics. It's the law," Shimon said. He gestured at Curtis. "What's with him?"

"He's pissed off and not talking right now."

"Oh, okay," Shimon said.

Sura 22, Verse 31. Worship Allah and not those who falsely represent him, or it will be as though one fell from a high place—then birds will snatch him away or the wind will carry him far away.

Book Two—Chapter Nine

Khostarak

ON THE THIRD floor of the Maakti Hotel, Major Karne had converted a two-bedroom suite into her meeting room and command center. The men were curious about her bedroom, but that door was closed and securely locked—they never saw her go in and out.

Lyle, wearing Bermuda shorts and a Cheshire cat's satisfied smile, smeared antiseptic goo to the ragged gash on his leg—and applied a new bandage. While Jimmy watched, he waggled his eyebrows and made a circle with his left hand and slid his right hand's index finger in and out. In response, Jimmy made a pistol with his right hand and shot Lyle in the eye. Karne caught their pantomime and scowled.

"You guys knock that fucking shit off and play nice," she said.

Harlan offered to refill Curtis's coffee from an elaborately-designed silver coffee pot, but Curtis ignored him. Shimon, typing rapidly and furiously on the touch screen of his vPad, whispered "aha," and made a victory fist.

When he noticed everyone looking at him, he said, "I didn't say anything," and went back to his typing.

Karne stood in front of Curtis and pulled on the bit of billy goat beard hanging a half-inch from his chin.

"I'm not sure I understand the look you're going for," she said. "You're starting to look familiar, but I can't place it. Who are you pretending to be? One of the doomed characters in Lawrence of Arabia? Some kind of Masai warrior? A used-camel dealer from Penttik Street?"

Refusing to make eye-contact with her, he pushed her hand away and sipped his coffee.

To Harlan, she said, "How long does he stay pissed off like this?"

Harlan shrugged. "I don't know. Never happened before."

She gave a final vigorous tug to Curtis's beard, then walked to the center of the living room.

"Listen up," she said. "This is important. You guys have your own pet theories about why we're in this shit-hole country and fighting this god-forsaken war, but I'm about to clue you in on something you don't get very often—the unvarnished truth. It's not oil, it's not opium, it's not uranium or hexavalent cadminium. It's money—cash money."

She handed a five-thousand dollar bill to Shimon, who set aside his vPad and took it—then examined it closely.

"You used to be able to buy a car, hell, two cars with five-thousand dollars, but now you're lucky if you can find a bicycle on sale at Wal-Mart—anyone know why?"

"Since the Federal Reserve Bank was created in 1913," Shimon said, "the value of the dollar has been deliberately devalued by ninety-nine percent by a cabal of Jewish bankers, sleazy politicians and crooked Wall Street manipulators—to keep the middle class in a form of indentured servitude."

Shimon passed the colorful bill to Jimmy.

Karne looked at Shimon with intense curiosity. "I don't

know about all that paranoid conspiracy shit, but I do know the government prints money and it doesn't buy anything like it used to. There's no arguing against that, but, that's not *our* problem. Do you know what the government hates more than anything else in the world?"

"A cheerful taxpayer?" Harlan said.

"Yeah, that's it," Jimmy said. They shared a fist-bump.

"No," Major Karne said with a bitter, unattractive twist to her lips, "it's competition—more than anything else they hate competition, gentlemen. And that's what that five-thousand dollar bill represents. You see, it's printed nicely on the proper Swiss multicolor-thread paper and it has the right ink and the right holograms and the right impressions in the texture and all of the other security features, but it was not printed by the Fed. It was printed right here in Khostarak by a team formed and financed by the former dear leader. That's the real reason he had to go—he was printing currency by the pallet-load. Our government wants to protect its monopoly on debasing the currency without competition from criminals and evil Middle Eastern religious-fanatic dictators."

"Does that mean there are no weapons of mass destruction buried in the foothills?" Harlan said.

"Shut up," Major Karne said.

"Why did they make up a bunch of shit about the dear leader? Why didn't they just tell the truth about why we're here?"

"They don't dare allow any doubt about the funny money they're printing," Shimon said, "its only real value comes from people's confidence in it. You're supposed to work hard producing shit in exchange for these colorful pieces of intrinsically-worthless fiat-currency bullshit pieces of paper. It's a law of economics—bad money drives out good. They need the 'good' to be worth something to pay for their private jets and Beverly Hills mansions and abortions for their supermodel mistresses."

"I thought I was the cynical one," Karne said.

"As long as it's an accepted medium of exchange," Harlan said, "and everyone agrees that one dollar is worth one chicken as a random example, then it's a great means of storing value and facilitating trade so we don't have to carry chickens around in our back pockets to support a barter economy."

"It works fine in theory," Shimon said, "but you can't trust the politicians and bankers with the printing presses. Those fucking, blood-sucking weasels will always twist things to their benefit—no one would care if they helped themselves to a few bucks from the cash register now and then, but they always push too far—pressing the withdrawal button on the global, metaphysical ATM as fast as they can until the system breaks down. They help themselves to one more trivial billion or one more trivial trillion, in effect raping and pillaging the economy until they destroy the productive class. It always ends with war and despair. Soup lines and tent cities. Every fucking time."

Major Karne looked at the team with wonder. "That's enough of this phony intellectual nonsense," she said. "Counterfeiting five-thousand dollar bills is bad juju…"

"Unless it's the government doing it," Harlan interrupted.

"…stop it! We follow orders and that's all we need to know. We're paid to *do*, not to think. Our job is to find the presses and destroy them. We're not going to turn this mission into a college economic-philosophy class. We're going to get out there and do our goddamned jobs. That's all there is to it. I'm afraid to ask—but are there any questions?"

Jimmy raised his hand and waved the counterfeit five-thousand dollar bill. "Can I keep this one?" he said.

Major Karne plucked it from his fingers.

"No," she said. "Now get out of here—and stay sober, we might make a run later this afternoon."

The team went downstairs for lunch. They had a favorite table by a window that looked out into a private courtyard—the courtyard was filled with potted palms and a couple of bedraggled lemon trees.

The hotel kitchen made a decent hamburger served on a hard roll—with a meat patty made from ground lamb or goat and flavored with garlic and onion and odd metallic-tasting spices. It was nothing like home, but was edible when washed down with cold bottles of watery Red Star beer.

"We been in this country for ten years," Jimmy said, "and just now get the real reason?"

"Karne is full of shit," Harlan said. "I wouldn't believe her if she said dog vomit tasted bad—I'd want a big spoonful to see for myself."

"Knock that off while I'm eating," Shimon said. "It's hard enough to choke down this dog-sausage—I don't need you guys turning my stomach."

With a grimace on his face, Jimmy pushed his plate away.

"You really think they grind up dogs in this?" he said.

"You see any stray dogs on the street?" Harlan said. "What do you think?"

"Moslem cultures don't like dogs," Curtis said. "They're considered unclean. That's why you don't see many dogs around here. They certainly wouldn't dream of eating one, or a pig either, for that matter."

Harlan reached across the table and pulled over Jimmy's plate to get at his dried figs.

"That don't mean," Harlan said, while chewing a fig, "they wouldn't grind up a dog to insult the foreign devils invading their country. We being the foreign devils, by the way. So, does this mean you're speaking to us again, your Excellency?"

"No," Curtis said. "I'm speaking to them, not you. I still hate your stinking guts."

"Just because you hate me doesn't mean we can't be friends," Harlan said.

"Go fuck yourself," Curtis replied. "And stop talking to me."

"Why won't Major Karne let us shave and take a shower?" Jimmy asked. "I'm starting to ferment in this infernal heat."

"That's obvious, ain't it?' Harlan said. "She wants us to blend in better. You watch—she'll make us wear sandals and caftans and those weird wool hats."

"If she wants us to blend in," Jimmy said, "she should make us wear dirty, five-year-old Nike shoes, rat-eaten Aerospatiale t-shirts and make us hang around street corners smoking cigarettes and doing nothing. It still wouldn't do any good—we stand out around here like flying nuns at a Mormon picnic."

"I got an e-mail from a guy named Duncan," Shimon said. "Duncan Fielder."

He stared at the other guys expectantly.

"Well," Harlan said. "Is there more to this story or are you simply sharing your GoGoBuddy best-friends-forever list?"

Shimon looked offended. "By my count," he said, "Karne ran at least five other in-country covert teams. Most of the guys in the teams are dead. Duncan is one of the few that made it home alive. If you're uninterested in what he has to say, I could stop wasting your time and go upstairs and take a refreshing nap."

"We apologize for being—a little skeptical," Curtis said. "Please, we're very, very interested in what this *Duncan Fielder* has to say."

Shimon leaned back in his seat and took a sip of beer.

"First of all, she's not a Major, or anything really. She's never been in the military. And, Karne is her married name—and regardless of the dick-dance she has going with her fuck-buddy Lyle, she's still married, believe it or not. You won't believe the name she was born with. Go ahead, guess. You'll never figure it out."

"She's a Kennedy?" Jimmy said.

"I'm not playing this stupid guessing-game," Curtis said. "Is she a Biden?"

"She's a Bush," Harlan said.

A crestfallen look washed across Shimon's face. "Have you been reading my e-mail?"

"She has a hatchet-face like a Bush, Harlan said. "In twenty years, she'll look like Grandma Barbara—wife of the first Bush president. It was just a lucky guess. Sorry."

"Well," Shimon said, "that's right. She's a cousin linked through Prescott—not a blood relative to Barbara, so you got there through the wrong train of thought, but your answer is correct."

"Story of my life," Harlan muttered.

"I don't think this is any surprise to any of us, but she's a spook—a well-connected, untouchable Foggy Bottom ghost—a wildcard, black-ops free-agent."

"A double-aught agent with a license to kill?" Jimmy said.

"You can scoff, but I'm serious. She's wired in. She's connected."

"A Bush, huh?" Jimmy said. "Well, I still want to see her tits, but not as much as I did. That kind of kills the buzz a bit."

"This calls for another Red Star," Curtis said. He raised his hand and flagged down a waiter.

Sura 022, Verse 39. To those against whom war is made, permission is given to fight because they are wronged. Allah is their most-powerful ally.

Book Two—Chapter Ten

Khostarak

CURTIS ORDERED THREE beers for the table. Harlan raised an index finger to make sure he got one too.

"Karne said we should stay sober," Shimon said.

"*Now* we're going to start doing everything she tells us to do?" Curtis said.

"That's the Curtis we know and love," Harlan said. "Welcome back, brother."

"Fuck you." Curtis said. "I'm still mad at you and we're still not speaking and you can buy your own goddamned beer."

"You're one stubborn boy," Harlan said. "Can we get back to the Duncan e-mail?"

"Right," Shimon said. "Duncan's team was six pulled out of a Ranger battalion—and he's the only one that made it home—minus three fingers on his left hand and with a bullet still lodged in his neck. Remember the King of Clubs? Mohammed Al-Renfro Kamiil? It was Duncan's version of Karne's team that took him down. They plowed through a hundred and seven militants in a warehouse by the river."

"A hundred and seven dead martyrs," Curtis commented.

"Right," Shimon continued. "The river ran red that day."

"Billy Ray Cyrus had a big hit with the song written about it," Harlan said. "The bloody red river of Khostarak," he sang.

"Don't quit the day job, kid," Curtis said.

"I knew it, you *are* speaking to me now," Harlan said.

"Go fuck yourself."

"Can I continue without this becoming a country and western concert?" Shimon said. "You're not going to believe this next part. The nuke[10] the Israelis used on the Golden Quran out in the desert in Iran? It was her idea."

"Bullshit," Jimmy said.

"Not only that, but they let her press the red button in Tel Aviv."

"It wasn't a red button," Harlan said, "it was a pickle switch—a toggle switch."

"That's not the point," Shimon said. "She dreamed up the idea, sold the Israelis on it and they let her launch the missile."

"I don't believe it, not for a New York minute," Jimmy said.

Curtis drained his beer. "When I see her, I'm going to ask her," he said. "Let's get to the end of Duncan's e-mail. What else did he say? Did she put the bomb in Willie Kennedy's car,

---

[10] Mossad stole a priceless a 16th century gold and jewel-encrusted Qu'ran from The Islamic History Museum in Cairo. The holy book was put on a pedestal in a remote section of the Iranian desert. They challenged Allah to protect the holy book if He could, and then launched a tactical nuke which exploded in the air and vaporized the book—and turned nearly a square mile of desert into a glassy mirror. There were violent riots around the world—twelve-thousand people died the following week—over five-hundred of them in the United States. However, the demonstration of power led to peaceful overtures by a few radical clerics and directly to more-open societies in Egypt, Libya, and Malaysia. To describe this as a controversial event in human history would be an understatement.

fire the missile that took down Pan Pacific Airways flight 922 and cause the Tokyo earthquake that killed all of those little yellow Japanese people?"

"No, but he said, if we get a chance, we should shoot her in the head. Twice to be sure. Otherwise, he thinks we'll all die out here. She's an expert at saving her own ass, but her teams have a lot of bad luck—or worse. Maybe she likes putting her men in impossible situations and doesn't care if they get shot to pieces."

"Christ on a southern cross," Harlan said. "Here comes that muscle-bound asshole. Lyle."

To Harlan's horror, Curtis got up and waved. "Come join us, Lyle, my man." He threw an arm around him and gave him a vigorous man-hug, then moved his chair and grabbed a spare one from an adjoining table. "Sit down—take a load off. Have a beer."

Lyle looked suspicious. "You guys drunk already?" He peered at his watch. "It's not even one o'clock yet."

"A few beers aren't going to make us drunk—not in this heat. Sit! We're shooting the breeze. Doing some male bonding—telling war stories. Tell us about yourself, Lyle. Where you from? Originally, that is. Where'd your snake egg hatch?"

"Bullshit. You guys hate me for being all up in Major Karne's female parts and I don't blame you. The previous dude, Lieutenant Gibson—well, I wasn't over-filled with sorrow when he took an explosive round in the belly. I get it. I've shot my love-juice into the promised land and sucked tits that taste like honeydew and it's as good as it gets. You guys will never get any of that, except a palmful when you're jerking off and thinking about me riding the slippery gash of heavenly glory. So, you guys fuck off and let me get my hummus and iced tea and enjoy a quiet lunch by myself in good company."

"Sit down," Curtis growled, "and talk to us for a minute or I'll shoot you in the knee, right here and right now."

Lyle looked down at Curtis's face for a moment.

"I don't think you got the spine to do it," Lyle said. "I think you're a mouthful of big-college words and that's all, coonboy."

Harlan showed the barrel of his Colt .45 under the table. "And I'll shoot the other knee," he said.

Lyle scratched his chin, and then laughed. He sat down at the table.

"Well, fuck me ragged, don't we have a fine batch of fresh meat? One thing about Karne, she has a keen eye for raw talent. The help don't last too long, but that's something you smart boys figured out already, ain't it? Fine. Ask your questions. When we're done, I'm going to get my lunch and eat by myself, like I always do. If you want to shoot me, then go right ahead, but make sure I'm stone cold dead, or I swear by my holy mother's ghost, I'll eat your livers with some salt and a little olive oil, and I'm talking about each and every one of you limp-dick cocksucker motherfuckers."

"Curtis laughed. "Maybe I'm not the only one with a mouth for big words. How long you been with Karne?"

"As a lover or on her team? She picked me out of a Navy Seal team almost three years ago and we retired a lot of enemy combatants since then. I've been rotor-rooting her plumbing for just over a year. In anticipation of your next question, she's more of a moaner than a screamer, but I've heard both come out of her when I push the buttons right-good."

"What's her original last name?"

Lyle stared at Curtis for a moment. "She's one of the Bush clan—a shirt-tail relative to the three presidents. Something tells me you already knew that, so what are you asking me for?"

Curtis shrugged. "Just to see if you'd lie about it. We heard a rumor—she pressed the button to launch the missile that vaporized the Golden Qu'ran?"

With a fingernail, Lyle scratched at a bit of dried food on the table.

"She told me it was the 'enter' key on a computer

keyboard—five people gathered around and pressed it at the same time. The Israeli president and the commanding officer of the missile command and I don't remember who the other two were. I wasn't there, but I believe the story the way she tells it. She also said it wasn't really a nuke, but I don't know about that. You guys don't know this yet, I mean really know it, but she's a great warrior—and school kids will be telling her story for generations after she wins this war. You were granted a great honor when she picked you guys. I'm dead serious about this. She will make history, hell, she already has—I know it with everything inside me. It's as real a fact as this table." He rapped his fist on the table's surface. He stood. "Now, please excuse me. I worked up an appetite upside-down and inside-out with Karne this morning—and my belly is empty."

"One last question, soldier," Curtis said.

"What?"

"What's Karne's first name?"

Lyle looked at Curtis, then at Harlan. "Call her Patty. Enough of this shit, you're wasting my time," he said.

He turned and walked away.

Harlan uncocked his .45 and slipped it back under his shirt.

Once Lyle was out of earshot, Shimon spoke first.

"Why didn't you ask me her first name? I can tell you."

Curtis shrugged and reached for a fresh beer. "I was jerking him around. I should have asked him a more intelligent question, but I couldn't think of one."

"It's Pat—Patricia. She hates being called Patty—she'd probably shoot you."

"Whatever," Curtis said.

Harlan leaned over the table and grabbed a beer. "Guys, listen up, I want to ask you something. Suppose we believed his line of bullshit and we did have a chance to make a real difference in this war. I think I'd go for it. What do you think?"

"What are you asking?" Jimmy said while lighting a cigar.

"It's simple enough. You in or out for turning the volume

knob to eleven?" Harlan said.

Jimmy leaned back in his chair—so far back he seemed in danger of falling over backwards. He blew a cloud of smoke at the ceiling. "In," he said.

"If you guys are in, I'm in," Shimon said.

"Curtis? What do you say, my black-African brother?"

"I'm still not talking to you, you rat-fucking cockroach," Curtis said.

Harlan grinned and gestured to Curtis with his beer.

"Ah, I knew I could count on you," he said.

"When do we get to find out why Curt is so angry?" Jimmy asked.

"It's a bit difficult to explain," Harlan said.

Sura 22, Verse 45. How many sinful townships have we destroyed, so, to this day, they lie in ruins? And, how many wells lie deserted and how many lofty palace towers lie abandoned?

Book Two—Chapter Eleven

Khostarak

LYLE, AFTER AN hour of reading a three-week-old edition of the New York Times Review of Books, finished scooping the last of his hummus on flatbread, tossed it in his mouth and drained his third iced tea. After signing the bill, he pushed his chair back and belched.

He called across the room.

"You ladies coming?"

Harlan and Jimmy were playing cribbage using a worn-out board with broken pieces of toothpicks for markers and cards so ancient and floppy they were nearly impossible to shuffle.

"Thank God," Jimmy said. "I can't beat this guy."

"We'll be up in a minute," Shimon said.

"What's up?"

"I still have passwords for the personnel system. We don't exist anymore."

"Hold on," Curtis said "What?"

"All the GIs have a status in the personnel database. You

know—active, on leave, sick, injured, AWOL, what-have-you. For every status, there is a code. We're code ninety-nine."

"What does that mean?" Harlan said.

"It means we're off the books."

"That's what Karne said already," Jimmy commented, "we're on a special, indefinite reassignment working for a secret group of the Department of Defense. I don't see the problem."

"No, the temporary duty assignment is code twenty-three. Twenty-four is assigned to an alternate service unit. Ninety-nine is missing—presumed dead, no rescue scenario. Written off—don't bother looking. She checked us into this hotel under fake names. We could disappear and no one would care. No one would come after us. Why would they? We're already dead. I don't like this."

"It does give one pause," Harlan said. "Should we talk to Patty about it?"

Curtis slowly shook his head. *No.*

"Yeah," Shimon said. "I agree."

"I don't want to be a ninety-nine," Jimmy said.

"Me either," Curtis agreed.

"I can see it working for us or against us," Harlan said. "Let's ride it out and see what happens."

"We're ninety-niners," Jimmy said slowly as if testing it on his tongue. He found the words sour.

Slowly, the team got up and headed to the creaky elevator.

Major Karne thumb-tacked a series of satellite photographs of a run-down brick and wattle house in a ramshackle neighborhood. She pointed at the streets and a trail through a field at the back of the house.

"You're coming in from both sides right after the evening prayers—Lyle and I will cover the back," Major Karne said. "The GPS will feed you driving instructions and show you where to park and wait for my command. We don't expect anything from this customer interaction; though our information tells us they have some of the counterfeit bills—we don't expect them to know anything about the printing location. But, we don't have any other leads at this moment. Lyle and I will run interrogation on the survivors if there are any. I want to make sure you know what to expect out there. We are not tied to restrictions on aggressive interrogation. We go with our best judgment based on the field situation. We're not messing around. These are known hostiles. Bad guys. Here's the way we roll—we shoot first and if there's anyone left alive, we ask questions later. Got it?"

"If they walk, they talk," Lyle said.

"So, we torture them and make them talk," Shimon said.

"We use aggressive interrogation techniques unrestricted by international law, congressional oversight rules and treaty conventions."

Shimon raised his hand. "That's what I said, we torture the prisoners, right?"

Navigating the living room furniture, Karne walked up to Shimon and stood directly in front of him.

"I'm not going to argue semantics with you, Corporal Shimon, but, no, we don't torture prisoners. We use aggressive interrogation techniques guided by the field situation. Perhaps there's an elastic line between the two—but we make the judgment call based on the field situation. Are there any other stupid questions? No? Then let's hit it."

Curtis insisted on riding with Shimon. Harlan shrugged and waved Jimmy into the passenger seat of their assigned Pathfinder—parked under the hotel. Shimon and Curtis piled into the adjacent Pathfinder. These vehicles were newer—clean and unscarred. They would stand out vividly on the streets compared to the battered truck-wreck Lyle and Major Karne drove.

"What's the sit-rep between you and Harlan?" Shimon said.

"It's kind of hard to explain," Curtis said. "He has a

deranged idea that I should work with the tribal leaders—
pretend I'm the second coming of some imaginary Islamic
legend. It's bizarre and weird and stupid."

"You're right, it does sound stupid."

"I really don't want to talk about it."

"I notice you haven't shaved off the beard."

Curtis turned his head and looked at Shimon. "I could easily
be angry with you too," he said.

Shimon raised both hands in supplication. "No, that's okay.
I'm just asking. Things are uncomfortable in the house when
mom and dad are fighting, that's all. If there's anything we need
to know, you'll speak up, I know you will, but you have to
admit it, the situation looks loco-loony-tunes-crazy from an
outside point of view. We're bound to be curious—you gotta
figure on that. You and Harlan can get all tied up in knots; I
don't feel any burning need to be in the middle and neither
does Jimmy."

"I want to plant my boot so deep up Harlan's ass that he has
the taste of leather on his tongue, but I won't let it affect the
job. Okay?"

"Okay," Shimon said.

When they emerged in waning sunlight from under the
hotel, the GPS display refreshed and zeroed in on their location.

Turn left, it said.

"Jimmy was talking to Harlan—he told him a crazy story
about a pretty girl…"

"Yeah, I met her," Curtis said. "Think of someone the
diametric opposite of Major Karne and you'll be headed in the
right direction."

"I wouldn't mind getting me one of those."

"Wouldn't we all," Curtis said. "Drive."

The neighborhood did not exactly look like the satellite photos.
The houses were two and three stories tall with repair shops
and miscellaneous open-air stores on the ground floors

displaying electronic equipment—prepaid cell phones, pirated DVDs, flatscreen monitors and old computers.

As the two Pathfinders approached each other and stopped about a block apart, there was bustle on the street—the shopkeepers locked up their roll-down doors and the shoppers slipped away down side streets and alleys. In thirty seconds, the moderately-busy commercial scene became deserted and abandoned.

"We might just as well paint targets on our foreheads," Shimon said, "or hell, why don't we save the hajjis the trouble and shoot ourselves."

Curtis checked the clip on his recoilless fifty-caliber chain gun. "You first," he said with a grin.

He pulled on his smart armor and wriggled his shoulders to settle the stiff fabric on his arms and across his back, then pulled the Velcro straps tight across his chest and around his neck. He pulled on his helmet and adjusted the chin strap. The smart armor calculated the speed and trajectory of incoming rounds and adjusted for the optimum deflection angle. It wasn't much good for a perfect ninety-degree assault vector, but they always tried to stand at an angle—it might look funny when they moved in a sideways shuffle, but they didn't care. Given a little help, the armor did an amazing job.

"Karne says armoring up is optional—we don't have to if we don't want to."

"She doesn't give a shit whether we're shot to pieces, but I do."

After a moment's reflection, Shimon also pulled on his armor. His rifle was a much lighter gun than Curtis's, a 4mm, high-velocity pin gun with computerized autosights. The stubby body was made with shiny carbon fiber laminates—it looked like a toy.

Karne's disembodied voice came through the Pathfinder's communicator.

"Pull up front and come in through the main entrance.

Flush the insurgents our way."

Curtis gestured to Jimmy and Harlan that he and Shimon would go in. Harlan and Jimmy spread out along the crumbling brick wall to cover the front door.

The massive wrought-iron gate could not be the main entrance to the house—it was locked with loops of fat chain and a shiny carbon-steel lock. Shimon cut through the lock in two seconds with a portable plasma cutter carried under a flap on his camo pants.

Curtis used a handheld scanner to search for explosive devices under the trash in the front yard. There was a small shaped-charge in a chunk of concrete—covered with rusty-nail shrapnel—on the left side of the brick-paved walkway. Curtis lit it up with a laser pointer—Shimon unfolded a small thermal blanket and gently tossed it over the bomb. When he stepped back, Curtis pressed buttons on a touchscreen controller and melted the bomb into a useless, red-glowing slag.

It was surprising, but there was still no sign of movement from inside the house—no flick of curtains and no sounds of inhabitants running around preparing for assault. Curtis and Shimon turned their backs and lay flat on the ground. When they were settled, Harlan and Jimmy fired flash-bang cartridges through the front windows—it was as if a nuclear bomb went off inside—the windows blew out and the house seemed filled with blinding sunlight for a fraction of a second. Curtis and Shimon got up and kicked their way through the front door.

They quickly checked all of the downstairs rooms, but the house was deserted. They ascended the stairs to the second floor. At the top, Harlan waved his hand to stop Curtis. He made a cutting motion—there was something in the doorway.

"Hand me up a broom or something," Harlan whispered.

Jimmy went to the kitchen and found a dust-mop. They handed it up the stairway hand-to-hand.

Harlan waved the handle in the doorway and there was a gleaming flash. In slow motion, a massive heavy blade embedded itself in the wall with a loud clunk.

Harlan peeked through the doorway, then climbed the remaining few stairs into the room. They searched the dark chambers.

In a top floor bedroom closet, Jimmy found two heavy bricks of plastic-wrapped currency. He tucked the bundles under his arm.

Once they'd inspected all the rooms, they slowly, with rifles held ready, walked out through the backdoor, down a short stretch of alley and into the center of the field where Lyle casually pointed his rotorgun in the general direction of four young men on their knees in the patch of dusty weeds.

Major Karne talked in Arabic with a very short, pudgy local who wore an elaborate wool hat and an off-white suit. It appeared as if he'd been doing car repairs in the suit—it was smudged with streaky black grease and dirt. His knitted necktie was tied loosely around his neck. He lifted the chins of the prisoners one-by-one and looked at their faces. The last one was nearly a boy, maybe thirteen, but no older. The rotund man, chattering rapid-fire, scolded the boy and hauled him to his feet. He gestured to Lyle and Lyle, with his heavy gun in the crook of his elbow, cut off the boy's flexcuffs with a large knife.

The round man kicked the boy in the seat of the pants; the kid raced off and in thirty seconds, was gone. The round man exchanged a ritual hug with Major Karne and slowly walked off, following the boy's trail.

Harlan put his head next to Curtis's.

"How much of that did you catch?"

"The kid is a police commander's sister's nephew?"

"Yeah, something like that," Harlan said. "Are we speaking now? Friends?"

"Not yet," Curtis replied.

Around them, as the sun set in the west, lights in the scattered houses began to come on. Around the field, the cautious heads of spectators peeked through window curtains and from around building walls.

"Good job, guys," Karne said. "They cleared out through the back door as soon as you guys rolled into view."

"You might have let us know," Harlan complained.

Karne shrugged. "I wanted to make sure the house was secure," she said. "We're taking these three to a remote location for questioning. The GPS will talk you in."

Jimmy dropped the heavy bundles of cash at Karne's feet. "What do we do with these?" he said.

She shrugged. "Bring them along," she said.

She turned and Lyle herded the young men toward their battered SUV. Harlan's team, a little more at ease this time, but still alert, walked back through the house to their vehicles.

When Harlan got to his Pathfinder, he found someone had drawn the capital 'A' anarchy symbol in dust on the driver's side door. He thought a second about wiping it off, but decided to leave it be.

They drove to the northwest for nearly an hour. The paved roads gave way to gravel, then to dirt, then to rutty tracks over raw earth that tested the four-wheel-drive and high clearance of the Pathfinders. Eventually, they stopped on the edge of a dry ravine—the only illumination was starlight and the SUV headlights.

Lyle hauled the prisoners out and arranged them on the edge of the gulch. He covered their eyes with duct tape wrapped all the way around their heads. With his wicked-sharp knife, he nicked their chins, one-by-one, until all three stood with blood dripping from their faces.

To Harlan, he said, "I like to mark them in case I ever see them again."

"You are truly a scholar and a gentleman—a credit to western civilization," Harlan commented.

Major Karne inspected the prisoners and pointed at the last one—Lyle wrapped another layer on duct tape on the man's head. She turned to Harlan.

"As I understand it, you speak some Arabic?"

"Some," Harlan said.

"And the other guys?"

Harlan shrugged. "They're hopeless."

Major Karne walked closer—until her face was six inches from Harlan's.

"Even Curtis? I get the sense he understands more than he lets on."

"He has trouble-enough speaking English. He can order a bottle of wine and find a toilet—otherwise you'd get more out of talking to a monkey."

"Are all hicks from upcountry Arkansas such ignorant racist stone age throwbacks?"

"No, some of my folk don't really care much for niggers. Me? I'm a little more open-minded. I wait until the man proves himself to be a worthless piece of shit before I judge him wanting."

"I don't think I understand the full nature of your relationship with Curtis—sometimes I think your racist bullshit is a bit of political theater—a smokescreen you funny guys find useful for some twist-fuck reason. In the end, the joke will not be on me, get it? You'll be the punchline. I don't advise you to underestimate me. We clear?"

"You like to hear yourself talk, don't you, Major?"

She raised her eyebrows and looked into his brown eyes, then removed her sidearm and clicked off the safety. She turned and shot the closest prisoner in the head. He collapsed over the edge of the ravine—his twitching body came to rest ten yards down the slope, near the bottom.

"Test me all you like, Sergeant," she said. "I softened them up, so let's see what you can get out of them, tough guy."

Harlan slipped his hand under his flak jacket and pulled out his .45. He pressed the weapon against the next man's head. The man was terrified, shaking and praying in a soft voice. Harlan pulled the trigger. The man jerked back and flew over the edge.

"He didn't know anything," Harlan said.

Major Karne looked pissed off, but clenched her jaw and did not speak.

Curtis turned away in disgust.

Harlan sidled to the remaining prisoner and spoke in halting, Arabic.

"I offer greetings and good wishes to you and your family in the name of the holy one, Allah."

After a few seconds of silence, the man spoke.

"God is great," he said.

Harlan searched for words. "The only thing we care about is the money—where it is printed and who is printing it. For any information you offer, we will be most grateful and will reward you in this life while Allah rewards you in the next."

"I don't know anything," the man said.

"I know you don't know anything, but it is my fond hope and desire that you might know someone who knows something so your life might be spared and you earn a great and generous cash reward."

The man, with tears streaming down his face, said a name.

Taleb al Hansaal Buhlibahn.

Harlan repeated it and the terrified man nodded. *Yes.*

"If we wanted to have tea—share a hookah and friendly conversation with brother Buhlibahn, where might we find him?"

The conversation went on for a few minutes until Harlan was satisfied, then he waved his hand to Shimon.

Shimon approached with one of the bundles of cash. Harlan took it and pressed it into the prisoner's arms.

"Go with God, my friend," Harlan said—then he pushed the man over the side. The prisoner slid to the bottom with an accompanying cascade of gravel and dust.

After a few seconds of absorbing the scene, they huddled by Karne's SUV. The air was crisp and cold because the afternoon heat dissipated quickly after the sun went down.

"Let him go?" Lyle said.

"If he can find his way out of here," Harlan said, "with the cash—barefoot, blindfolded and flex-cuffed, then he deserves a break." To Shimon, he said, "The bundle tracker is online?"

"Five bars—all green," Shimon replied.

"We're tracking the bundle, so if he does get out of here, we'll know where he goes."

"You good with all this?" Lyle asked Major Karne.

"I got to where I am today by delegating authority when possible. Harlan's plan is worth a shot. They'll find the RF tag eventually, but we might learn something about its travels in the meantime. Yeah, we're good—this encounter was productive-enough." She looked at Harlan with focused intensity. "I think we set a proper foundation for the remainder of our relationship."

"Fine," Lyle said. "Let's roll back to the bright lights. My belly thinks it's dinner time."

Jimmy walked toward Harlan's SUV, but Curtis tapped him on the arm and pointed to Shimon. Jimmy cocked his head in curiosity, but turned to jump in Shimon's Pathfinder.

Curtis didn't speak until they were a few miles down the road back to the city.

"I don't think you should have plugged that hajji."

"Maybe not. I guess I was still pissed off because of the scimitar thing. They know our body armor has trouble with low-velocity, high-mass things with razor-sharp edges. They were, all of them, camel-cock sucking scum or they wouldn't set boobytraps like that to hack open our bellies and leave us dying with our guts hanging out. Look, I never made any secret about it, I joined the Army because I wanted to kill me some fucking brown-skinned, medieval sandpipers. One day, it will be my turn and they'll hang my flayed body over a bridge, but until then? I'm taking as many with me as I can. We've talked about this. We will not win this war if we play by effete, wussy western rules. They respect power—a strong man willing to swim through a river of blood if that's what it takes. Fuck them and fuck you if you don't like it."

"All I'm saying is—you don't want to get in a mano-y-mano pissing match with Karne. Head to head? She'll beat you silly."

"I get your point," Harlan said. "When she shot that kid, I almost shit a paver. I needed to make a point and I didn't think about it, I went with my gut instinct. Too bad for the hajji, but they're expendable as far as I'm concerned. Ninety-niners, each and every one of them—and us too. That's the sad reality of the world. So, we're talking now. We good?"

"I think so, you white-trash, trailer-park son-of-a-syphilitic bitch."

"What about the thing with Telleh's grandfather?"

"I don't want to talk about that yet," Curtis said.

Yet, Harlan thought with a surge of elation.

Yet.

Sura 22, Verse 51. To those who thwart our message—they shall be inmates of the flaming fires of hell.

Book Two—Chapter Twelve

Khostarak

CURTIS AND HARLAN began spending all of their free time at a nearly-microscopic mosque. They met near a market in an abandoned warehouse with a bombed out roof, transferred to a Mercedes panel van and got out in a garage so small, the van barely fit in it. From there, they could open the van's sliding door and enter the mosque without being seen.

Inside, Curtis studied selected passages of the Qu'ran and sahih Hadith and practiced pronouncing the foreign words properly. The old man hit him with a stick once to correct an egregious pronunciation, but Curtis grabbed the stick, broke it in four pieces and tossed it aside—and that was the end of that form of the old man's guidance. Daily, the old man still pulled on Curtis's chin-beard as if that would make it grow faster.

After a few days, Curtis stood behind a lectern and practiced projecting the words with force and authority—and he got better at it.

He wouldn't admit it out loud, but he liked it.

It felt good.

The week passed slowly.

The money-pack found its way out of the desert. Shimon found it amusing to mark its progress—it was obvious the man was lost in the wilderness for a while, then he hitched a ride on a something slow, like a horse-drawn wagon, then a car, and then the packet stopped moving for a while in a house—where it sat for a week before being moved again.

In the meantime, Shimon and Karne studied the information they could find on Buhlibahn—he was a former officer in the Republican Guard and spent a few years in prison, but was released. Though lurid, horrifying rumors about his role in the dear leader's military police were abundant, there was no evidence against him and no witnesses stepped forward to testify about his crimes. It was an easy story to read between the lines, it was a story as old as human nature.

Money changed hands.

Witnesses either shut their mouths or disappeared.

It takes a few years, but a very bad guy walks.

They gathered information about Buhlibahn and watched the location of the money-pack, but they did not have a plan. So, they waited for inspiration.

Major Karne played with Shimon's affection. Sometimes, when he came up with an interesting fact from his deep-subsurface interweb data-diving or drew an interesting conclusion from scattered, disparate information, she would run a finger up his arm or touch his thigh, but it was obvious she really cared about Harlan and Curtis—no matter what else she and Shimon talked about, the conversation always ended up back on the two men and their odd-couple relationship.

Jimmy struck up a relationship with a waitress at the hotel restaurant; she was a loud, brassy, red-headed woman from Australia about six inches taller and forty pounds heavier than him. Her name was Raquel Balboa, but everyone called her Rocky.

On Saturday, the money-packet moved. On a flatscreen

terminal, Shimon watched its progress as it wound around the city streets. It landed at an old-city location, where it sat for a half-hour, before the RF tag signal—a blinking red dot on Shimon's computer screen—abruptly disappeared.

Tandiin Emergency Medical Center.

The satellite array could detect the altitude. Third floor.

Gotcha, Shimon whispered to himself.

When the assembly call came, Harlan was performing a magic trick with an antique silver dollar and a handkerchief for an audience of a dozen little kids, who watched in fascination as the dollar appeared behind this ear and that ear and disappeared into thin air with a wave of a hand.

Across the room, Curtis sat head-to-head with the old man, going over holy passages again and again.

Harlan flipped the coin in the air, but it did not come down. Waving his hands in mock panic, he pretended to look for it—then it appeared in the hand of a gaunt little girl with a sad expression on her dirty face.

Perhaps the dollar is good for a decent meal, Harlan hoped. It looks like she needs it.

He met Curtis at the van; they piled in and the driver took them back to Harlan's little Toyota. In the Toyota, the dashboard communicator yapped. It was Lyle's tinny voice.

Harlan made a talking expression with his hands—blah, blah, blah.

"Mama's getting impatient—are you guys going to check in for our exciting tour of the city? Guys? Do we have to wait until Curtis comes in your ass before it's convenient for you to check in?"

Harlan pressed the talk button.

"Don't be so jealous, Lyley. Curtis will service you when it's your turn. He's got enough jizz in him for everyone."

The next voice was Major Karne's.

"I'm glad to hear you homos are saving us some spunk, but

even while enjoying nonstop gay sex parties, you're supposed to keep your ears on. Come to the hotel, grab your Pathfinder, and get your dick-sprung asses to the target location," she said. "Pronto, if not sooner."

Before the connection was broken, they heard her muttering. "Goddamned millennial slackers," she said.

Harlan and Curtis grinned at each other in delight for irritating the Major.

The bottom floor of the Tandiin Emergency Medical Center was a pharmacy, but not a prosperous one. Inside, the shelves were nearly barren. A clerk, with a long beard wearing a filthy-looking cotton turban sat behind the counter on a stool watching a soccer match on a tiny, flickering flatscreen TV set. A hanging sign said the place was open, but no one appeared to go in—apparently uninterested in hemorrhoid suppositories on sale two for one.

Curtis drove the Pathfinder.

"Let's roll around back and see if we can catch anyone scurrying out the backdoor," Harlan said.

Curtis angled the SUV into the entrance to the narrow alley. It was lined with black garbage bags. Curtis took a quick look and then backed out.

"No way I'm driving in there before its scanned," he said. "Besides, I think these guys split the instant they saw the RF tag. I'll bet we don't find anything upstairs except empty falafel containers and porno magazines."

"And cigarette butts—lots of cigarette butts."

Parking was nonexistent, so Harlan tapped a knuckle on the driver's side glass of a parked motorist. The driver argued his case vehemently, but Harlan showed him his .45 and the driver, still cursing, eventually moved out. With a few back-and-forths, Curtis crammed the SUV in the empty space. They adjusted their body armor and walked to the pharmacy. The clerk, flex-cuffed and bleeding from a ragged gash on his head was face-down on the dirty floor, cursing.

"This is what happens when you're late to a party," Curtis commented. "You miss half the fun."

They walked up two flights of crude concrete stairs and found the team assembled and ready to break through the door.

"Good of you faggots to find time in your busy schedule to join us," Lyle said.

He raised a boot to kick down the door.

Shimon held up a hand to stop him.

"Hold on. There's something that bothers me. If I was trying to fry an RF tag in a bundle of cash, I'd toss it in a microwave oven and press the popcorn button. As the insurgents unpacked the money and uncovered the tag, the bit-error-rate would improve and then, as the tag melted down, it would transmit a few bad packets before dying completely. I looked over the raw datastream and that's not how it happened. The tag switched off like a light, bang, no more. It reeks of something more sophisticated—like Russian RF-sniffing technology or something. I think we should run in a mobile sensor, scan for surprise packages they might have left us, then go in light."

"No," Jimmy said. "I knew it would come to this. Shit."

Jimmy was the smallest member of the team. When going in light, it meant he would get undressed, apply sensor-invisible smart-skin and be the one to explore.

"Get nekkid," Harlan told him.

"You guys are insane," Lyle said. "This is a lot of speculation—I'm willing to take the chance. Russians? I don't see how they play in this."

Major Karne put a hand on his arm. "Let them run this round their way. We'll mock their useless caution later."

Jimmy repeated himself. "Shit."

He began taking off his clothes.

Shimon cut a small hole in the corner of the door with his plasma cutter, then pulled a small bundle from a flap-pocket of his flak jacket and unwrapped a three-wheeled contraption.

"You're one of my favorites, aren't you sweetie," Shimon said. He slipped the mouse-like robot-sensor unit through the hole and pressed a series of buttons on his touchscreen controller.

"Where do you get these fancy toys?" Major Karne said.

"They're easy to make from kits I order online. They're really smart and the sensors are getting really good. You can program them with new hyper-aware code modules or teach them by manipulating their omni-aware servos. They learn and they can understand good-bad fuzzy context-sensitive emotional programming paradigms…"

"That's enough, Shimon," Harlan said. "Focus on scanning the rooms for now." To Karne, he said, "He can go on and on all day about this stuff. This is not the right time for a robotics class."

Jimmy was nude—his stubby cock was mostly hidden in a red bush of pubic hair. Karne openly inspected him.

"I'll give you a closer look later," Jimmy said. "It's big enough to get the job done, don't worry about that."

He held up his arms and turned while Shimon sprayed him with a silvery mist.

"The next person on our team better be smaller than me," Jimmy complained. "I'm tired of this. The smart-skin stinks like skunk cabbage and burns like nettles."

Shimon rotated his index finger so Jimmy would spin one more time—when the final inspection was done, Shimon nodded.

"You're ready," Shimon said, before returning his attention to his flatscreen controller unit. "We'd be dead had you kicked down that door," he said to Lyle. He walked to a large patterned-glass window. "We can go in this way."

He ran the plasma cutter around the edges and eased out the glass, which he carefully leaned against the back wall. Jimmy eased through the opening, taking care not to disturb the thin, glossy sheen of the smart-skin.

"Stay on the right side—tell me where you want to go and I'll get you there by the best route. We have three warm bodies in the far left bedroom, but they look like harem girls. They don't look hostile."

Jimmy nodded and disappeared into the room. Room-by-room, and step-by-step, Jimmy, invisible to any sensors, dismantled the boobytraps—there were four. On intrusion, the building would have been turned to smoking rubble.

"Okay, we're clear," Shimon said. "Good job, Jimmy."

"Am I green-light for showering this shit off? It burns."

Shimon looked at Harlan—Harlan nodded.

"Go ahead," Shimon said via the communicator.

Harlan gestured at the door and spoke to Lyle. "If you're determined to impress the lady, you can smash the door down now."

Lyle frowned. "You guys are assholes, each and every one of you—each in your own unique way." He tried the knob, it was unlocked. He opened the door and politely gestured for Karne to enter.

"That's okay, you first," she said.

Once inside, Shimon inspected the main room boobytrap.

"I was right," he said, "Russians."

"Generally, the Ruskies are like cockroaches," Karne said. "You might see one or two, but you know there are thousands of them everywhere."

"You don't see them because you're not looking in the right places," Harlan muttered.

From the hallway, Curtis brought in Jimmy's clothes and threw them on the steamed-up bathroom's floor.

"Take a look at this first," Shimon called out.

Curtis and Harlan walked to the kitchen. On the center of a cheap, rickety dinette table was a large rifle cartridge, standing like a sentinel gleaming in the harsh overhead light.

"This is an ugly piece of work," Shimon said. "Jimmy knows

85

more about this stuff than me, but I know this thing; it's a low-velocity, high throw-weight, compound, depleted-uranium charge. It would drill through our armor like it was nothing."

"Russian mil-tech?" Harlan asked.

"Yes," Shimon replied.

Karne poked her head into the room.

"Is that thing supposed to scare us?" she said.

"If you're not scared, you're stupid," Harlan said. "Let's check out the harem."

The lights didn't work in the far back bedroom. Inside, in dim, filtered light, three young women stood against the wall as if waiting for inspection. They were clothed, but in baggy dresses that could be pulled over their heads in a hurry. The room smelled rank and musky. Each girl had a collection of bruises on their arms and legs and cuts and contusions on their faces. They did not look directly at Curtis and Harlan. Major Karne looked over the men's shoulders.

"Give them some of the money and chase them out of here," Harlan said.

"Bullshit," Major Karne said. "We can't throw the counterfeit money around like that."

Harlan cupped the chin of one of the girls and raised her head. The girl still would not look at his face—she shifted her eyes left and right.

"These houris," Harlan said, "have been through a living hell. Let's give them a fighting chance to reinvent themselves. We're gonna do it whether you like the idea or not."

"Excuse me?" Karne said.

"You heard me, Major." Harlan spoke in Arabic to the girl in front of him. "We're letting you go home. Pack up your things. Five minutes."

The girl chattered to the others and they quickly scattered and pulled clothing and jewelry from their hiding places around the room. They threw on makeup and veils and were ready in minutes. They looked quite different. With their modesty refreshed and restored, they wouldn't get a second glance on the street.

To Lyle, Harlan said, "Peel off a few of those funny-money notes and give them to the girls."

"What notes?" Lyle said.

"Are we going to dance?" Harlan said to Major Karne. She considered for a moment, then nodded to Lyle.

"Do as he says," she said.

Lyle reached in his jacket and pulled out a thick sheaf of bills. He peeled off one for each girl and handed them out as they bustled from the room.

"I still don't see the point of this," Lyle said.

Harlan stood by the front door and patted each girl on the arm as they left the room. The last one stopped and handed him a tightly-folded piece of paper. In another instant, she was gone.

With Lyle looking on, Harlan unfolded the paper. It was a drawing of a man's face expertly drawn with a pencil like a police artist's sketch. The man had a wide face and his cheeks were covered with short, dark, stubbly beard. His head was covered with short, bristly hair. He had thick eyebrows and a large, flat nose.

"What is it?" Lyle said.

"I think this is our Russian." Harlan showed the picture to Curtis, Shimon and Major Karne before carefully folding it back up and securing it in a flap-pocket of his flak jacket.

"Excuse me," Jimmy said. He was dressed again—his damp hair stood up in spiky clumps. He came in from the hallway outside the apartment. "I'm almost done."

"Done with what?" Major Karne said.

"Give us a few more minutes to look around," Curtis said.

"Search the place and grab anything that looks interesting," Harlan said.

"You got it, boss," Jimmy replied.

"I don't know what is going on," Major Karne said. "I don't like not knowing what's going on."

"We're taking this building down."

Inside, in the main room, Jimmy looked happy, which was unusual, because, generally his face held a taciturn, stoical expression. He whistled while hauling a bundle downstairs.

"What are you doing?" Major Karne said.

"A building like this," Jimmy said with a wide grin, "has four central reinforced concrete supports. Take them out and the whole building collapses under its own weight. Take them out in sequence and it really gets interesting—it will corkscrew into the ground. It's frickin' awesome."

"I don't recall ordering you to blow up this building, Corporal."

Harlan walked up behind Major Karne.

"It's just something we do. Once we find a snakepit, we make sure it can't be used against us again. It's one of our rules of engagement."

"Wait a fucking minute," Major Karne said. "Did you guys blow up the Sevraal central tower? For about five minutes the top brass were very interested in finding out who did that."

"Didn't they finally decide it was one of the Islamic Triad splinter groups? We have plausible deniability on that one." Harlan raised his voice. "We about done, guys? No loitering."

Shimon threw tattered magazines into a pile in the center of a pile of trash in the main room.

"It's the perfect trifecta, boss. Porno magazines, take-out falafel containers and about a million cigarette butts."

"What a surprise," Harlan said. "Let's clear out."

On the ground floor, Harlan tapped Shimon on the shoulder and walked with him to the mouth of the alley. They looked up the narrow corridor at the scattered trash bags.

"Right," Shimon said. "They're not even trying to be subtle."

"I'm curious about what's in there. Run one of your sensor-robots in."

"No, don't ask me to do that. Come on, get real. These

robots cost me hundreds of dollars of my own money out of my own pocket and take hours and hours to put together. I don't mind losing one if there's a point, but this is just a waste. No, I won't do it."

"Shimon, my man, please humor me, will you?"

"I already know what you're going to say, so forget it. These robots are my friends."

"Please, I wouldn't ask if it wasn't important, you know that. Please."

"Shit-fuck," Shimon said. "All right."

Shimon pulled off his backpack and removed a little robot the size of a toaster. He flipped its power switch to ON and ran diagnostic tests using his flatscreen controller. The robot wheeled back and forth, and then rolled into the alley.

Shimon spoke a running commentary.

"Clear so far. Okay, got one, an IED, the usual claptrap, 155 millimeter cartridge, now another, same thing. Wait, what's this? Crap, look at the X-ray. What is this? It looks like a—wow, I think it is—yes—Russian; absolutely, no question about it. A chem bomb against the center wall, shit, maybe kilotons with a mass disturbance trigger. These guys were taking no chances, they wanted a big boom and no survivors coming out of this alley. Fuck a duck, that's a lot of throw-down. Wow."

"I want you to light it up," Harlan said.

Shimon turned to look into Harlan's face.

"No way. Not going to happen on my watch, boss."

Harlan waved to Jimmy. Jimmy walked over.

"What's up?" he said.

"We got a big Russian bomb in the alley. We're going to light it off, then I want the whole building to disappear. Can you work with that?"

Jimmy's eyes lighted up.

"Yeah, no problem. The bomb will push the building to the east. As it oscillates back, I can set off my charge sequence, and there will be nothing left but old postcard photographs and bricklayer's memories. We need to be a long way off, though— it's going to make a big noise."

"Perfect," Harlan said.

"I see why Curtis was pissed off at you," Shimon said. "You're a prize-winning fucking asshole."

Harlan activated his communicator to broadcast to the team. "Let's get a few blocks between us and this building," he said.

After everyone checked in clear, Harlan gave the command to Shimon.

The blast rattled the windows and activated car alarms— then Jimmy's sequence charges went off and the earth shook and rolled like a 6.8 shaker earthquake. Dust and smoke rose in the air three hundred feet.

Over the communicator link, Jimmy laughed.

"It worked," he said. "I'm too good at this shit."

Sura 22, Verse 75. Allah chooses messengers from angels and men; he hears and sees all things.

Book Two—Chapter Thirteen

Khostarak

IN THE WAR room at the hotel, Lyle leaned against the wall and cleaned his teeth with an ivory toothpick. Major Karne stood in front of the group and paced back and forth.

"We seem to be getting off track," she said. "You guys have lost sight of who runs this operation and owns your hairy asses. The Army gave you to me and you'll do what I say, when I say it and the way I say it—nothing more and nothing less. Now, who here is confused? Unsure? Puzzled? Who here has an unclear grasp of the situation?"

Curtis made eye-contact with Harlan. Barely perceptible, Harlan shook his head.

No.

"We're very sorry, Major," Harlan said. "We survived on the streets by doing things our own way with our own set of engagement rules. We promise on our sacred honor not to do it again."

Lyle snorted.

"I see more sacred honor on my toilet paper when I'm done with it," he said.

91

"Stow it, Lyle," she said. "For now, we'll take them at their word until they act out again. Then we'll deal with them very directly and the consequences will be uncomfortable and unpleasant. Does anyone here doubt my words?"

"We understand you completely," Harlan said. "We did a good job for you today, Major. I formally request another week of R and R. We earned it. We deserve it."

"What? No," the Major said. "We need to dig into the Russian situation and make a plan for shaking down Buhlibahn."

Harlan stood up. "Thank you. Okay, that's it then, we'll report back here at oh-nine-hundred hours on Monday morning—refreshed and ready to get back to work. You have our gratitude, Major, you won't regret this."

The four men got up and shuffled to the door. Harlan was the last to leave the room.

"See," he said to Lyle. "All you got to do is be nice to her and she'll be nice to you."

Once the door was closed, Lyle looked at Major Karne.

"How quickly could we replace these guys?"

Lyle put away his toothpick.

"It would take a couple of weeks," he said.

She spoke quietly, as if to herself. "Right, and there's four of them and two of us."

"I noticed that."

"At first, the idea of them joined together as a unit seemed like a benefit, something different, something we hadn't seen before—cute and refreshing. They work together very efficiently. It didn't occur to me they might work against us."

"It doesn't help that there's four of them—to retire this team, we'd need to get rid of all of them at once. I don't think it would be a good idea to leave even one of them standing."

"Well," the Major said. "When the time comes, don't mess around. I like Shimon and I have the feeling he could be saved and useful, but let's not outsmart ourselves. Take them all out." She stretched her arms into the air. "It's too early for lunch.

Why don't you grease up that cattle prod between your legs and ride me hard."

"Yes, ma-am," Lyle said.

Shimon played this recording for Harlan.

"You'd think they'd get tired of being so predictable," Harlan said. "You sure they won't find the bug?"

Shimon shrugged. "It's spread-spectrum and transmits packets masked by an FM radio frequency. I probably couldn't find it; draw a conclusion from that."

"They could be doing the same thing to us."

"Maybe, but I zap all the best masking frequencies with wide-band countermeasures. There's no evidence they are that smart."

"Let's not make it easy. We'll run two-by-two with the four of us never in the same place at the same time until we sort this out."

"Got it, boss."

Shimon packed his equipment into a Kevlar flight case.

"How's locating Buhlibahn coming along?" Harlan said.

"Give me another day and I think I'll have it."

"What's your sense of him?"

"I think, at heart, he's a businessman. For the right price, he'd sell his mama's virginity to a camel."

"So, you suggest *Let's Make a Deal* instead of shock and awe?"

"Yeah. With pistols loose in their holsters, of course."

Harlan put his hand on Shimon's shoulder. "Be careful with the Major. She's a clown in an officer's suit, but..."

"I know," Shimon said. "I just want to see if I can ride the pony once to see what it's like. I'm not going to fall in love like that meatball Lyle. I'll be careful."

"If you want to know what happens, I can tell you. You get a nice nap with a smile on your face and cream sauce drying on your dick while she lays awake and wonders if that's all there is to it. You're a quiet one, but you've always been the horniest guy I know. That reminds me, were you bullshitting about getting all up under Mary-Catherine's habit?"

"She was no virgin, I can tell you that much. Sweet, creamy thighs, yes. Innocent? No."

"How'd you get her? You were fourteen, for God's sake."

"No big mystery, she got real friendly after a few cups of sacramental wine. In my wildest dreams, I never saw us coming from Saint Peter's Boy's School to this pimple on a rat's ass. Khostarak. One thing hasn't changed over the years, if we stick together and hold together, we win."

"You're right about that, cowboy," Harlan said. "Good luck and let me know if the Major says anything interesting."

"Shit," Major Karne said. Topless, she sat at a desk in her panties tapping keys on her netbook computer. "I thought these guys did not hook up until they met in boot camp?"

"Yeah," Lyle said. "That's what the deep-brief report said. Why? What did you find?"

"They go back a lot further than that. Curtis and Harlan and Shimon were students at a Catholic school for troubled boys. Saint Peter's in Bethesda. Shimon's family is loaded, so he came in through the front door. Curtis and Harlan won scholarships, Curtis because he aced the SAT; Harlan because the Jesuits wanted him for their championship wrestling team. Jimmy's dad was a janitor, guess where. These guys have been a gang-unit since their public hairs could be counted on one hand. We're not going to split them up easily."

Lyle got up and stood by her side. She turned her head and his limp cock was right there.

"Put that thing away, Lyle. When I want it in my face, I'll let you know."

Whatever you say, boss."

He picked up free weights and, while watching himself in the mirror, began working on the tone of the knotty muscles in his arms and shoulders.

"It bothers me that our bugs and spy devices don't work. Why is that?"

"It's Shimon. He gets the latest Jew-tech from Israel. He's years ahead of us, that's why. Everything we put on those guys just stops working or feeds us live coverage of Fort Lauderdale greyhound races."

Karne turned on her seat to watch Lyle work with the weights.

"It might be interesting to take a smart lover just to see what it's like."

Sweat caused Lyle's taught skin to take on sheen. Perspiration dribbled down his face.

"Your husband is smart—you said it a hundred times."

"Yeah, you're right. Not smart like Shimon, though. I'm feeling the itch. Go take a shower and report back to me under the covers."

Sura 23, Verse 14. Then we made the sperm into a clot of congealed blood; then we made that clot into a fetal-lump; then we made bones from that lump and clothed the bones with flesh; creating a new creature. Truly, Allah is the very best creator.

Book Two—Chapter Fourteen

Islamidahd

HARLAN PULLED THE SUV to a stop in an area clearly-marked with signs that shouted their strident, unequivocal message.

No Parking

He took a deep breath and let it out slowly. "That was fun," he said.

After weaving through truck traffic that swerved and honked and stopped and went with only a vague concept of staying in a lane, they'd driven west two hours on a new four-lane highway paid for by U.S. taxpayers to the next largish city, Islamidahd. It held a half-million people and was not quite as big or as prosperous as Khostarak—there was only one big building in the business district, but taller than Khostarak's at twenty stories. A window washer, who appeared to dangle from a string, bellowed to the men pulling the rope who moved him up, down, left and right. The shirtless man wore cut-off jeans and tennis shoes with no socks. His safety equipment consisted of a turned-around-backwards Boston Red Sox baseball hat.

"When you think you have the worst goddamned job in the world…" Harlan commented.

Curtis finished his sentence.

"…you find the guy who hangs from a thread and cleans birdshit off a twenty-story Islamidahd office building with a bucket of dirty water and a rag on a hundred-ten degree day."

Harlan grunted. "Right. And he probably makes four cents an hour."

Curtis craned his neck and looked at the damp streaks the man made in the dust on the windows. "And worth every penny of it," he said.

Harlan spoke to Shimon through the dashboard communicator. "We're onsite and going off-grid now."

"Take it easy out there," Shimon replied.

They removed all of their toys and weapons from pouches and pockets and stacked them on the backseat of the SUV. Harlan was dressed in an off-white business suit with bare feet in leather sandals. Curtis wore a caftan and thin-wool skull cap.

Outside, an Irakkistani soldier with a plastic burp gun hanging from a leather strap around his shoulder shouted and gestured for them to move the SUV. Harlan showed their military ID, but the man remained angry and gesticulated until Harlan palmed him a thick roll of new-dollars. After glancing at the wad, the man turned and rapidly walked down the street—past his plastic chair under an umbrella.

"Valet parking," Harlan commented while locking the doors with a few touches to his communicator keypad.

"Where do you think he's going in such a hurry?"

"Late lunch?" Harlan said.

They walked to the main entrance of the building—a man in a service uniform opened the front door for them, and then led them to the elevator. He looked at the two men with the question in his eyes.

"Buhlibahn," Harlan said.

The man punched in codes on the elevator controls and stepped out. Harlan tossed him a coin and the man pressed it to his forehead before dropping it in his pocket.

When the elevator doors slid open, they looked into the barrels of a pair of twelve-gauge, slide-action riot guns. The two guards motioned for them to raise their arms—then Curtis and Harlan got a rough pat down from two other guards.

"If you touch my junk, I'll have you arrested," Curtis said.

Harlan laughed. "Yeah, and don't taze me, bro."

The guards stepped back and gestured with the shotguns. Harlan and Curtis came out and walked down a plush corridor on thick Persian carpets. The glass doors had *International Global* etched on them. A guard swiped a keycard and the doors slid open. A pretty receptionist dressed in an elegant, western-style pantsuit with a massive strand of white pearls around her neck smiled at them and offered them bottles of cold water.

They walked through a boiler room filled with men typing on computer keyboards and talking on telephone headsets.

Buying? Selling? A little of both?

It was impossible to tell.

They walked into a corner office—the view to the north and east was stunning. A short, round man dressed in a natty suit, came around his desk and shook their hands vigorously.

Harlan started an elaborate greeting in Arabic, but the man held up a palm to stop him.

"Please," he said. "I appreciate your courtesy, but your accent grates on my ears. Wouldn't you be more comfortable speaking in English?"

His accent was one-hundred percent perfection.

English.

Mayfair in London, to be more specific.

"What exactly do you do here, Mr. Buhlibahn?" Harlan asked.

"Isn't that the American way—to skip all the polite formalities and get right to the point?" He gestured for Harlan to approach and pointed down at the ground. The SUV, parked all alone on the street, could be seen. Dirty, it stood out like a canker on a supermodel. "How much did you pay the guard?" Buhlibahn asked.

Harlan shrugged. "About a hundred new-dollars."

"A year's salary. In a way, I understand the irresistible temptation, but I stress to them the importance of keeping the street clear so I can worry a little less about car bombs—now, whether I want to or not, I have to send a team to the man's house to visit him and his family. If he's at all clever, he'll be gone by then. In cases like this, the people—and my rivals—would see me as a weak horse if I did anything differently. If it pleases you, could I have the keys so one of my men can move the vehicle. I assure you, we have safe, secure parking down the block."

Harlan reached in his pocket and pulled out the keyfob. He tossed it to a guard.

"I'd be disappointed if any of our personal effects were—molested or came up missing."

Buhlibahn laughed. "As would I," he said. "Is there anything about driving the car that we should be aware of?"

"No," Harlan said. "As long as they stay out of our backpacks and leave our belongings in the backseat alone, there will be no problem."

"Excellent." Buhlibahn chattered staccato words to the guard, who immediately left the room. "Can we at least introduce ourselves properly and enjoy English tea and biscuits before we converse about my business and the self-evidentiary importance of your visit?"

He shook hands with Harlan. "I am Mr. Taleb al Hansaal Buhlibahn, the president and chief executive officer of this humble company, International Global," he said.

He walked up to Curtis and hugged and kissed him in the

formal way of the Irrakistanis. He held Curtis at arm length and tugged Curtis's beard. "You almost look like someone— someone who tickles a childhood memory. If only the beard on your chin was a little longer..."

"I know," Curtis said, "and it irritates me more every time I hear it."

Buhlibahn tilted his head back and laughed. His mouth was filled with white, perfectly-aligned teeth.

"One thing you can count on with Americans—and that is an excellent sense of humor. Please, sit. Esmeralda will serve us tea and then we can discuss your business."

"I hope we can discuss our mutual business, Mr. Buhlibahn," Harlan said.

"And you can count on my full attention and serious consideration for anything you have to say," Buhlibahn said.

They sat before a low, polished-teak table. Esmeralda served tea from a silver chalice along with a platter of cookies sprinkled with brown sugar. With silver tongs, she placed three irregular lumps of golden sugar into Buhlibahn's cup. Harlan held up two fingers—as did Curtis. Once the men were served, she bowed her head and left the room. From a small china creamer, Buhlibahn added milk to his tea.

"That's a special woman," Buhlibahn said. "She's so lovely and charming, even my wife likes her and that's my first mistress who enjoyed that honor."

""What exactly do you do here, Mr. Buhlibahn?" Harlan repeated.

"Ah, persistence," Buhlibahn said. "Another delightful and enviable trait of Americans." He leaned back against a satin cushion and sipped his tea. "When I worked for the dear leader, I had several duties and one was to run a team of geologists. Geologists have a tough life—it seems romantic and pleasant to a college student, but the reality of it is much less prosaic. They spend months in hostile places digging little holes in the ground and assaying endless samples, most of which are useless, worthless dirt. However, if you want to know where minerals and other valuable things are, this is what must be done. I find it ironic—a hundred years ago, the world was interested in our rubies and sapphires which remain among the most beautiful on earth. Fifty years ago, the world had an endless hunger for materials like our tungsten and tantalum. Now, industrialized countries in Asia, Europe and North America are more interested in rare earths like hexavalent cadminium, iridium and other materials needed for chemical batteries and magnetic motors. The world finds a way to reward those who know where to find these rare materials. And, in this part of the world, to my great fortune, they have me they can turn to for assistance and I am always willing to help where I can."

"You didn't mention the Russians."

Buhlibahn looked at Harlan with a barren expression. "Did I neglect mentioning them?" he said, "It's true; the Russians are among those who enjoy the benefit of my humble knowledge. Now, I have been frank with you—completely transparent and fully informative. I request of you the same. What exactly do you want, Mr. Farris and Mr. Washington?"

The men did not react, but they wondered.

How did Buhlibahn know their last names?

"Here's what we were told when we came over here, Mr. Buhlibahn, that our fighting was for a noble cause to defeat the backward tyrants of the middle ages, the evil, backward, fundamentalist Muslim enemies of progress and our rich, modern way of life. To root out and destroy the source of terror in the west, to stop the toppling of buildings, to extinguish the flaming cruise ships and save the commercial airplanes that crash to the ground. The reality of the situation is different than the slogans and jingoism, but none-the-less, we're here to fight this war and, if we can, to win."

Buhlibahn looked toward a far corner of the room. When he finally spoke, his voice was soft and quiet. "What does it mean to you, Mr. Farris, to *win*? To the peoples of Irakkistan, what does that look like?"

"I imagine a place where people can work and enjoy the fruits of their labors. Where people can live and love and worship the God, gods or no God as they choose. Where people who disagree on religion or lifestyle can agree to disagree and work side-by-side for a better future for their country and their children and their children's children. A place where girls can walk to school in their neighborhoods without worrying about being whipped or raped—or worse—by psychotic, Talibani fundamentalist shitbirds. A place where women can vote and wear the head scarf, chador, burka, or nylons and a miniskirt, if they choose it. I imagine a place safe for business with fair levels of taxation and minimal bureaucratic graft, extortion and baksheesh. A place with good toilets, soft toilet paper, sidewalks and streetlights—a prosperous place where there are more BMWs on the street than goats."

As if catching up to what he'd been saying, Harlan looked embarrassed. Buhlibahn laughed heartily. Under his vest, his belly shook in rhythmic waves and on his face, his cheeks turned rosy.

"While we're dreaming the big dream, can we get a Wal-Mart and a Starbucks on every street corner?" Curtis said.

"Fuck off," Harlan replied.

"You'll excuse me?" Buhlibahn said. "Your wish list sounds more like a John Lennon song than a serious plan for my troubled country. Are you an impractical idealist? A hopeless romantic and dreamer, Mr. Farris?"

"Well, I'm willing to burn the whole fucking country to the ground and send all the women and screaming children straight to hell and start over with bare, scorched earth, if that's what it takes," Harlan said. "I don't know how laughable and idealistic that makes me."

There was a knock at the door and one of the guards came in and whispered into Buhlibahn's ear. The round man got up and walked to his north-facing window. With a wave of his hand, he gestured for Harlan to join him. After exchanging a glance with Curtis, Harlan got up. Curtis sat back in his seat and inspected his fingernails.

At the window, Buhlibahn pointed. A couple of miles away, a ragged plume of dirty smoke rose into the air.

"When my men got there, the man, the street watcher and his family were gone. Still, I can't be seen as weak. My orders must be obeyed and there must be consequences for disobedience. We burned his house and we'll kill him if we find him—though we probably won't find him, I suppose." Buhlibahn sighed. "So, you can see, a generous gift from you results in destruction and death for others. I'm not sure if there is a larger parallel that can be drawn to the unwanted foreign war you bring to my poor country, but maybe there is."

Buhlibahn moved to his desk and sat down.

"As you can imagine, Mr. Farris," he continued, "I hear a lot of ideas and plans from people who visit me. Important people from very far-away places around the world who represent vast political powers and huge financial resources. Most of these ideas are stupid or the potential for profit is limited and I must regretfully decline. In your case, you and your men and your plan pique my interest. So, as an opening gesture to begin our potential future working relationship, I will not order my men to kill you and bury your bodies deep in a poppy field—a situation you can consider permanently in place until it changes."

"Outstanding," Harlan said. "Wonderful. Thank you. On another topic, I wonder, sir, if you've thought about the proper, most-effective way to rule in Irakkistan? Democracy is no good answer for the Irrakistani people."

Buhlibahn looked thoughtful. "Mob rule always devolves into societal breakdown and anarchy."

"But, a theocracy also has fatal problems. The west will not allow it."

"I'm listening," Buhlibahn said.

"It seems to me that a coalition of sorts would be the best. A partnership. A friendly cooperative between a strong religious leader with an effective alliance of military and police forces—and a businessman. Perhaps a businessman like yourself, Mr. Buhlibahn."

Buhlibahn glanced at Curtis's beard and robe and then back into Harlan's eyes.

"This," he said slowly, "is an idea with merit; one that deserves full and honest consideration. You have done something which surprises me, Mr. Farris. You *intrigued* me and I find myself pleased that you thought to come up here to see me."

"You're welcome," Harlan said.

"I hope you won't take this wrong, Mr. Farris, but our meeting has gone on quite a lot longer than I anticipated, which I do not regret a bit. However, my duties call and demand my attention. Is there anything else, Mr. Farris, or shall we declare this a constructive and productive conclusion to our meeting?"

"There is one more small matter I beg your indulgence on, sir," Harlan said.

"Very well," Buhlibahn said while shooting a look at his watch. "What is it?"

Harlan pulled a counterfeit five-thousand dollar bill from his inner shirt pocket and smoothed it on Buhlibahn's desk.

"You might have heard something about your dear leader's printing operation. There are those who say this is the real reason—the secret reason—for the unfortunate war that came to your country."

"I believe I have heard vague, unsubstantiated rumors about this horrible thing," Buhlibahn said.

"For an honest businessman—like yourself as an example— men who make their living with commissions on honorable, voluntary contracts and legitimate business transactions, the printing of American currency is unhelpful. A hindrance. Even counterproductive. It upsets the powerful leaders of the west and brings unwanted attention and meddling from abroad. Any assistance—even a name, or a location, or any useful information at all would be very much, gratefully and humbly appreciated."

Buhlibahn held out his hands palms up. "As a small, powerless fish in a vast sea of tiger sharks and manta rays, I am unsure what I can offer. But, in the spirit of friendly cooperation between you and me—though I can make no promises—I am willing to make a few phone calls and ask a few questions on your behalf."

Harlan bowed his head. "I can ask no more from you, sir, and I thank you sincerely from the very bottom of my heart."

He pulled a photograph from his inside pocket, then unfolded it and put it on Buhlibahn's desk.

"You might get a visit from these two," Harlan said.

With an index finger, Buhlibahn moved the photograph across his desk and leaned over to look.

Major Karne and Lyle.

"Should I consider them friends or foes?"

Harlan grinned. "I really don't know yet, sir," he said.

Buhlibahn's phone buzzed. Harlan smiled—that meant their twenty-minute audience had expired.

"Please. I know we have asked too much already," Harlan said. Buhlibahn gestured for him to continue. "We are looking for this man."

Harlan pulled the illustration from his pocket, unfolded it and placed it on Buhlibahn's desk.

Buhlibahn picked it up and examined it carefully.

"Yes," he said, "I believe I *have* met this man—perhaps at a party or maybe I passed him on the street at time or two."

"If you see him again," Harlan said, "and find it convenient, perhaps you'd let him know we are looking for him and are very much looking forward to enjoying a conversation with him."

"Of course," Buhlibahn said. "I will do that. You will find your vehicle parked near the front entrance of the building. I bid you good day, sirs."

Buhlibahn picked up his telephone as Curtis and Harlan left the room. At the elevator, the guard pressed the buttons for them and let them ride down alone.

The SUV idled at the curb in front of the building.

"Mr. Buhlibahn seems like a nice-enough man," Curtis commented once they were in the SUV and moving.

"Yes, an excellent and honorable person I am delighted to become acquainted with." They drove for a mile, and then pulled over by a roadside stand that sold prepaid telephone cards.

"Now?" Curtis said. "Here?"

Harlan nodded. "Sooner is better, I think. I feel dirty and don't want to wait until we're on the highway."

Curtis crawled around the cabin and ran one of Shimon's sensors inside the vehicle while Harlan walked around the outside and worked his way under the truck on his back. There were three sensor/transponders inside and one outside. They were all killed with focused, near-field electromagnetic pulses from emitter wands.

Harlan brushed dust from his shirt and pants, and then hopped back into the driver's seat.

"What did you conclude from our conversation with Buhlibahn?" Curtis said.

"That he's not going to kill us. Not right away, anyway."

"That's a good start, I suppose."

"Could be worse," Harlan said.

Ignoring a bleating horn from an oncoming taxi, he pulled the truck onto the road and pointed it back toward Khostarak.

Sura 23, Verse 24. But the chieftains of his folk who disbelieved said, "Noah is only a mortal like you who would make himself superior to you. Had Allah willed, he surely could have sent down angels, but we heard not of this from our fathers of old."

Book Two—Chapter Fifteen

Khostarak

CURTIS'S FIRST AUDIENCE was a small one consisting of five men in the living room. Three of the men were old and two were young. The old men wore traditional garb—robes and long, gray beards. The young men wore suits with open collar shirts and lots of gold—gold chains around their necks, gold bracelets, Rolex watches with gold bands on their wrists and glittering gold rings on their fingers. The old man gave Curtis no advanced warning and provided no information about this first audience.

Curtis wondered.

Were they important? Or, were they the opposite—a safe, inconsequential group gathered in case Curtis fell completely on his face?

He did not know.

The preparation was embarrassing. The old man pressed him back into a chair and Telleh removed his shoes and dirty socks. Then she carefully trimmed his toenails and sliced off horny sections of thick, black skin with a small, very-sharp curved knife. She washed his feet with a soft cloth, umber soap and warm, scented water from an ornamental basin. He didn't understand any of it.

Telleh would not meet his eyes, but he had the sense she was intrigued by him—perhaps even interested. Her hands were gentle on his feet and there was sexual tension and warm affection in the way she soaped his insteps, stroked his ankles and heels and worked her trim fingers between his slippery toes.

She was Harlan's girl and no good would come of Curtis wooing her or taking up with her, but he could not prevent his eyes from peering down the loose folds of her outer blouse and imagining her soft, slender body in his arms. As usual, she wore blouses in many layers and any view of her intimate skin was one-hundred percent imagined.

But, what skin. Brown skin. Velvet skin. Young, smooth, unblemished skin. With every cell in his body, he hungered to possess it. With her hands on his feet, he felt delicately balanced between heaven and hell.

The sermon was a generic one, nearly completely metaphorical and allegorical. Strong lions of war this and gentle fawns of paradise that. Curtis had stage-fright—he was scared and started out weakly and hesitantly. He had the young men's attention for about ten minutes, and then they glanced at their Blackberries and tap-tapped text messages. One of the old men appeared to be asleep or dead—he leaned back in his overstuffed chair with his head back and his mouth hanging open.

It was disrespectful.

Curtis became angry and then grew angrier. Raising his voice, he threw his body into the presentation with waving arms—he paced back and forth like a wild animal. With unleashed fury, he glared at the young men until they put away their communicators. The old man returned from the dead; he sat up and paid attention. Curtis improvised by mixing the few hundred poetic words he knew and the memorized words the old man hand-wrote on yellow, crinkly paper. By the end he bellowed and shook his fist at the sky. When he was done speaking, he was drained and empty.

There was nothing left in him.

The men lined up and gave him a hug and the traditional dry kiss on the cheek. He had the sense they were impressed and excited, but he could not tell for sure. After the visitors left, the old man made him repeat some of the words he bungled. Finally, at the end of the evening, the old man said nothing, but his face held a small smile and a satisfied expression. Telleh motioned for Curtis to sit and led the old man from the room.

The children, released from captivity, ran into the room and noisily played a game with a set of colorful plastic blocks. The game appeared to be related to how tall and complicated a design could be constructed. After ten minutes, Telleh came back and sat in a chair across the room. She didn't say anything and she didn't look at him, but Curtis sensed this was a courtship ritual. It was generally inappropriate for an unmarried woman to be alone in a room with a man. The implication teased him. He wanted to tear her clothes off. He wanted to marry her. He wanted to bury himself in her. He wanted her hands on his feet again.

"So, you like David Bowie..." he said.

Involuntarily, she smiled, just a little, but did not look at him or speak.

There was a knock on the front door. It was Harlan—one of the kids let him in. He stood in the middle of the small room and looked back and forth between Curtis and Telleh.

He knows something is going on between us.

Harlan reached in his pocket and pulled out a small, paper-wrapped package. He handed it to Telleh. She took it, but, as if filled with guilty shame, did not meet his gaze.

Harlan gestured for her to open it.

It was a delicately figured silver bracelet with flush-set rubies. Red rubies.

From across the room, Curtis could tell it was expensive.

Telleh held out her arm and allowed Harlan to put the bracelet on her; it was an act as intimate as the foot-washing ritual.

Still, she would not look into Harlan's face. She sat and stared at the floor. "Thank you," she whispered.

Harlan leaned over to kiss her cheek, but she pushed his head away. It didn't seem to bother him. He got on his knees and helped the kids with their construction project for a few minutes, then stood and gestured for Curtis to go.

They didn't speak until they were in the SUV and rolling down the avenue.

"How'd it go?" Harlan said.

"It's hard to say for sure, but I think I pegged the ball out of the park. The old man didn't say anything, but he seemed pleased."

"Good," Harlan said. After a few minutes of driving, he spoke again. "Ever notice how much you really, really want the things you can't have?"

"Shit, Harlan. Isn't that the sad, hard-edged truth, my brother." A minute passed before Curtis spoke again. "Harlan. This thing with Telleh—between her and me. It might be getting out of my control."

With a face made of stone, Harlan drove with his fists clenched on the steering wheel for a few seconds, but he couldn't hold it in. He laughed.

"Curtis, you crazy motherfucker, do you think I'd leave you alone with her for two minutes if it wasn't a done deal between us? Her grandfather already gave her to me, we'll be married in a month. Hell, just accepting the bracelet is a dead-serious intimacy which would never happen unless we were engaged to be married, idiot. Besides, at this point, if she tossed me aside and took up with you, then she's not the woman I think she is. You'd be doing me a big favor. I'd sure want to know now, not later. If you think you have a chance with her, then have at it, moron. Take a shot. Unleash your irresistable charm. Romance her. Knock her off her feet."

"Uhh," Curtis said.

"Besides, the legendary black warrior riding to the rescue of this country on a black stallion does not have a wife. Mistresses, sure, a dozen if you want them, but no wife. He rides alone. You and Telleh? No way. Not going to happen, dimwit."

"So we're clear, fuckhead," Curtis said, "I have your permission to turn on my overwhelming Curtis Washington allure. Full bore. One-hundred percent."

"Sure, knock yourself out, dumbshit."

"Good," Curtis said. They drove for another minute in silence. "She really is a pretty little thing. Those bright eyes. That soft skin. She's special."

"You're hopeless," Harlan said.

They drove the rest of the way back to the hotel in silence.

Sura 23, Verse 35. Does he promise that when you die and become dust and bones, you shall be brought forth again?

Book Two—Chapter Sixteen

Khostarak—Curtis

THE NEXT SERMON was different, though it again started with Telleh washing his feet. On her wrist, Harlan's gift, the delicate ruby bracelet, gleamed and flashed and mocked him, but her soft hands and sensuous stroking still seemed to hold erotic promise.

When she reached the rinse and repeat part of the wash cycle, he reached in the pocket of his robe and pulled out *his* gift, a larger bracelet, with twice-as-big blood-red rubies. He dangled it in front of her face, but she, as if afraid to touch it, pushed his hand and made him put it back in his pocket.

"No," she said. "Not now."

Not now? Did that mean there would be a proper time later?

Curtis grasped at the hope. She stood and pushed something into a large fabric bag. He leaned over for a closer look. They were shiny golden slippers with pointed toes.

"I'm not wearing those." In response, she smiled a little—just a hint. The ends of her mouth curled upward slightly. "No, really. I'm not wearing those gaudy things."

The robe he wore was a little fancier—with a silk sash and

gold-embroidered collars that matched the absurd genie slippers. It was still plain, but richer than the previous robe they gave him.

There was a tap at the door. Harlan. As he came in, he leaned over to kiss her cheek, but she gently pushed him away.

Curtis squelched a grin.

These two married in a month? No way.

"Let's move out, amigo," Harlan said.

Telleh pointed at flip-flop sandals. While Curtis slipped them on, Telleh handed Harlan the bag with the fancy shoes.

They didn't talk much in the car. Soon, they pulled up beside an old brick wall covered with graffiti. Dead plants spilled from old terra cotta bowls. The roof was covered with broken red-clay tiles. There was a shabby door on the street. The place looked abandoned.

"What's this?" Curtis said.

"You'll see," Harlan replied. He opened the cloth bag and handed Curtis the slippers. "Put these on."

"No. They're hideous."

"You can't go inside wearing flip-flops."

"Shit. You suck." He slipped his feet into the fancy slippers and studied them on his feet. "Hey, they're comfortable."

"Shut up," Harlan said. He walked to the dilapidated door and banged on it hard.

Inside, two men looked out. One had a stubby sawed-off shotgun; the other carried an old revolver.

"Showtime," Harlan said.

Inside, the house was lavish and lovely. They walked through an entry area, then into a thick-carpeted lounge and continued into a plush central courtyard. Curtis tried not to stare, but it was hard. The place was fit for a king.

Twenty chairs were arranged around a tall table. One of the young men from the previous meeting chattered and kissed his hand as if they were familiar. Family.

Men slowly gathered and settled in their seats.

The sermon was different too. After a few words of introduction, words he read went directly to the war talk. Storms on the horizon, raging bulls in the streets and rivers running with infidel blood. Curtis did not understand every word, but he could follow the main ideas.

He raged. He shouted. He stared at his audience as if they were devils and he was the last decent man on earth. When he turned to the last page of the script, he found the sweet lambs, and gentle, honorable lions and the soft rain on the beautiful garden. He lowered his voice more and more and basically whispered the final words, then stood with his head bowed and his arms hanging loosely at his sides.

The silence stretched for almost a minute. Then the old man stood, put his arm around Curtis's shoulders and kissed his cheek. Soon, he was surrounded with well-wishers and back-slappers.

Curtis was spent; he just wanted to throw the stupid slippers in the garbage and go to his room and sleep for a week or two. Instead, he stood and listened and uttered a few words of encouragement and wisdom or the best that he think of off the top of his head with his limited vocabulary.

Apparently, it was close enough. Strong tea was served with figs, dates and clumps of pungent, crumbly yellow-brown cheese. To be polite, Curtis nibbled.

He noticed a teak chest open on a side table. The men as they were near it dropped in jewelry—bracelets, jeweled rings, watches, gold coins and gold necklaces with shiny, colorful stones. And diamonds. Curtis was no expert jeweler, but some of this stuff looked expensive.

Very expensive.

At the end of the evening, Telleh closed the box, closed the clasp on an elaborate silver padlock and carried it away.

Finally, it was time to go. Harlan guided him to the little

Toyota.

"That was so good, even *I* started to believe it. Well done, my friend."

"Fuck off," Curtis said.

"You can thank me later. It's not easy, you know. First of all, everyone is skeptical of blacks. They don't see you dark people very often. As middle easterners living on the historic frankincense trail, they are reasonably worldly and open-minded, but the stereotype is that black folks are stupid and steal. Like monkeys."

"If I wasn't so tired, I'd beat the living shit out of your racist ass."

"On the other hand," Harlan continued, "we have the legend of the black prince who unites the tribes and kicks off the next caliphate. That works in our favor."

"I don't know what you're going on about."

"And there's the moral code to deal with."

"If you're not going to speak plainly, then just shut the fuck up. You're pissing me off."

"Go inside. Follow Telleh's lead and you'll be fine."

"I don't want to see your ugly face ever again," Curtis spat the words. "We're not friends. Eat shit and die, cocksucker."

After Curtis got out of the little Toyota, Harlan slowly drove away.

Curtis trudged to the front door.

Wait. What? Telleh? Follow Telleh's lead?

Curtis fingered the heavy bracelet in his pocket and allowed himself to feel hope.

Telleh.

As Curtis approached, the front door swung open. Telleh took his hand and led him to his usual chair. She gently pulled off the fancy slippers, brushed them off and put them away.

I hope she washes my feet again.

"Aalmah has had a tough time," Telleh said.

Huh? Aalmah? Who's that?

Telleh continued. "She is alone with her two children and has not seen her husband for more than three years. We fear the worst. That he is dead in the war."

What the fuck?

"You should offer her a pretty gift with the hope that it will bring a little joy to her sad heart—a tiny ray of sunshine for the dark night of her soul." Telleh reached into Curtis's pocket and pulled out the bracelet. "One hopes that a strong, powerful man could have sympathy for poor Aalmah and be gentle with her broken heart and treat her with respect and kindness."

A figure entered the room. She was wrapped in a long dress trailing silky, billowing scarves. Her head was covered, but her face was visible in the faint evening light. Perhaps ten years older than Telleh, she was pretty, but more weathered. Her hair, framing her face around the edges of the head scarf, was hennaed reddish-purple in the dim room's light.

"Tell her she is pretty and give her your gift," Telleh whispered.

She pressed his hand upward. Aalmah bowed and took the bracelet.

"You're very pretty," Curtis said.

Telleh looked at him expectantly.

"Uh," Curtis stumbled, before discovering confidence, "when the sun shines on Irakkistani rubies, they glitter in a way that pleases Allah, but a smile on your lovely face pleases Allah more."

Telleh nodded.

Now what?

"I believe Aalmah would like to show you how the bracelet looks on her arm," Telleh said. "In privacy, which would be proper. Upstairs. With your kind permission, will you allow her to lead the way?"

Why not?

Curtis got up. Aalmah took his hand and tugged gently. She walked to the back of the room and stood by the stairway until

Curtis approached. Then she ascended and Curtis followed.

At the top of the stairway, there was a hallway. At the end of the hall was a door. Behind the door, there was a small bedroom where candles flickered and the air was filled with a flowery perfume. She guided and pushed him until he sat on the bed.

There was hardly room to move.

She pressed a button on a cassette tape player and the room filled with music. Snake charmer music with keening pipes and tabla drums.

Under her dress, her hips swayed. She plucked off the scarves one-by-one, starting with the one that restrained her wild hair.

Was it five minutes or an hour?

She was completely naked—shadows flickered on her body. She pulled the robe over his head and pushed him back on the bed. His penis was not large, but it was not small either. She weighed it with her hand and pretended to be shocked at its size and heft.

"I beg you, kind sir, to be gentle with me. It has been so long since I have been with a man—I am very nearly a virgin."

What are you talking about? I should be gentle? You're the one on top.

She pressed a breast into his face.

"Do you like me, kind sir? Do you find me attractive? Will you allow me please and comfort you?"

Yes.

From the month of intensive study, his mind was saturated with the language and culture. When she finally stopped teasing him and let him come in waves of heaven-touched bliss, it was Allah he praised—it was Allah's name on his lips.

God is great.

In the morning after more vigorous sex, Aalmah washed herself with a basin and got dressed. As she put her clothes on, she grew more and more modest and shy. With a hand-mirror she applied lipstick and eye shadow. She pushed his face away when he tried to kiss her and did not meet his eyes as she left the room.

He pulled on his clothes and enjoyed a long piss in a chamber pot before wandering downstairs. The two women in headscarves did not look him in the eye as they served him a breakfast of cold toast, dark coffee and honey-sweetened yoghurt. He noticed the lovely bracelet peeking from under the long sleeves of Aalmah's blouse.

He sipped his coffee and watched the women wash the breakfast dishes. From outside, he heard the peep of Harlan's Toyota's horn.

Telleh touched his arm.

"It would be a blessing," she whispered, "if you left a small gift for Aalmah, some money to help her feed her children."

Curtis looked in his wallet. He pulled out fifty new dollars and showed Telleh.

"More," she said.

He worked another fifty out of his billfold and held it out.

Telleh smiled.

Her smile was spectacular—like a cool breeze on a hot day.

She pointed at a small table in the living room. Curtis placed the money on that table.

As he stood by the front door, he looked back and caught Aalmah and Telleh watching him—openly and frankly studying his ass—though both immediately looked down and away. This made him smile.

They were looking.

Outside, he scratched the long fuzz on his chin and breathed cool morning air while the hungry sun bit into his bare head. He thought he heard a bird singing, but it could have been his imagination.

Were there songbirds in Irakkistan?

118

He didn't remember hearing one before.

"Good morning, sunshine," Harlan said as Curtis worked his large body into the small car.

"Okay, we're friends again," Curtis said while staring straight ahead and trying to maintain a stern, angry look.

Harlan laughed as he restarted the car.

"I can tell when you're angry," he said, "and I can tell when you've been well and good fucked by a good woman who knows what she's doing."

"Drive," Curtis said.

They drove.

Sura 23, Verse 41. So the mighty blast overtook them with Allah's justice, and made them as rubbish left behind by the torrential stream of time. Thus, the unjust were washed away.

Book Two—Chapter Seventeen

Khostarak

THEY WERE ALMOST back to the hotel when the communicator blatted.

"Where are you guys?" Shimon said. "Get your asses back to the hotel. Jimmy's room. We got trouble."

"Give us two minutes," Harlan said as he downshifted and hammered on the horn. The car jumped around a rusty bus—an oncoming motorcycle swerved out of the way.

"I thought things were moving suspiciously smoothly."

"Quit yapping and pay attention to the road," Curtis said while holding onto his armrest.

Harlan tapped a knuckle on the hotel room door. Shimon opened the door a crack, then ushered them in.

The wall across from the window was covered with splattered blood. Jimmy's body was on the floor.

"Shit," Curtis said.

"Stay away from the window," Shimon said.

Curtis and Harlan looked at Jimmy, but his body seemed

untouched.

"No shit," Harlan commented. "Jimmy's blood?"

"No," Shimon said. "His girl. Rocky Balboa. It looks like she got in the crosshairs—the Russian lost patience and took his shot."

"What happened to Jimmy?"

"Ah, hell, I took him down with Hibernation-three. He'll be down for about four hours. That's about all the time I could buy. I didn't want to hurt him, just lay him out until we could make a plan. He liked this girl, and you know how he is—he wanted to race over there with six-guns blazing. I didn't think that was a good idea."

"Race over where?" Curtis said.

"I got a vector on the line-of-sight. The shooter was four-hundred yards out in an apartment window. Second floor, third window from the left."

"Where's Lyle and the Major?"

"I haven't seen them. That's another thing. Jimmy thinks Lyle set us up."

"What's that? Lyle? That's out of left field."

"There wasn't time for a conversation before I took him down. Man, he's going to be pissed when he wakes up."

Rocky's body was sprawled across the bed with her head pressed against the wall at nearly a right angle. There was a perfectly circular one-inch hole in the window.

"What a mess," Harlan commented.

"Those goddamned compound shells—that's what they do. Subtle, they ain't. So, boss, what's the play? I hate to think about what the Russian left for us at the apartment, but I suppose we need to take a look anyway."

"This might seem odd," Harlan said, "but how about if we hang out in the bar—let the Major run this one and see what she does with it?"

Curtis shrugged. "I'm not sure I see the point, but okay, if that's how you want to do it," he said.

Harlan continued. "Shimon, how about you go over and clean up that apartment. While you're at it, see if anything catches your eye. Give us the green light when it's okay for us to stop by for a look-see."

"You guys will hang out here—drinking—while I go into that apartment and see if I can get myself blown up? That's the plan?"

"You have your little robots, right? You'll be fine."

"I appreciate the vote of confidence," Shimon said, "but if your clever plan gets me killed, then maybe Jimmy had the better idea. What are we going to do with him?"

"Curtis and I will haul him upstairs. Go."

"I'm gone," Shimon said.

Upstairs in Curtis's room, they arranged Jimmy's body on the floor so he was comfortable. They made sure there was no firing angle that could get to him in case there was a way the shooter could see through the aluminum foil on the windows.

Then they took the elevator down to the bar. The place was nearly deserted with only a couple of media stringers deep into their Cutty Sark at a corner table, otherwise the place was empty.

"I'm not sure what we did to piss off the Russian," Curtis said.

"Let's talk it out over a beer," Harlan said. "Maybe we can figure it out."

He gestured to the bartender with two fingers.

"Okay, but your plans always seem to include beer."

"What's wrong with that?"

While waiting for the Red Stars, Harlan typed a text message to the Major suggesting she take a look at the situation in Jimmy's room, then meet them in the bar.

The response was quick.

Ten minutes, she said.

"Jimmy's not known for coming up with wild ideas," Curtis

said. "I hate that fucktard Lyle as much as anyone and wish he'd dry up and blow away, but I don't get this tie-in with the Russian."

"Jimmy doesn't come up with wild ideas? Are you nuts? That's all he does."

"Yeah," Curtis said. "You're right. Still, I'll bet he has some reason to think whatever it is he's thinking. You seem to be taking this calmly. Are you mellowing in your old age?"

Harlan took a sip of his beer. "Just keeping my eye on the big picture," he said. "Jimmy will find another girl—she was irrelevant to our mission."

"That's cold, even for you, Harlan. And, regardless of what you think, when Jimmy wakes up, he'll spill blood by the gallons—including yours if you get in his way."

Harlan seemed offended.

"I know that. We have a couple of hours before we have to worry about that, so let's play out this hand and see what happens, okay? Here's Karne. Look sharp."

Lyle sat down and gestured for a beer. Major Karne remained standing. "That's an ugly scene you guys left up there," she said. "Is Jimmy okay?"

"Yeah," Harlan said. "Jimmy's fine. Pull up a seat, Major."

"No," she said. "I want to know what you intend to do about the waitress. Are you tracking down the shooter? Have you contacted the local police? Who is going to call her family? There's a lot to do and you useless creeps are drinking beer and not doing it."

Harlan looked up at her. "We're still on our holiday. We'll be back on the clock Monday morning. You're the one on duty, what are you going to do?"

"Oh, no," she said, "you're not laying this on me, Sergeant."

"What can we do," Harlan said, "that you can't do better, Major? You make a few phone calls, coordinate with the I-K police, get a cleanup crew in, get the window glass replaced and have the body cremated and prepared for shipment home. If I tried to do any of that, we'd have a big, complicated difficult-to-explain international-diplomatic mess on our hands."

Karne sat down.

"Crap. You're right. Fine, I'll do it. That reminds me, what were you guys doing in Islamidahd?"

"What? We didn't go all the way to Islamidahd. We took a wrong turn."

"You were on the highway to Islamidahd when the transponder failed."

"Being on the highway to Islamidahd is not the same thing as making a trip to Islamidahd. I told you. We took a wrong turn."

"You," the Major said, biting her words off as if they were beef jerky, "really think I'm stupid, don't you? Bozo the clown. Ronald McDonald. A pointy-headed geek."

"Don't you have phone calls to make, Major?" Harlan said with a bland, toneless expression.

She reached over, plucked Lyle's beer from his meaty hand and took a large drink. "Yes, I do," she said. She stifled a belch. "But, when I'm done, we're going to have a look at where that sniper was holed up. All of us. That includes you two worthless fucks."

"Thank you for inviting us, Major," Harlan said. "We'd be delighted to join you on a field trip. It sounds like fun."

While Major Karne fumbled with a pocket to remove her communicator, Lyle took back his beer and finished it off, then held up four fingers to order more.

Beep. Harlan glanced at his communicator. It was an *all-clear* message from Shimon. He put his communicator away.

He exchanged a glance with Curtis—who raised his right arm with his watch on it a fraction of an inch.

Harlan nodded. He knew.

Three hours until Jimmy wakes up.

They stood in front of the apartment's main entrance.

"You sure this is the one?" Major Karne said.

Harlan nodded. "Yeah," he said. "This is the building. Second floor."

"Where's your little buddy with his fancy toys?" Lyle said.

"I don't know. Around somewhere with Jimmy, I guess. Who knows?"

Lyle looked at Harlan intently, then at Curtis.

"I can smell it. You guys are fucking with us. What's your game?"

"Major Karne, don't you think it would be a good idea if Lyle took a look around upstairs before the rest of us go up? Make sure it's clear. Safe."

"Me?" Lyle said. "No way. Send one of these jerk-offs up. Send Curtis. Better yet, we should get a long way away in case there's something big wired up there."

Karne looked at Curtis and Harlan. "Don't you get it, Lyle?" she said. "They already know it's clear and are playing one of their stupid-ass games. For what conceivable reason, I don't know, but I'm getting pretty tired of it. Fuck you guys, I'll go. Second floor? Which apartment?"

"Third one in from the west," Harlan said.

She opened the wrought-iron door of the apartment complex. "Assholes," she muttered.

Harlan smiled at Lyle, ushered Curtis in, and then followed her himself. "You can stand out here and wait for the Russian to zero in on you if you like," he said.

Lyle scanned the tops of the surrounding buildings, then followed them into the complex.

On the second floor, Karne tried the door. It was open. She turned to Curtis, who followed close on her heels, and kicked at the mouse hole Shimon had cut in the door. The piece he'd stuck back in flew out. "You guys upset me," she said before entering the room.

Inside, there was a ball of explosives the size of a basketball—with a melted-down detonator module laid on top.

All the other rooms were empty except for a huge heap of shit in the toilet and the single cartridge standing up on the bathroom counter.

Karne reached out to flush the toilet, but Curtis put his hand on her arm to stop her. "I wouldn't," he said.

She looked at the mess in the bowl with distaste, but left it.

"Disgusting," she said.

"Can I make a suggestion?" Harlan said. Karne nodded. "Let's have a sit-down meeting in Curtis's room and clear the air. Get some things straight."

"Fine," Karne said. "See you there."

Shimon waited outside Curtis's hotel room.

"Why didn't you go in?" Curtis said. "You couldn't manage a hotel room door?"

"I could, but I didn't want to be rude," Shimon said.

Curtis keyed the door open and they all went inside. Karne seemed a little nonplussed to see Jimmy sleeping on the floor.

"What's with sleeping beauty?" she said, but no one answered her.

"Drinks?" Curtis said. "I have Red Star—lots of it."

He passed them out. Lyle turned a chair around backwards, settled on it and twisted the cap off his bottle. "We need to stop the games and secrecy. We're a team. We need to work together, or you guys are going back to your unit minus a few stripes."

"Shut up, Lyle," Major Karne said. "Let's hear what the guys have to say and we'll go from there."

"You can't be taking these peasants seriously," Lyle said.

"Shut your face, Lyle. I'm not saying it again." To Harlan, she said, "Your show, Sergeant. What's on your mind?"

Harlan smiled. He stabbed his knife into the hardwood table top where it swayed back and forth as if it was alive. "Shimon?" he said. "Please bring Jimmy out of hibernation."

"Zap him?" Shimon said.

"Yeah."

"He's going to be pissed," Shimon commented. He dug through a medical kit and pulled on blue, sheer latex gloves, then found a plastic packet which he zipped open. "You don't want to get any of this shit on you."

He unfolded a small white patch and took a deep breath, then slapped the patch on Jimmy's upper arm.

The effect was almost instantaneous. Jimmy's body convulsed and he sat up. Shimon handed him a cold bottle of water from Curtis's minibar. "Hydrate. It will help with the headache."

Jimmy guzzled nearly the whole thing. He wiped at water dripping down his chin.

"What did you do to me?" he said with fury. "And what is this asshole doing here? He got Rocky killed." Lizard-quick, he grabbed the knife and lunged at Lyle, catching the front of Lyle's shirt with the tip as Lyle jumped back. A button flew off the shirt and bounced on the floor. Curtis and Shimon tackled Jimmy and held him down.

"Hold on, Jimmy," Harlan said. "We want to hear what evidence you have against Lyle before we let you kill him."

"Evidence," Jimmy said. "I don't have any evidence, just a feeling. I just don't like the fucker. Never did. I talked to Rocky and she said Lyle stopped by for a minute looking for me. He was in the room. You know me, I would never leave the drapes open, not even a crack. I think he came in, took a look out of the window and left an opening, maybe an inch, that's all that was needed and when Rocky pulled the drapes closed, tight, the way I taught her, the Russian took the shot."

"Hold on," Lyle said. "It's true that I stopped by and took a quick peek out the window…"

"Shut your mouth, Lyle," Karne said. "Sit your ass down."

Jimmy looked up. His eyed overflowed with tears. "I'm okay, guys. Let me go, I won't do anything." Harlan nodded. Curtis and Shimon stepped back. Jimmy buried his face in his hands and sobbed.

"He's crashing already," Shimon said. "The pseudo-adrenaline wears off fast."

Jimmy stood up. "There's something I noticed," he said. "The curtains were closed when we left, but someone opened them a little bit. The Russian waited. When Rocky was in the firing zone, the Russian took the shot."

"That leaves one question, Harlan said. "Is Lyle stupid or working with the Russian? Either way, I say we let Jimmy have him."

"Patricia," Lyle said.

To silence him, she held up her index finger. "Don't," she said.

Shimon clasped and unclasped the hooks and loops of a Velcro strap on his holster. The harsh noise was loud and annoying in the small room.

Harlan picked up the knife and held it an inch from Lyle's eye. "You're right, Shimon. Strap him down."

Shimon securely taped Lyle's feet and wrists to the chair. Unless he was strong enough to break the chair, he wasn't going anywhere.

"Major…" Lyle said.

"I'm tired of hearing his voice," Harlan said. "If he says one more word…"

"…Karne."

With a quick motion, Harlan picked up a plastic bag of pistachio nuts and shoved it in Lyle's mouth. Shimon applied a foot of duct tape over the top of it. Lyle could wriggle and grunt, but that was all.

Harlan put a hand on Jimmy's shoulder and pressed the knife into his hand. "Okay, Jimmy. Do what you want."

Jimmy looked up. "I'm not like you guys. Killing and death bothers me. It wears on me. I'm through with it. Really. I can't walk around here with so much sadness and brutality and pain and destruction and pretend it doesn't touch me. It does. I just want to go home where I can be a real human being again. I don't want to let the team down, but please, we don't exist anymore as far as the Army is concerned. I want to go home."

"There's no one, Harlan said, "who enjoys blowing things up as much as you, Jimmy." To Shimon, he said, "Is this just the drugs?"

"I don't know," Shimon said. "He talks like this when he's been drinking. My sense? He's telling it straight. He's burned out."

"Okay, Jimmy. Let's take a day to think on this. If you feel the same way in the morning, then we'll figure out a way to get you out of here. You served your country and have been a real asset to us and we'll miss you, but every man has a limit. If you've reached yours, then, that's it and it's cool. Take him to your room, Shimon."

The two men shuffled off. When the door closed, Curtis spoke. "What are we going to do with Lyle?"

Harlan reached over, picked up the knife and admired the keen edge in the harsh hotel light.

"Let's set Lyle in front of the window. If the Russian takes him out, then we know he was innocent. Stupid, but innocent. If he's still alive by nightfall, then he's in league with the Russian and I'll come up here and cut his throat. You have a problem with that plan, Major? Either way, you'll have another mess to call in for clean up."

Karne looked at Lyle. His contorted face was red. He clearly did not like the plan; he grunted and vigorously wriggled in the chair.

"No, I guess not," she said.

Grunting, they moved Lyle to a spot in front of the window, and then carefully tore down most of the aluminum foil. Curtis crawled to stay under the window and they gathered by the door. Lyle's view out of the window was majestic. He could see the city skyline, such as it was, the streets baking in the cruel sun and the cars, trucks and motorbikes weaving in and out as the people went about their daily business.

Harlan tore off another strip of duct tape and covered Lyle's eyes. Looking on with no expression on his face, Curtis unconsciously tugged on his beard like everyone else did.

Outside in the hallway, after Harlan hung out the *Do Not Disturb* sign and eased the door shut, the Major spoke.

"That was needlessly cruel," she said.

"Then go back in and rescue him," Harlan replied.

She took a deep breath, then turned and walked down the hallway toward the elevators.

Curtis and Harlan looked at each other. Curtis shrugged. Then, they followed her.

Sura 23, Verses 45-46. Then we sent Moses and his brother Aaron to visit the Pharaoh and his chiefs with our seals and manifest authority, but they behaved insolently—they were an arrogant people.

Book Two—Chapter Eighteen

Khostarak—Shimon and Major Karne

DOWNSTAIRS, IN THE hotel lobby, Curtis and Harlan headed toward the stairs to the underground parking garage. Major Karne followed them, but Harlan waved her away.

"What am I supposed to do?" she said.

"Sit with Shimon and Jimmy," Harlan said. "We'll be back in a bit."

She grumbled under her breath, but stayed behind, watching the two men walk away. After they were out of sight, she waited a few seconds, and then walked into the bar. Jimmy was hunched over a beer. He didn't look up when Karne sat down. Shimon waved a finger and ordered her a beer.

"Is he going to be okay?" she said.

Jimmy looked up. "I'm sitting right here, Major. You want to know my status? Ask me directly. Does Harlan think I'm going to change my mind? Well, I'm not. I've been thinking about this for a long time. I don't know what we're doing here. I don't care about these people and their problems. They've been fucked up for thousands of years and they'll be fucked up for another thousand as far as I can tell. If they're not fighting off invaders, then they're fighting amongst themselves. That's what they do. Fight. And they're good at it. No one can build anything here. Five years from now, this mullah or that Imam or some fresh new cold-blooded dictator backed by Russia or the U.S. or Pakistan or Iran or India or China will blow it up. My step-uncle Jimmy has a bagel shop in Brooklyn. He already told me he wants to retire and move to Fort Lauderdale and he'll sell it to me cheap. That's what I want to do, make bagels and argue with customers over the Yankees and the Knicks. Rocky wanted to join me. She really did, that was no bullshit. A guy like me never finds love. You guys get all of the luck and there's nothing left for me. Honest to God, you are my brother, Shimon, and I love you, but I hate you too, all of you."

He hunched over his beer and wept.

"Is he going to be okay?" Karne said.

"He'll be fine," Shimon replied, "once he's home."

They sat for a while and drank in silence.

She slid her index finger across the table until it rested an inch from Shimon's arm. He pretended not to notice, but he did.

"Four is a good number for a team," she said. "You think?"

Shimon considered. "It's more important *who* is in the team," he said.

"You guys want to talk as if I'm not here?" Jimmy said. "Fine, screw you both; I'll go take a dump—a leisurely one with the newspaper." He scooted out of the booth. Shimon and Karne watched him go.

"You might have influence with Harlan," she said.

Shimon laughed. "Maybe. Maybe not. He might listen, then he might do the opposite of what I suggest. Harlan's Harlan. Who knows?"

"I can help you guys. I want in. Help me with Harlan."

She slowly moved her finger until it just barely touched

Shimon's brown arm.

"I'm happy to throw my opinion in the mix," he said. "Though it might be helpful if I got to know you a little better."

She leaned back in her chair and laughed. When she was done laughing, she took a pull off her beer.

"Let's move this party to my place," she said.

In her room, Shimon checked. Her curtains were drawn tight; not even a sliver of light came through.

She walked to the bathroom door. "Give me a minute to freshen up," she said.

He looked through her minibar. After filling two water glasses with ice; he poured Baileys Irish Cream for both of them and sat in her guest chair. Waiting.

To her, 'freshening up' apparently meant taking off all of her clothes. She stood in the bathroom doorway—striking a pose—with light pouring from behind her.

She walked across the room and straddled Shimon's lap. After sipping her drink, she put a finger in it and then dribbled a few drops of the ivory fluid above each of her pert, brown nipples.

"Damn it," she said. "It appears I've made a mess."

With pillows fluffed up behind their backs and their naked bodies stretched across the bed, they drank and watched the ceiling fan spin in lazy circles. From the nightstand drawer, she found one of Lyle's Guantanamera Cubanos and lighted it for him.

"What do you think?" she said. "Did I meet all of your manly expectations?"

Shimon considered. "You certainly don't leave much in a man, I'll say that much."

"I'll take that as a compliment," she said. "If you're ready again in a few minutes, we'll go again, but at some point we should go back down and see if Jimmy is done with his shit."

"I'm no teenage boy any more, but I'll be happy to scrub your back in the shower."

"It's a deal," she said.

After Shimon finished his little cigar, they took a shower, but there was not much back scrubbing that went on.

Back in the bar, Jimmy had switched to black coffee and seemed to be in a more cheerful mood. Shimon and Major Karne's wet hair and rumpled clothing did not faze him one bit.

"Taking a shit seems to have agreed with you," Karne said.

"Getting my ass out of this hellhole fucking wart on a horny toad's ugly ass of a country agrees with me," Jimmy said. "There's something you can do for me, Major."

After she waved her fingers for two beers, she turned her attention to Jimmy.

"What?" she said.

"I want Rocky's ashes. I'll take the long way home and stop in Perth to scatter her dust in the wind. That's the least I can do in her memory."

She put out her hand to cover Jimmy's. "Done. I'll have the guys bring her by tonight," she said.

Jimmy raised his glass. "To Rocky, she was a fine woman."

"To Rocky," Karne and Shimon repeated.

Curtis walked into the bar. Major Karne looked behind Curtis.

"Where's the boss?"

"He went up to check on Lyle. You know, to see if he needs anything, like a cool drink or something."

"Bullshit," Karne said.

"It turns out," Curtis said, "if you stand at the proper angle out on the street, you can see an new hole in the window. The perfectly round little hole those rounds make without shattering the glass is amazing."

"Compound shells," Jimmy said, "melt and vaporize the glass ahead of themselves as they pass through. It's not just the

Russians—the French and the Japanese figured it out too."

"I'm going to miss you, Jimmy," Curtis said. "You're good company when you're in the right mood."

Harlan joined them at the table.

"What did you find?" Major Karne said.

"It's such a god-awful mess that it's hard to say for sure, but it looks like Lyle's throat was cut *before* the Russian shot him. This is pure speculation—I think someone slashed Lyle's carotid artery and the Russian caught a glimpse and took a bad-angle shot at the cutter. Unless the shooter just missed this time, but the shell took Lyle in the upper left arm, not dead center, which leads me to think the Russian was shooting at something else. Either way, Lyle's deceased. Expired. Dead and the devil's problem, not mine."

"I'll drink to that," Jimmy said.

"You're moving on?" Curtis said to Jimmy.

"Yeah. I called in a favor and hooked a lift on a Constellation to Kuwait. I'll play it by ear from there."

A corpsman in dress uniform approached the table and placed a colorful, ceramic cookie jar in the center. He saluted, turned on his heel and left without saying a word.

"Perfect," Jimmy said. "Now Rocky joins us." The bartender, with a glass in his fist, approached their table. "All of my friends are here. Can we have a moment of silence?" They bowed their heads for just a second before Jimmy spoke again in a boisterous voice. "Screw it. She hated silence." He raised his coffee cup. "To Rocky," he said.

Everyone in the room, including the drunken wire service stringers, raised their glasses and repeated the toast.

They drank into the early evening, though Major Karne ducked out a few times to coordinate Lyle's cleanup. About seven-thirty, everyone said they were ready for bed.

"Before we split up," Major Karne said, "I think Shimon has something he wants to say."

Shimon looked into Harlan's eyes. "Deep inside, I think Karne is good people. I think you should bring her in and make her a full partner in the team."

Harlan stared at Shimon as if horns had sprouted from his head, then he nodded. "Coming from you, Shimon," he said, "that means a lot. I will give your suggestion the full consideration it merits."

Karne beamed and winked at Shimon. "Starting tomorrow," she said, "I'm looking forward to a new, more intimate phase of our working relationship."

Jimmy, swaying, stood up too.

"I also have something I want to say. You guys ever find yourself in Brooklyn with a hankering for a genuine, first-quality New York bagel; come see me and get half off for life because I really love you."

"If you loved me, you'd give me a free bagel—at least the first one," Curtis said.

"Hey," Jimmy said, offended, "you want a free meal, go listen to the sermon on Seventy-Fifth and Hudson with the other worthless bums."

Harlan pulled a bundle of the counterfeit bills from under his jacket and slid them across the table. "Don't spend these directly, run them through a good fence."

"You have to stop doing that," Major Karne said. "I get chewed out when these bills keep showing up."

"Blow me," Harlan said to Karne as he reached across the table to shake Jimmy's hand.

"Thanks," Jimmy said. "This will help a lot."

"Jimmy," Shimon said, "I'd like to talk to you about your bagel store. My uncle Hiram ran a successful shop in Boston and he taught me a few things."

"It already has the right sign. Jimmy's Authentic New York Bagels and, so you know, there's no room for another name. As an added benefit, there are no Russians shooting at you there, just fat women from the old country trying to get discounts."

"*That* can be dangerous," Shimon said.

Karne leaned over and whispered in Shimon's ear. "You coming up?"

"Maybe later," he said. "We'll see."

Sura 23, Verse 49. We gave Moses the Book, so his followers might follow the true path.

Book Two—Chapter Nineteen

Khostarak

IT WAS A typical Irakkistan morning; by nine o'clock, the sun was done playing and angrily blazed in the sky alternately baking and broiling the bustling city.

Curtis was bleary-eyed and when he came down to meet Harlan at the Khostarak Serena Hotel coffee shop where they'd landed after abandoning the Hilton.

"My head hurts," Curtis said.

"My belly feels like a rat ate a hole in it," Harlan replied. "Another day with the requisite drinking afterward will kill me dead."

Major Karne, looking dapper in her uniform with her hair pulled back tightly in a French roll, seemed to be okay, not nearly as hung over as the men.

She pulled out a chair and sat down, then immediately reached for the carafe of coffee in the middle of the table.

"Good morning, team," she said, while looking around the room to see who else was around. "I halfway expected Shimon to visit me last night, but he must have been too tired."

"He's gone," Harlan said.

"What? Up and already out of here? That would be a surprise. He was keeping up with you guys drink-for-drink."

"No," Harlan said. "He caught the cargo bird with Jimmy. They're in Kuwait by now unless they got lucky and caught another southbound plane already. They could be halfway to Manila by now, who knows?"

"You're kidding, right?" Major Karne said. "Shimon is my friend. I can't believe it. After the day we shared, he'd leave me without saying goodbye?"

Curtis shrugged. "He said goodbye, but you weren't paying attention. Can you imagine Shimon-the-Jew letting Jimmy run a New York bagel shop without butting in and telling him how things were done in Beantown? They're probably arguing over the right kind of lox as we speak."

"I have something I want to get off my chest," Harlan said to Major Karne. "When I prove to myself you are working with the Russian, there is going to be trouble between you and me. Understand?"

Karne looked wounded. "Lyle..."

"...wasn't running rogue," Harlan interjected. "He wouldn't whip out his dick and use the pisser without you telling him to."

"I promise you..." she said.

Harlan held up his palm to her face. "Don't even bother. If it is, it is and I will find out. If it isn't, then I will apologize. If and when..."

"I understand," she said.

"This Russian is pissing me off," Curtis said. "I don't like the idea of him lurking out there with his fancy rifle."

"It's worse than that," Harlan said. "He's toying with us and I'd like to know why. Have any ideas, Major?"

She quietly stared into her coffee.

"No," she eventually whispered. "I don't."

"So, we agree," Harlan said, "Our number one priority is to take out the Russian? Curtis?"

"Yes. I already told you—the guy is pissing me off."

"Karne?"

"Fine," she said, "that's a good short-term, tactical mission. Take out the Russian. Okay. But, what about the bigger picture? It's better if we work together, right? Pull the rope in the same direction. I can't do that unless you tell me what the big play is."

Harlan tugged Curtis's beard. Curtis swatted his hand away.

"Curtis is the emissary for the big Kahuna Twelfth Imam. With the help and backing of international business interests, the local military and police, and cooperative religious leaders, he's going to ride into Khostarak's old city square on a black stallion with a huge sword and unite the disparate tribes of Irakkistan."

"The horse and the scimitar part," Curtis said, "are figurative, not literal."

"Woah, woah, what?" she said. "You can't be sober."

"And you're going to help us with your badge, the secret codes on your communicator and your spook connections back in D-C. Whatever you *can* bring to the party, you *will* bring— that's the way a team works together."

"I have a more modest mission," the Major said. "All I care about is shutting down the printing press."

"Compared to uniting a whole country," Harlan said, "that part will be easy. We're going to help you with that and you're going to help us. See how that works?"

"I can't believe you guys are serious."

"He's a little more serious about his plan than I am," Curtis said. He noted the stricken expression on Harlan's face. "But I'm pretty serious too."

"So," she said, "you'll help me unless you decide I'm working with the Russian, then you won't help me—you'll kill me."

Harlan touched his temples. "Not only that, but I have a

vision of you screaming in pain for a long time before you die, if that helps."

He grinned from ear to ear.

To Curtis, she said, "I can never tell if he's completely serious."

"Good luck," Curtis said. "I've known him half my life and I have the same problem."

Sura 23, Verse 52. And verily your brotherhood is a single brotherhood, and I its Lord and protector. Worship and fear me and no other.

Book Two—Chapter Twenty

Khostarak

AT BREAKFAST THE next morning, Curtis slipped a piece of paper across the table to Harlan.

"Got something from Shimon," he said.

Harlan opened the paper and read it. "Great," he said.

Major Karne, after filling a plate with sausages, flat bread and dried fruit from the buffet, joined them.

"Don't hide it. What's the paper say?" she asked.

Harlan considered for a moment, then shrugged and pushed it over to her. "It's from Shimon," he said.

"Where is he?"

"I don't know, that didn't come up. Kuwait? Manila? Perth? What difference does it make? His terminal works anywhere there is a high-speed data connection. And, where ever he is, he's still helping us out."

She chewed a date, daintily spat out the seed into her napkin and unfolded the paper. It was an e-mail, with header, footer, and security codes all printed out on cheap, smudgy paper.

I might have to give them the Russian.
—PKarne

"I can explain this," she said. "It will make sense once you know the context."

"Excellent," Harlan said. He leaned across the table to study her face. Grinning, he seemed genuinely amused and deeply interested. "This should be good. Go ahead."

She swallowed her date and speared another with her fork and examined it as if she'd never seen one before.

"Actually," she said, "no, I can't. It's too complicated to easily explain. Tell me what you think it means and I'll correct you when you go wrong."

"It means you know how to find the Russian and you're jerking us off. Maybe he doesn't work for you, but you have influence over what he's doing. It means you're a lying, conniving bitch and we were right not to trust you with the full details of our strategy."

"Okay," she said. "You got me. That's about right. But, can we make a deal? I'll give you the Russian if you don't kill me. And, whether you know it or not, you can still use my State Department connections. In fact, I have some news."

"News," Harlan said. To Curtis, he said, "She has news for us. I can't hardly wait."

"It's probably the important news we've been waiting for," Curtis said, with a flat, dry tone.

"You guys running around this country playing stupid games are good at one thing. Stirring up trouble. And, you're such outstanding third-rate comedians having a lot of fun at my expense. At your country's expense. Causing *diplomatic* troubles, get it? Lyle was right, the best way to describe you? Clowns, circus clowns, bad-joke midgets riding in circles on clown bicycles, tripping over your own two feet and interpreting the crowd's guffaws as encouragement."

"I think we get the *clown* part of your monologue," Harlan

said. "Can we move on to the *news* part?"

With a controlled dignity, she refilled her coffee cup. Her hands were steady, she did not slosh a drop.

It was an impressive, masterful performance.

"It's a mystery I can't explain," she said, "but your plan has been approved. Green lighted, one-hundred percent. This can't be public, of course, but you have the full support and cooperation of the military, the state department, the White House, the CIA, the NSA and our friendly sock puppet supporters in the media. Full funding. Blanket authorizations. Diplomatic and justice department immunity for all of your war crimes. Someone, high up the food chain, thinks your plan has a chance of succeeding. Now, it even has an official name. Operation Sandcastle. I came up with that. Pretty good, huh? So, that counts as news, right? This is big. We should celebrate."

"What do you think, Curtis?" Harlan said. "The geniuses in the government want to help us."

Curtis picked up a raisin from his plate and looked it over carefully before sticking it in his mouth. "I think, considering how they bungle nearly everything they lay their hammy hands on, that we should politely decline accepting their help."

"That's pretty much the way I see it too," Harlan said. "There're only two things we want from you and you're going to hand them over now, or we're going to kill you and take them from your cold, dead body. We want the fancy gold badge you show the local police to get their cooperation and we want the secret satellite communicator we're not supposed to know about—the one you carry on an inside hip pocket."

Her eyes flicked between Harlan and Curtis. She pulled the badge from an inside jacket pocket, placed it on the table, then lifted a Velcro flap on her trousers and slid the communicator across the table.

"The communicator will be useless in an hour," she said.

"I don't understand all this stuff," Harlan replied, "but

Shimon says you guys are too cheap to make custom electronic chips. Once he figures out how you configure the commercial-grade chips you use and copies the encryption algorithm, we can make our Chinese communicators act the same way. You can take down the whole system and reprogram everything, but Shimon doesn't think that will happen. Personally, I don't care. As long as it works for a little while, that's good enough."

Harlan stuffed the badge and communicator into his backpack.

"Are you going to tell her about the Russian?" Curtis said.

Harlan snapped his fingers. "Hell, you're right, I almost forgot. We got a bit of information about the Russian—Viktor Maksimovich, that's one of his names, anyway. He seems like an interesting man and I'd love to sit down and trade war stories with him someday, but I guess that probably won't happen. Too bad. We don't know where he is or exactly why he's fucking with us, but, through a mutual acquaintance, we were able to pass a message to him, your message, Major, the one where you suggest, how did you put it? Giving him up to us? That's bound to irritate him, don't you think?"

Harlan and Curtis got up.

"Keep your hands on the table until we're out of sight," Harlan said. "And there's one more thing."

With her hands spread flat on the table, she took a breath and pretended to be bored.

"Okay, what is it?" she said.

"I don't ever want to see your ugly face again," he said. "If I see you, I kill you."

Rotating their heads, they kept an eye on her as they left the room. They walked out the front door and almost immediately disappeared in the crowd.

"You shouldn't have called her ugly. She'll never give up now."

"I don't like being called a clown."

"But you *are* a clown," Curtis said.

"From you, I'll take it. Not from her."

A block from the hotel across from a twenty-four-hour real estate office, a massive, shiny Hyundai SUV pulled up to the curb.

Harlan and Curtis got in and pulled the door shut behind them. The car pulled out into traffic and vanished.

Sura 23, Verses 53-54. They cut their unity into pieces—with each group rejoicing in its own tenets. Let's leave them in their confused ignorance for now.

Book Three—Chapter One

Steve Stephens

DISTURBED BY A polite knock at his door, Steve glanced at his wall clock. Unlike the other clocks in this section of the building, his was a high-quality Government Services Administration (GSA) National Stock Number (NSN) 4919814 atomic clock with radio-controlled quartz movement, twelve-inch diameter black clock with white face.

12:33 it said, very nearly the dead-center of his lunch hour. He read a tattered, second-hand copy of *The National Review* while leaning back in his chair with his flat, shoeless feet splayed on his desk. He ate a peanut butter and raison sandwich made with twelve-grain bread and drank a peach Snapple made from 'the best stuff on earth'.

It was a grand mystery. How did they find the best corn syrup on earth? After retirement, perhaps I'll have time to solve this perplexing brain teaser.

Whoever was at the door would not take the hint. There came another polite knock.

He wrapped up the remaining half of his sandwich and

slipped it into a desk drawer. Removing a lint roller from his side drawer, he rolled it over his shirt-front and necktie until the sandwich crumbs and stray gray hairs were removed to his satisfaction. He tugged at the cuff of his long-sleeved shirt. The bulk of a bandage was barely visible under the fabric. For almost a year, he'd been cutting himself. Usually when you think of cutters, you think of bulimic, angst-ridden teen-aged girls, but black, depressed, nearly-retired law enforcement officers did it too.

For cutting, he used a razor-sharp KA-BAR knife. This KA-BAR was a hand-me-down U.S. Air Force #1262 knife, a semi-valuable collector's piece Steve carried in the third version of the Iraqi Desert Storm assault; he used it in place of the plain-edged, black, cord handle Ontario knife the Air Force issued. The KA-BAR's compacted-disk leather handle was stained and the dark, powder-coated blade was faded by years of redundant sharpening.

The cutting started by accident. He'd been honing the ultra-keen carbon-steel edge when the blade slipped. The resulting cut wasn't deep—just a little crease in the dark skin of the inside of his arm. The knife was so sharp that the wound didn't hurt. Blood oozed nearly black under the harsh fluorescent lighting of his apartment.

It struck him. Here at the trailing end of his useful life, everything seemed like bullshit except the harsh reality of sobering pain and the blood seeping from his arm.

He knew he was depressed and should get professional help, but he thought he could handle it.

Pills?

No.

He was no pathetic housefrau-hypochondriac; he was a field-toughened law enforcement professional. Besides, the hypocrisy was too ironic. He'd spent fourteen years tracking and prosecuting drug dealers, now he would throw himself into their world of mind-altering pharmaceuticals? Xanax, Paxil,

Zoloft, Celexa, Elavil and old-school Prozac? How was that different from cocaine, heroin, marijuana, roofies, uppers and downers? He could not face it. He only had thirty-seven more days to live anyway, so why bother?

"Okay, come in," he called out, mostly avoiding any hint of annoyance in his tone.

His voice was smooth like deep, rich dark chocolate. His hair was cropped close; a quarter-inch of gray mat. A husky man, he was in his mid-fifties and retired from the Air Force after a twenty-four year hitch. Assigned to a Drug Enforcement Administration Regional Enforcement Team, he marked time until his second retirement kicked in. Literally. On a GSA NSN 7892455 Wall Calendar Board, he'd been neatly marking off the days with elaborate red X's; he had precisely thirty-seven days left.

He did not recognize the woman who poked her head in.

The first thing he noticed was an array of wounds scattered around her left eye, butterfly bandages and black knots of stitches.

Something nearly took her head off.

The surgeon's work was excellent—the artificial left eye was a near-perfect match for the right.

"You get anything from that artificial eye?" Steve said.

"Thirty-percent vision, they tell me. Shapes. Colors. It's better than nothing."

The question was a cliché, but he couldn't resist it. "What happened?" he said.

It appeared that she considered a range of answers before picking one.

"Irakkistan," she said. "Russian sniper."

"Ah."

After stepping into the room, she stood at attention before his desk.

She wore a crisp, formal Army uniform—her brown hair was pulled back in a bun so tightly that it gave her eyes an Asian cast. Approving, Steve noted she wore her standard Army beret properly with the brim a precise one inch above her carefully plucked right eyebrow and with the flash over the left eye folded to the right front with excess draped over right side down to the top of her ear with the dip behind the flash. She wore a Field Service Uniform (FSU) AG 489 and the belt of her skirt was dressed properly to the right, opposed to the male's belt regulation. The hem of her skirt was centered exactly on the back fold of her knee.

After taking note of her brass shoulder blobs and nametag, Steve spoke.

"What can I do for you, Major Karne?"

"I'm sorry to bother you, Agent Stephens. I know it's your lunch time."

"Therefore this must be important."

There was the slightest hint of threat in his voice.

"Of course," the Major replied.

She reached over and pushed the door closed behind her, then extended her hand for a shake. Steve carefully wrapped it in his monstrous fingers and shook it firmly.

"Please take a seat," he said, gesturing.

Favoring his stiff back, he eased backward into his chair. He folded his giant hands on his desk and tried to imagine what she'd come to tell him. After thirty-five years of by-the-book service and with only thirty-seven days to go, he had nearly nothing to fear, but still a warning tickle teased the back of his mind.

Unredeemably, the routine boredom of his day was disrupted.

"Thank you," she replied, while looking around his office. His desk, completely clean and uncluttered, displayed only a NSN 2866954 Binder, Note Pad, Springback, Aluminum, 8.5 X 11, a yellow pencil (Pencil, Number 2, 100% Recycled) sharpened to a perfect point and a 4588210 8.5 X 11 Picture Frame, Clear Glass. She pointed at the picture with a question on her face. Steve nodded slightly. She picked the picture up and studied the soldier's images carefully.

"Balad Ruz?" she said.

"Yes," Steve answered.

She put the picture back and adjusted it with a painted fingernail. Steve glanced and approved. She'd positioned it properly; just exactly as she'd found it.

"I'm sorry," she said. "This is very uncomfortable."

"I have a very busy schedule this afternoon."

"I understand. I'll get to the point. I'm really sorry to say—it's about your nephew. Curtis."

All strength flowed from his body. He wilted.

"Oh, no," he said while pressing on his stomach as if that was the only thing keeping his guts from spilling out.

"I'm truly sorry," she said gently.

Sura 2, Verse 33. He said, "Oh, Adam. Tell them about their natures."

When Adam told them, Allah said, "Did I not tell you that I know the secrets of heaven and earth? I know what you reveal and what you conceal."

Book Three—Chapter Two

Steve Stephens

RETURNING FROM AN invented quest to give Steve a few minutes to find his composure, she bought a soft drink from the hallway vending machine. She carefully folded a paper towel to act as a coaster and set a cold can of Mountain Dew on the center of his desk. Steve was hunched over pressing his massive palms against his temples. She pushed a handkerchief across his desk. After leaning back in his chair, he used it to blot at dampness in the corners of his eyes.

He cleared his throat and managed to speak.

"Tell me," he said.

Major Karne settled in the guest chair. She unfolded a sheet of paper and read from it.

"The Department of Defense today announces the death of a soldier supporting Operation Irakkistan Liberation. Specialist Curtis Aaron Washington, 24, of Herndon, Virginia died in Khostarak, Irakkistan, on December 28 when an improvised explosive device detonated near his HMMWV during combat operations. Specialist Washington was assigned to the 1st Battalion, 67th Armored Regiment, 2nd Brigade Combat Team, 4th Infantry Division out of Fort Hood, Texas."

"Spare me the military jargon—skip the bullshit."

She folded the paper and put it back in her purse.

"Okay. I-E-D. Roadside bomb. Improvised Explosive Device."

"I know what an IED is, Major."

"I'm sorry. While on driving in convoy on the Khaliid Bin al Waliid Expressway, a remotely detonated 155mm artillery shell hit their HMMWV. Three soldiers lost their lives. Your nephew suffered extreme head injuries and was killed instantly. He was declared dead on the scene by Army medics."

"Did they get the fucking Islamo-Taliban fascist dickheads that did this?"

"I understand your grief, Agent Stephens, but I would appreciate professional restraint with regard to your language." Steve stared at her passively until she continued. "We are continually tracking down, killing or detaining insurgents, but we have no specific information on the makers of this specific weapon. I will say, in general, sir, they are losing the battle and we're winning."

"He was a great kid. Smart and focused. He could have been a Senator or a General if he'd set his mind to it. All he cared about was serving his country."

"His family will be awarded his Purple Heart."

"John-fricking-Kerry got one of those for a sliver of metal up his ass," Steve said bitterly.

"I don't know how you expect me to respond to that, Agent Stephens. Senator Kerry served his country in Vietnam with honor."

Steve slapped his hand on the desk.

"Don't fucking patronize me, I was fucking there and I know first-hand what kind of soldier Kerry was."

"I apologize if I offended you. There's something else we have to talk about, but perhaps this is not the right time."

Steve covered his eyes. "I'm sorry, Curtis was a great kid. I loved him. Everybody loved him. This is a great shock. The Lord should have taken me instead. I'm at my end and he was just starting out." He picked up his #2 pencil and twisted it until it shattered. He dropped splinters on his desk. "Okay, I'm composed. Don't jerk me off. What else do we need to talk about?"

"As I said, sir, there are a few things I can't go into right now, but the Army would be grateful if you come with me to Virginia to tell his mother."

With the palm of a massive hand, he swept the remnants of his mangled pencil into his medium-sized, GSA-approved black mesh wastebasket.

"Okay," he said. "I'll do it."

Natalie Curtis lived in a neighborhood of nearly-identical concrete block houses in a decommissioned Navy housing project. The streets were run-down, but not slummy. The cars that lined the streets were old, but none were gutted or abandoned. Major Karne drove the Army Ford Explorer (for official use only) and pulled up to the house, checking the numbers to make sure they matched her computer printout. The curtains in the house flicked.

"This never gets any easier," she commented. "I have Restoril if she needs it."

"You're ghoulish," Steve commented as he unfolded himself from the SUV. "She's not going to take drugs to mask the loss of her son."

"I'm just trying to do my job, sir."

A heavy-set black woman, wearing a bathrobe and colorful scarf in her hair, ran out the front door.

"Oh, no, Steve, please," she cried, "not my baby Curtis."

"I'm really sorry," Steve said as she collapsed into his arms.

"Ask her to make us some tea. The kitchen routine can be helpful," Major Karne suggested.

"I'm beginning to not like you very much," Steve said.

They sipped bitter black tea from a diverse collection of cups. Steve's was a chipped Air Force recruiting mug. Major Karne's was a flowery teacup. Natalie sat on a threadbare couch, sobbing and holding her Winnie the Pooh mug between her knees. Subtly, the Major rattled a pill bottle in her purse, but Steve waved her away. Karne read from the news release to make sure the details were accurately communicated, then stood and pulled on formal white gloves to present the Purple Heart medal.

"Your son is an American hero and on behalf of the United States Army, the Department of Defense and the United States Federal government, I extend heart-felt condolences for your loss."

Dazed, Natalie accepted the medal and clutched it to her chest. Watching an afternoon soap opera on a muted TV, they sat in silence for ten minutes until Major Karne cleared her throat.

"This is uncomfortable, but I need to ask. It's simply military routine, but if you collected any letters from Curtis, I need them for a judicial review. I assure you, they will all be returned, undamaged, in a day or two. This is purely a routine request."

Natalie nodded and got up. "I'll get them," she said.

"Excuse me," Steve whispered. "I've never heard of anything like this. What's going on?"

"It's a routine review of his correspondence."

"No it isn't, Major."

She shushed him as Natalie came back with a shoebox filled with letters. She handed them to the Major.

"I'll take them," Steve said.

He tugged the box, but Major Karne held on tightly.

"I have it," the Major insisted.

"It's alright, Steve," Natalie said. "She can have them. I'll get them back?"

"Yes, all of them, right away." To Steve, she asked. "Can I drop you back at your office?"

"No, I'll stay until Auntie Grace gets here. I can get a ride back."

"Very well." The Major stood by the front door. "Again, on behalf of the military, I offer sincere apologies on your loss. Your son is a true American hero. May God bless you and your family. There will be an arrival ceremony for his cremated remains at Washington National Airport and a burial service at Arlington National Cemetery. Other details, including his death benefit settlement, will be taken care of later. For now, I bid you goodbye. Please call me on my cell phone, day or night, if you need anything."

With the box under her arm, she left the front room.

Moving the curtain aside, Steve watched Karne walk to the SUV and waited until she drove off. He turned and put a hand on Natalie's shoulder.

"I'm very sorry about Curtis," he said.

She gestured for him to follow. They went to the kitchen where she turned on a radio—loud—and turned on the kitchen faucet.

What?

She whispered in Steve's ear. "Curtis is fine, I heard from him yesterday."

"What?"

"Do you think my performance convinced her? Curtis wasn't sure, but he said she might show up."

"You convinced *me*. My heart was breaking."

"Sorry about that, Steve." She gave him a kiss on the cheek.

"You shouldn't have given up those letters," he said. "Something doesn't seem right about all this."

Natalie looked up at him with her eyes brimming with tears. "Oh, I didn't give them *all* to her," she said quietly.

Sura 2, Verse 42. And cover not truth with falsehood, nor conceal the truth when ye know it.

Book Three—Chapter Three

Steve Stephens

STEVE'S HOME WAS not much to look at; he lived on the second floor of a nondescript three-story apartment building. It was too many painful stop-and-go commuting miles from his office in Washington DC, but the rent was within reach of his General Schedule 15 Grade Step 6 paycheck.

The complex was built in the 1970's but had been refurbished in the 2020's and was easy walking distance to the Lake Forest Mall. Except for the divorced wife of an airline pilot whom he occasionally shared a bed with; he didn't know many people in the complex. The ones he did know mostly worked in the many DC bureaucracies and he often shared the same subway with them in the morning and the evening.

On his coffee table, he'd made a shrine. In thirty-seven days—after signing the last of the retirement paperwork—he was going to kill himself, Marilyn Monroe style.

Accidental overdose, alcohol and barbiturates.

A fifth-gallon bottle of Bacardi 151 rum sat precisely in the center of his coffee table. 75.5% pure alcohol. Warning: Flammable, the label on the front advised.

No shit.

Arranged to the left of the bottle, he'd placed four Dramamine tablets in a line. Chewable, orange-flavored. They would reduce nausea—the job would be botched if he vomited up the rum and the pills. The final course was Nembutal, oral pentobarbital. Twenty-four capsules arranged in three columns to be washed down with fresh orange juice from the refrigerator. He'd selected a DEA coffee mug for mixing up his last and final drink.

A Cuban cigar—illegally imported by his some-time lover—completed the shrine with wooden matches and a ceramic ashtray. The apartment complex was a non-smoking facility, but Steve kept the windows closed and paid his rent on time, so no one bothered him about an occasional cigar.

He sat, drinking a cold bottle of Miller High Life. The rum called to him, but Steve was afraid of it. Hard liquor was a trap. A one-way ticket to hell. He'd been there and knew alcohol was no good answer to any question—no matter how difficult. Still, he could visualize pouring it into a glass. He knew how it would taste on his tongue, how it would burn when coursing down his throat and how the warm glow in his belly would spread.

Also on the coffee table, he'd placed Natalie's letters from Curtis. Still unread. Steve stared at the wall. There were no decorations except a photograph from his time in Vietnam. Looking at this picture, he could feel the oppressive humidity and the smell of decay, the nauseating motorbike fumes mixed with rotting vegetables.

Sewage and vomit.

The picture showed Steve and some of his men on a Saigon street. Staring into the lens, a too-young Steve Stephens, with his typical, old-man's dead-serious expression. Chip Porter, holding up his arms as if he'd just scored a goal, was now dead from a car accident in 2002. Orrin Gallo with his hands in his fatigue pants pockets, now repaired pickup trucks in Montana or Wyoming or some damned place. Jack "Chopper"

Reynolds—stoned on opium and staring into space. The last he'd heard, Chopper was down in Florida. Veterinarian? Finally, there was Glen Wilson bearing a crooked, toothy grin—smoking a cigar and flipping his middle finger at the whore operating Steve's old rangefinder camera.

Goddamned Glen Wilson.

During Steve's work with the DEA, he'd crossed paths with Glen a few times over the years. More honestly, Steve kept track of Glen as he traveled. It was a complicated mystery.

How could a former drug dealer win a congressional race in Alaska?

How could he recover from having it ripped from under his feet like a Turkish rug? How could one man survive when he'd made such powerful enemies? What was the nature of Glen's engine? What sustained this bizarre agent of chaos?

The vision of his nephew bleeding to death on a Khostarak highway kept intruding into Steve's thoughts.

In one world, dear, sweet Curtis was dead.

In another, he was well, but up to something crazy in Irakkistan.

It was absurd, but—what would Glen do?

Running his thumbs over the colorful stamps on his nephew's small bundle of letters, Steve wasn't ready to read them.

Really. What would the mad man—the wretched, insane jester in God's court—Glen Wilson, do?

He tried to visualize the face of Buddha to calm his mind, but Glen's grinning face drifted into the picture.

We're autumn leaves stirred by the invisible hand of God. Seek oneness with the way, where nothing is lacking and nothing is in excess. Undisturbed shall our mind remain, no evil words shall escape our lips; friendly and full of sympathy shall we remain, with heart full of love, and free from any hidden malice; and that person shall we penetrate with loving thoughts, wide, deep, boundless, freed from anger and hatred.[11]

Feeling forlorn, sad and stupid, Steve reached for his phone and worked the keypad. After a persistent hour of long-distance phone calls and the promise of returning a few favors, he had Glen's cell phone number. While staring at it, he'd unconsciously twisted the top off the rum bottle.

What am I doing? Losing my feeble grip on reality, that's what.

He pressed the numbers into his phone.

"Wilson here, who is calling?"

"Steve Stephens."

There was a short silence on the connection.

"Huh, how about that. What's on your mind, Sarge?"

Glen seemed unsurprised.

Over twenty years since they last spoke and Glen picks up the thread of a conversation as if they'd talked yesterday. This was no big deal to Glen?

"Hey, my man, how are you?"

"Reducing small talk. It wastes time. Life is short. Please get to your point or hang up, thank you."

"Busy, eh? Okay. You never met my nephew, Curtis, but he's a great young man. Irakkistan. Army. Operation Irakki Liberation. Today, an Army Major tells me he's dead. His mother says she talked to him yesterday and he's alive."

"Operation Irakki Bullshit, you mean. Not to be rude, but what has this to do with me, Steve?"

"The whole thing stinks. The Army Bereavement Consultant lies to us and acts weird. What would you do?"

Glen snorted. "Army Bereavement Consultant, that's a good one. Are you drunk, Sarge?"

"Not yet."

"Well, I'd go fucking non-linear, that's what I'd do."

Steve thought about the suggestion.

"Excuse me, but what the hell does that mean? After all

[11] From Buddha's Eightfold Path, 500BC.

these years, I track you down and ask for your help and you tell me to go *non-linear*. Pardon me all to hell, but I don't know what you're talking about."

Glen sighed and it was like a sad, bitter wind in Steve's ear.

"I'm not sure you've ever done anything for me except jerk me around." There was silence on the connection for a few moments. "Okay. What's the kid's name?"

"Curtis Washington."

"Okay, I got it. Now, if you don't mind, I'm in the middle of someone."

Click. Dead air.

Steve stared at the cordless phone's handset. He stifled an impulse to throw the handset across the room. However, he'd paid forty-five dollars for it at Best Buy and wasn't inclined to buy a new one. It wasn't the phone's fault Glen was an asshole.

Go non-linear. Right.

He looked at the bottle of rum as if he'd never seen it before; then screwed the top back on. From the coffee table, he picked up an armload of empty beer bottles and took them to the garbage bag under his sink. The bag was full, so he put the bottles on the counter. He opened a fresh beer and stared out the back window at the apartment complex swimming pool. It was filled with dry leaves.

Walking back to his couch, he picked up the oldest of the envelopes. While opening it a five-thousand dollar bill slipped out. Holding the bill up to the light, he examined it.

Why was a five-thousand dollar bill in the envelope?

Dear Mom.

I know you worry about me, but I'm fine. Some friends started a soccer competition. Football, the Aussies call it. We oiled down a patch of sand and built goals out of cargo nets. We play early in the morning or late at night because it's too damned hot during the day. We've won a game or two, but the Croatians kick our ass. There are only twenty Croatian soldiers in our camp, and they all damned well play good soccer. We have fun.

Yesterday, I guarded a pump station and little kids came around. We gave them balloons and Tootsie Pops and they taught us a little Irakki slang. One of them brought a dead camel spider—big as my hand and ugly as hell. Maybe I'll bring one home for you. Ha!

We've been watching DVDs. Have you seen that movie Jarhead? With the Donnie Darko guy? Stupid movie (Jarhead, not DD), but turn off the sound and just watch the pictures and its okay. Maybe someone will dub in real jarhead dialog and a patriotic storyline, and make something way-cool out of it.

We buy movies from a market on Siina'aa Street for a few dollars; they have crappy video quality and noisy sound because they're usually recorded in Kuwaiti theaters with hand-held cameras. It's a joke, but what do you expect for two new dollars?

We laugh at the news programs. Don't pay any attention to the alphabet networks, they really don't know shit. Sometimes Fox gets it right, but even them? Not always.

Hey, I met a guy who worked near the dear leader's oldest son's cell—says he was a senile old man who ate Doritos and talked to himself all day. He still thought he was still president and offered my friend a position in his government if he'd help him bust out. Maybe I could be ambassador to the UN or something? That's silly, of course. He couldn't walk anywhere on the street because he'd be torn to pieces by a mob in five minutes. Maybe ten minutes, max.

None of the locals I talk to wants him back in power.

PS: I'm enclosing some currency. We found a stash of them in a bombed-out garage. Don't try to spend it! It's counterfeit. I could get in serious trouble, so don't mention it in return mail or e-mail, they read everything that comes in. Sometimes they read out-going mail, but I know a guy who knows a guy, know what I mean?

PPS: I love you, mom. Just a couple more months here unless they extend us. It will be nice to have a real shower and sleep in my old bed. And beer, I'm going to drink lots of cold beer when I get home. Until then, I'll be thinking of you. Draft beer and bacon-cheeseburgers, I'll be thinking of them too. They make them here (lamb burgers, not the beer), but it's just not the same. Did you know beer was invented in Irakkistan? Well, in Baabiliin, the cradle of civilization, you know? I'll try to write again tomorrow or the next day.

Love, Curtis

There were three more letters, Steve skimmed the bodies of them and just read the PS sections where Curtis mentioned the money.

PS: There are four of us, mom, who found this stash. It's in a crashed-in garage buried under rubble courtesy of a Navy cruise missile. What's it doing here? I don't know. We haven't counted it all, but there are millions in plastic-wrapped bundles. We're rich, right? If we could get it home. I don't want to do anything illegal, but maybe this money is real. We can't tell. Finders = keepers? We talk about it all the time, but no one has a good theory. It's not far from one of the Dear Leader's palaces. And we found a dead guy, one of the guys on the most-wanted playing cards, I think the six of hearts, you know? No reward for enlisted folks, too bad.

Love, Curtis

PS: We're really pissed off, but one of our friends, I'd rather not mention his name, spent some of the bills. He bought a satellite dish from a shop on al Ruubayee Street. The vendor looked at the bills carefully, but took them. The serial numbers are sequential, but they look like good money to everyone that's seen them. There's over ten million and I'm a little scared. As time goes on, more people know. How can we keep a secret this big? If I could just forget about it, I would. Then I think about how cool it would be to buy you a nice house and a car. Like a Honda or something.

Yours, Curtis

Steve fanned the bills, ten of them, all crisp and fresh-looking. Playing by the book, he'd turn in the letters and the money and let military intelligence do their job.

Dammit, Curtis, what bee's nest did you stick your combat boots into? What would Glen do?

He'd dozed off with his head at an awkward angle. Waking with a start, he rolled his head on his neck to loosen the kinks.

Making a decision, he flipped the top off the Bacardi bottle. Standing at his sink, took one of the bills, rolled it up and stuffed it in his sock, then soaked the letters and remaining cash with rum. Holding them at arm's length with tongs, he lighted them with flame from his gas stove. Blue flame flared up instantly—the heat warmed his face. After washing the ashes down the drain—followed by the suicide pills, he crammed a perfectly good head of lettuce into the grinding garbage disposal to flush the ashes and drugs deep into the plumbing.

After opening a sliding window, he lighted a cigar to cover the smell of the fire. Puffing, he watched the wind ripple dead leaves in the swimming pool.

What would Glen do?

He pulled a pair of beer bottles from his refrigerator, then walked to the wall and stared deeply into the Vietnam photograph. Lifting it off its nail he took it back to his couch.

So young, yes they were, but not innocent, not even then. How could he help the people who risked everything to escape after Saigon fell in 1975? The newspaper photographs were etched in his mind; old men, women and children in flimsy boats, begging for help and drowning. What did he do to help his lover escape the horror of a communist re-education camp? Guilt washed over him. Now, as an old man, the battles moved to the deserts of the Middle East, what could he do? He drained a beer.

In all of his years of public service, he'd never taken a dirty dollar or cut a lucrative side deal. Fellow soldiers smuggled home weapons and dope, but he didn't. He knew DEA agents with secret homes in Florida decorated with thick carpets and young girls. Agent Carlyle had a young Cuban boyfriend stashed in Miami. Steve had a pension, a broken-down Buick station wagon and a portfolio full of underwater technology stocks.

By-the-book Stephens. Square-head Stephens. Over the years, he'd heard the nicknames and paid them no mind. Now, at the end of his life, he was prepared to throw it all away because something about a situation smelled bad. Did he owe something to Curtis? What was Curtis up to?

He held the photograph close. Goddamned Glen *non-linear* Wilson and his irreverent, evil grin, still disturbing after all these years. Slowly, he slid down in the couch cushions and dozed.

"Agent Stephens?" A hand gently shook his shoulder. Startled, he sat up. Beer bottles were strewn about. The Army Sergeant, wearing white gloves, stood in the kitchen doorway and shook the empty rum bottle. Major Karne nodded her head and looked at Steve with distain. "Do you mind, sir, if we look around your apartment?"

Steve rubbed his eyes. Three men opened drawers and riffled through his stuff.

"You're already doing it."

"For the record, we prefer to have your permission, sir."

"Well, you're not getting it."

"Very well, sir, we'll make a note. This search is involuntary. You can file a formal complaint and request a hearing."

A Sergeant appeared in his bedroom door with Steve's battered Colt .45. Major Karne took it and looked it over.

"Old school, Agent Stephens? That does not look like an agency-supplied weapon, sir. Is it registered with the state of Maryland? Have you been issued a concealed-weapon license? Do you have a *good and substantial* reason for it as demanded by the Secretary of the Maryland State Police?"

"You're not really a Bereavement Councilor, are you, Major Karne?"

Laughing, she idly flicked the safety on and off.

"You surprise me, Agent Stephens. Most of your people are dumb, but not you. You're a clever man, are you not?"

"My people? Black people?"

"No, deadweight, D-E-A D-C bureaucrats. Did you think I'd made a racial slur? Will you call the Equal Opportunity Task Force and report me?"

"Major?"

She turned. "Yes, Sergeant?"

"The place is clean."

"Thank you." Turning back to Steve, she sat the .45 on his

coffee table and spun it using her index finger. "How would it look to the police, Agent Stephens, if they found you here with a bullet in your head? With all these empty bottles strewn around—a despondent old man eating a bullet? It happens all the time, even to a guy with only thirty-seven days left to retirement."

"Thirty-six days."

The Major glanced at a wall clock. "Yes, you're right, it's after midnight. Thirty-six days left to go, then a comfortable double-dip from Uncle Sam's pension funds unless you fuck it all up by putting your nose into matters that are best left alone."

She sat back and stared at him. Picking up the Vietnam photo, she glanced at it briefly.

Tapping a gleaming fingernail on Glen's grinning face, she asked, "Who is this mad-dog soldier? His face looks familiar. Have I seen it in the newspaper?"

"Some people say he looks like James Woods. You know, the actor with the high IQ?"

"Yeah, I see that resemblance." She sighed and pulled off her beret. "I can only imagine what you think of me, Agent Stephens." After pulling out her hair clip, she ran her fingers through her hair and loosened her bun. Her short brown hair framed her face and covered some of her wounds. "But, I'm just a fellow soldier. Like all of us, I simply follow orders. If I seem abrupt or impatient, it's because I've been on my feet for too many hours and I'm extremely tired. Your nephew seemed like a great young man and I'm truly and deeply sorry that he died in service to his country. In addition, you seem like a good man, so I'll offer you free advice. Bury your nephew and honor his memory by waiting out your thirty-six days. Then you can retire and drink yourself to death in comfort and peace."

Instead of answering, Steve reached slowly out for his .45. The Major picked it up and held it outside his reach.

"I don't think so. With your permission, sir, we'll take this fine old weapon and the hard drive from your computer. In accordance with Army Regulation 195-2, you can fill out a form at Army Criminal Investigation Command headquarters at Fort Belvoir to retrieve your personal belongings once we've finished our investigation. We promise your request will be carefully reviewed by the Commanding General's staff before being rejected. Don't be your own worst enemy—relax and go with the prevailing winds. The direction shouldn't be hard to detect for a clever man like you, sir."

She stood and held out her hand for a shake. Steve grasped it and shook it passively and limply.

"Goodbye, Major Karne."

"Yes," she said. "You have yourself a good day, sir."

Curtis? What are you mixed up in, boy?

Sura 2, Verse 72-74. Remember ye slew a man and fell into a dispute among yourselves about the crime, but Allah brought forth what you hid. Henceforth, your hearts were hardened; they became like a rock and even harder. For among rocks there are some from which rivers gush forth; others, when split asunder, send forth water; and there are others which sink in fear of Allah. Allah knows of what you do.

Book Three—Chapter Four

Steve Stephens

OPERATING ON AUTOPILOT, he swallowed an uncounted palmful of Advil capsules, guzzled from a cold bottle of water and did his morning exercise walk around the mall. Afterwards, he showered, shaved and rode the Metro to work. Sitting at his metal desk, he sat and drank coffee while rubbing his tired eyes. He studied his count-down calendar.

It was a deliberate, well-thought-out plan. Thirty-six days, then he had vacation days, comp time and sick leave to cash in which took him to the fourteen-year mark and gave a good bump to his pension.

Of the thirty-six days, one was a holiday and ten fell on weekends; that left twenty-five working days to slide through.

Twenty-five easy days.

All he had to do was sit at his desk and let voicemail take

the phone calls and forward e-mails to young agents who still gave a shit about crime and punishment.

Easy days to cross off his calendar one-by-one.

Making a decision, he grabbed the calendar and walked down the hallway to his boss's office—Robert Campbell, Assistant Administrator of the Operational Support Division. Bobby sat at his desk carefully studying brackets for the inter-office football pool.

"The Redskins are going to get their asses kicked. What do you think, Steve? Twenty-two points?"

"Sure, boss, that sounds about right."

Bobby scrawled his initials on the grid and slipped his five dollar bill in the envelope and dropped it in his interoffice mail (out) basket.

"I heard about your cousin, that's a damned shame. We're losing too many good boys over there. What's the count-down?"

"He was my nephew and I have thirty-six calendar days left. Boss, I came to ask a favor."

"Sure, Steve, bereavement leave? I thought you might ask. We don't usually approve it except for close family—dads and moms, sisters and brothers, certified same-sex life partners and the like, but I can call in a favor and get this request signed off in H-R. We fudged a little and got Karl a couple of days off when his dog died. He loved that old mutt. What if I can get you three days off? Will that give you the time to do what you need to do?"

"Thanks, Bobby, I appreciate it, but that's not the favor."

Bobby leaned back in his chair. "Okay, hit me."

"I want a field assignment."

"What? Oh, boy, that's a doozy. You could get your ass shot off, why do you want to take the risk? Okay, I can get you a week off to mourn for your boy, plus a little travel time for the funeral, how about that? Human Resources will buy it if I get departmental approval."

Steve leaned forward.

"No," he said, "I want an assignment with international undercover authorization. Full diplomatic coverage. State department paperwork. All clearances and embassy red list. The full shooting match."

Bobby looked around the room as if seeking an escape route.

"Wow, that's a big bomb out of left field," he said. "I expect this high-spy nonsense from Allman or Gethesman, but not from you, Steve. Are you aware of what you're asking? This is absurd. Can I give you a short answer? No."

"Yes, Bobby, I'm deadly serious. There's been a lot of morphine base coming out of Irakkistan through Turkey. Maybe we should step up our effort to shut it down."

"You've always been one of our best special agents. Remember that bust in El Paso? We got primetime network exposure for the suits on *20-20* and *Sixty Minutes*. The Director really appreciated that. I can call in chits up the food chain and get you the rest of your time off. Thirty-six days? No problem. By the end of the day, go ahead and walk down to H-R, sign their forms—I'll take care of everything." He stood up. "Way to go, Steve, well-played. It's been a real pleasure working with you and on behalf of everyone in the department, they don't make good men like you anymore and we'll miss you."

Non-linear.

"Deep cover with an unlimited black American Express card for expenses, a ten-thousand dollar cash advance and field coordination on the ground."

"You're insane, Steve. I can't do all that. It's impossible. I'm sorry."

"Yes, you can, boss. Don't make me say it. Remember the Gomez-Maya situation? Would the director like to see that on *Sixty Minutes*? I have photographs locked up at a secure location. How do you think *those* would look on Fox News?"

"Steve, please, don't bring that up. Even if I wanted to, I

can't authorize a blank check."

"You not only can, but you will. I'll give you until the end of the day."

Steve got up.

"Have you been drinking?" Bobby said. "Are you off your meds? Losing your mind? This kind of thing can cause a lot of problems for the Agency."

"I expect the paperwork by the end of the day, boss."

Bobby leaned back in his chair and pulled at his ears. He did this when under stress and there was much speculation in the office as to why.

Perhaps a grandmother pulled his ears when he misbehaved?

"Alright, I'll look into it. I expect this crap from some of the others—Levine and Gonzales, but never you. At least give me a good code name for cover."

"Let's call it Operation Sandstorm," Steve said, before leaving the office.

As he walked down the hallway back to his office, he noticed his knees were loose. Disjointed—as if his lower legs were not quite connected to his thighs. At any instant, he expected his pieces to fly apart and scatter across the room.

In his chest, his heart trembled like a scared, shivering rabbit.

That was a stupid move, Steve. Insane and—non-linear.

The remaining hours of the day passed glacially. Steve kept his office door closed and no one bothered him. His laptop computer was not supposed to have a 5G modem and he was not supposed to bypass the department firewall and directly link to an Internet service, but he did it anyway.

He signed up for a free Hotmail account using phony, made-up information and surfed around. Searching with his nephew's name didn't bring up much. Curtis had won a Montgomery College golf tournament a few years back and there were a few newspaper announcements of his various

Army postings. Boot camp, tech school and assigned duty in Irakkistan. The news of his imaginary death was not public yet.

Switching to his DEA computer, he did a background search. There were more Curtis Washington's than he thought there would be, but he found the right one. Except for a marijuana bust several years back (the judge signed off on a youth offender program, so all Curtis got was a fine, forty hours of community service and his record was expunged after a trouble-free year), his record was clean.

Various routine parking and traffic tickets. Who cares?

On impulse, turning to his DEA computer and the databases he had authority to search, he did a background check on Major Karne. There were details from early in her career; her Master's degree was from Princeton in International Diplomacy. The last few years, her records were sketchy with many sections redacted or hidden behind screens requesting additional passwords, agency approval and biometric identification.

Steve smelled spycraft.

CIA or NSA.

He switched back to his private computer and spent the remainder of the day immersed in news updates from Irakkistan. Despite several presidents promising immanent victory, Irakki takeovers of police and internal security forces, and coalition troop pullbacks, the war with drug lords and radical fundamentalist Islamic fascists was still hot.

One-hundred and twenty-eight people, including women and children, were killed by a suicide bomber in a van detonated in a crowd gathered in response to an announcement of offers of work. One-hundred and seventy-three people were wounded. A Mormon missionary was beheaded on camera; the video was all over the internet. A mass grave was uncovered near Taakric when ditches for laying sewage pipes were excavated—hundreds of female skeletons, all with small caliber bullet holes in the back of the skull were found in a cassava field. This mayhem was the usual background noise from mountains and plains of Irakkistan.

Finally, it was 4:30. Steve sat and watched the door, knowing Bobby would come. The door flew open at 4:37. Bobby was flushed—as if he'd been running.

"Here you go, Steve," he said. "Everything you asked for. I hope you know what you're doing. Don't do anything to embarrass the Director or the department, that's all I ask."

Steve stuffed the credit card into his wallet and looked at the thick bundle of petty cash. He thought about stuffing it in his lunchbox, but decided against it.

I don't want to carry this stuff around.

Filling an overnight express envelope with the cash and a copy of his orders, he addressed it to a private mailbox he kept at the mall and dropped it off at the mail room. He charged the express mail charge to Bobby's general office account.

"We'll get this out to you right away, Steve," the clerk said. He reached over the counter and patted Steve on the shoulder. "We're all really sorry to hear the news about your nephew."

"Yeah, thanks," Steve replied. "He was a great kid."

Sura 2, Verse 119. Verily we have sent thee in truth as a bearer of glad tidings and bringer of warning. Of thee no question shall be asked of the companions of the blazing fire.

Book Three—Chapter Five

Steve Stephens

THE COLD WIND flowing off the Potomac River smelled of exhaust from heavy traffic on the Jefferson Davis Highway. It whipped at the lapels of Steve's coat. The Army Old Guard, the Third United States Infantry Regiment, was busy this day with twenty-two funerals.

The timetable was tight; the cremated remains of Specialist Curtis Aaron Washington were scheduled to be interred at 11:25. His plastic urn rode on a horse-drawn caisson with remains of three other soldiers. On his own, Curtis did not warrant the caisson, he was hitching a ride with a top—a commissioned officer.

With slow, solemn formality, his urn was turned over to the casket team who walked it to the columbarium.

Gardens of Stone—the Arlington National Cemetery. Rolling hills of sad, bloody history. Curtis was assigned the center niche on the fifth row of the northwest Project 190 columbarium. The Army chaplain, the right Reverend Amos Anthony, read from a printed sheaf of notes, but Steve could not concentrate on the words.

A fine young man struck down in his bountiful years.

A patriot called to duty in an honorable mission.

An American soldier of first order.

God this and God that.

Snippets of the practiced speech drifted through Steve's mind while he studied the hollow words etched in the white marble of Curtis's tomb marker.

Curtis Aaron Washington, Specialist, U.S. Army, Purple Heart, Operation Irakkistani Liberation.

Natalie leaned against him with a silky white handkerchief pressed against her face. It made a sharp contrast to her black skin, dress and hat. He scanned the thin crowd—comprised of the three members of the Old Guard, a few VFW servicemen in historic uniforms, a hard-faced young man in a wheelchair, a civilian dressed in a suit with black raincoat lapels flapping in the breeze, and a few others.

I'm sorry, Curtis. There are more who care, but they just couldn't be with us today.

Major Karne, with the wind ruffling her wool overcoat, stood fifty yards away—partially hidden under a tree.

Watching.

She waved a white-gloved hand, but Steve ignored her. The bugler, wearing a sharply-pressed uniform with his black and tan buff strap wrapped on his shoulder, played taps. The casket team leader and assistant performed the burial flag folding ceremony and presented Natalie with the memorial flag folded in a tight triangle. An Arlington Lady dressed in black handed Natalie a condolence card and patted her on the shoulder. With that, the service concluded and the mourners drifted back to their cars parked along the curb. The civilian walked away briskly, but Steve caught up with him.

"Excuse me. I want to thank you for coming out for my nephew's service," Steve said, slightly out of breath.

"It was the least I could do," the man said.

He turned and began walking again.

"I didn't catch your name," Steve called out to the man's retreating back.

The man scowled briefly over his shoulder, then stopped and turned toward Steve.

"McDonald."

Steve studied the man's face—he was about forty and the only white person beside Major Karne at the funeral service. Clean shaven, he wore a military-style haircut and wire rim glasses. His face was pudgy and his eyes darted left and right.

Fucking intelligence agency spook.

"Could I have a business card, sir? I'd like to chat with you later at your convenience."

The man sighed. "I suppose," he said.

He brought out a silver case and extracted a card. Steve glanced at it. William McDonald, Commodities Broker, it said. Stewart Brothers Financial Services. Steve slipped the card into his coat pocket.

"Thank you again for coming, it means a lot to the family."

A procession of marching activists appeared on the access road—a single line of protesters carrying miniature cardboard coffins. In front, a line of pudgy college-aged girls displayed a rippling banner. The wind tugged at it, but it could be read.

Neccon Rivers of Blood.

There were other signs and Steve caught their messages in psychedelic flashes.

Burn down the Puzzle Palace
Wilson-Brown: War Criminals
Wars cause Death not Love
The Angels are crying in Khostarak
Cures, not Wars

Most of the members of the procession were clad in black jackets and jeans. They chanted.

There is one thing we all know,
Wilson and Brown have to go.

With his strong arms working furiously, the man in the wheelchair rolled toward the procession.

Trouble.

Steve scurried across the wet grass. Wheelchair-man grappled with a protester and soon both writhed on the ground surrounded by a milling crowd. Steve pulled the protester out of the mêlée—his face was bloodied and his clothes were soaked.

"Get off me, you fucking fascist bastard."

"Hey, cool out. Give peace a chance," Steve said, handing the kid his torn sign.

Meet Mr. Reality, it said.

The image was a bloody skull overlaid on President Wilson's face.

"I have a right to peacefully protest. I'll sue for assault."

"Good. You can explain to a judge how you got your ass kicked by a man in a wheelchair." Steve raised his arms and addressed the crowd in a booming voice. "There's nothing more to see folks, move it along."

A group of military police vehicles—with colored lights flashing—converged. The protesters formed ragged columns and continued their march. Steve reset the wheelchair upright and helped Natalie ease the man into it. Still under her tree, Major Karne watched with amusement evident on her face.

Thanks for your fucking help, bitch.

"I'm sorry, Natalie. I lost it with these damned assholes," the man in the wheelchair said.

Natalie smiled. "I suppose I should introduce y'all. Steve, this is Carter Smythe. He's a friend—he served with Curtis in

Khostarak."

After brushing leaves off his coat and shaking hands with Steve, Carter rolled toward the parking area. Unlocking his van with a remote, he heaved open the driver's door, hauled himself out of his chair and settled behind the steering wheel. Folding up the chair, he maneuvered it into a slot behind the driver's seat. His knuckles were calloused and his tattooed arms were knotted with muscle. After walking over, Steve made a motion to help, but Carter waved him away.

"I've done this a thousand times, I can get it."

"I'd like to talk with you about Curtis. Can you meet me at Evan's Coffee Shop?"

"It ain't called that no more," Carter said.

"But you know the place it used to be?"

Carter chewed his lower lip, and then nodded.

"I need to run Natalie home," Steve said, "but I can meet you there in an hour."

Carter appeared uninspired by the idea, but relented.

"Okay, fine," he said.

On the way home, Natalie stared out the window. When they pulled into her driveway, she finally spoke.

"They tore the place apart searching. I told them not to, but they had a warrant."

"I know," Steve said.

"I'm glad I don't know anything—those people scare me. Will you find out what's going on? I need to know that Curtis is safe, but I can't go. You have to go over there."

What? Me?

Irakkistan?

The reality hit him. It was no place for him. It was still a hot zone—forty or fifty soldiers, mainly Irakkistani security forces now, were killed every day. He knew enough to order a beer in five or six languages, but not Arabic. He could not chase ghosts in Irakkistan.

"Natalie, I loved Curtis too, but me going to Irakkistan? That's crazy-talk. I'm taking some time off to look into things here, but over there? I'm an old man."

He hugged her and kissed her cheek.

"I know. I'm sorry. That just popped out. You'll help, I know you will. Maybe we can figure this out without you going there, I don't know. For now, I don't have anything to do but to keep on living."

"That's all any of us have."

"I have not been thinking straight. Whatever the meddle Curtis was in; it's not worth death in the family. More death—that's not what *he* wants. Please be careful."

"I will," Steve replied.

As he drove away, she stood in the driveway and waved. Steve quickly maneuvered through traffic—watching for any sign that he was followed. It was hopeless, traffic was snarled and too many plain-looking cars looked suspicious.

He found the coffee shop. Carter's van was already there—parked in a handicapped space. Evans Coffee Shop was a converted house, the old-fashioned opposite of fancy shops like Starbucks and Peets. The tables were old and scarred with cigarette burns. A cup of watery drip coffee ordered with a sandwich was twelve new dollars. Steve ordered a bacon sandwich.

"The only reason I'm here is because you're Curtis's uncle."

Carter seemed needlessly hostile and defensive. Steve's cop senses were alert.

"I understand and I appreciate your meeting me on this tragic day. What happened to your legs?"

Rubbing the stubs, Carter said, "Mine sweeping operation in a poppy field."

"Gives you a good excuse for not running the marathon."

Carter stared. "Was that supposed to be funny?"

"I'm sorry. That didn't come out right. When did you get back to the world?"

"Six months ago after too damned many long nights in a Walter Reed luxury suite."

"Now *you're* making a joke."

"I left both feet in towel-head central. I have the right."

Steve was tired.

Non-linear? I can do non-linear.

"Shall we pull out our dicks and see which is prettier? I concede—you win. I did my time in Saigon and in forward operating bases in the rice paddies and jungle. Then Iraq. You did your duty in the desert with Talibani goat-fuckers. Life sucks ass crack—then you die. What are you going to do about it? How did you meet Curtis?"

Carter stared and his clenched his knuckles until they were white—bleached-bone white. He looked out through the window at the cars in the parking lot and took a few deep breaths.

"Forgive me. I know you're not the enemy." Carter took a deep breath and sipped ice water before continuing. "Curtis was in my platoon—we rotated outbound together. He wasn't like the rest of us niggas, he was smart. He could have been a Senator or something. I'd be dead except—when some hajji was shooting up a street market—Curt pulled me under a truck to get me out of a line of fire. Sniper. Not much of a sure shot, but still, those guys hit a target every now and then. Sniper got his. Apache chopper. Thirty millimeter cannon turned him into sausage. One less Moslem camel-jockey and the world became a better place."

"Most Moslems are good, peaceful people."

"Bullshit!" Carter slapped his hand on the table. "Until they separate themselves from the radicals and help us, they're all the same to me. What are they doing to clean up their own fucking backyard?"

The waitress hovered with the steaming food—Steve gestured to her that it was safe to approach.

"Please excuse my friend."

"Meal's on the house for wounded soldiers, but keep a lid on it, will ya?"

"We're sorry," Carter said.

Steve took a bite of his sandwich and wiped his lips before speaking.

"Did you hear anything about Curtis getting into anything hinky?"

Carter considered the question. "No. It was against regulations so he wouldn't even take advantage of the tent girls. One in particular, a hillbilly E-2 private from West Virginia, she'd polish Curt's knob any time, but he wasn't having any of it. He was on tap for promotion—he'd passed the tests with lots of margin and was just waiting for the quota numbers to post. Earning his Sergeant's stripes, that's all he cared about."

"I want to run a name by you. A guy named Jimmy?"

"That would probably be Jimmy O'Connelly. He and Curt pulled patrol duty together. There were four of them that ran around together. They lifted weights, played cards and watched movies."

Steve pulled a folded piece of paper out of his pocket and scribbled down the name.

"Who were the others?"

"Shimon Goldfarb and Harlan Farris. Shimon was okay for a Jewboy, you know how they are, smart, but not going to risk a bullet in his ass. Watch out for Harlan, he's a mean son-of-a-bitch. Came from some up-river redneck KKK backwater in Arkansas and thinks it's still 1850, know what I mean? He called Curt his favorite darkie. Why Curt put up with that shit, I don't know. A mick, hymie, cracker and nigger, what a team they ran, huh? Diversity in action? Harlan was a platoon leader and had input on Curt's record; he'd have to sign off on the promotion. Curt was the smart one, he didn't care what names they called him as long as he got treated square. If Harlan ever disrespected me, I'd cut off his nuts with my Buck Knife, but Curt said, 'don't sweat the small shit, boy.' One day, they all disappeared and that was all I heard about them until this news about them getting killed."

"Do you know what happened to them?"

Carter shrugged. "I don't know. You know how the Army is, but there weren't even rumors. It was a complete black-out."

Steve tossed the last fragment of sandwich into his mouth. "I guess that's it then," he said.

He stood and tossed a few bills on the table.

"The lady said lunch was a freebie."

"She still deserves a tip." Steve handed Carter a business card. "If anything else comes to mind, give me a call and leave a message at the main number—they'll know how to get in touch of me. Oh, one last thing, do you know a Major Karne?"

A thunderstorm rolled across Carter's face. "Yeah, I saw her lurking under that tree at the cemetery. She was in-country. There was talk." Carter looked over his shoulder. "C-I-A," he whispered.

"My sister wants me to go over, but I can't," Steve said.

"To Irakkistan? I don't mean no disrespect, but you're old."

"Yes. I know that. You're right. But, Natalie's right too. There's a nasty smell to things. Did you know she told them not to cremate Curtis, but they did it anyway? Things stink of deception and cover-up. I wish I was ten years younger—I'd go over in a flash."

Carter studied Steve's face.

"Deep inside, you're a crazy motherfucker—I can see it in your eyes. I'll give you some free advice, if you want freedom to roam, go over as a contractor. They do whatever they want. If you go over as a Fed or DEA agent you'll get nowhere."

"I just said I can't go."

"I heard what you said, but I'm not buying it. That guy at the funeral. McDonald? He's wired in at Halliburton–KBR. He can grease the wheels for you."

"KBR? The civilian contractors? What do they have to do

with anything?" Steve said.

"Thanks for pulling me off the protesters," Carter said. "I woulda killed one and then I'd be in jail. That wouldn't serve the plan."

There was something disturbing in Carter's tone.

Plan?

A hint of madness lived in Carter's wry, crooked smile.

He's up to something.

What plan?

I should sit back down and explore this.

But, Steve didn't. Instead, he glanced at his watch.

"I have to roll. You take care, soldier," Steve said.

Sura 2, Verse 174. Those who conceal Allah's revelations in the Book and purchase a miserable profit—they swallow nothing but fire; Allah will not address them on the Day of Resurrection, nor purify them. Grievous will be their penalty.

Book Three—Chapter Six

Steve Stephens

WHILE DRIVING, STEVE thought about his conversation with Carter. There were questions left unasked and the storyline was incomplete. He felt sorry for Carter, but there were others far worse off.

The imaginary Curtis for example—his body shattered by a roadside bomb and now resting with tens of thousands of others at the Arlington Cemetery. Or Steve himself—old, used-up and at the very end of his days on earth.

With what to show for his labor?

Memories. An apartment. A double-dip pension.

Nothing but empty veins.

He pulled into the Lake Forest Mall. He locked his door and started across the parking lot when he saw Major Karne hop out of a large black SUV. Steve altered his course to get closer.

"Hello, Steve," the Major said coolly.

"Major."

"You don't mind if we take a look through your car, do

you?"

"No problem. Show me the warrant and it's all yours."

Major Karne laughed. "Charlie, show Steve the warrant," she said.

Charlie grinned and showed off a thin strip of metal. Slim Jim, the car prowlers call it. In five seconds the car door was open and the men began throwing his books and magazines and music CDs around the parking lot.

"Did you have a pleasant lunch with Carter?" the Major asked calmly.

"Sure. I didn't know you were stationed in Irakkistan. You're a girl who gets around."

"I'm a girl who doesn't convey a message properly. Was I unclear? Mourn your kin and move along with your life."

A part of Steve willed him to obey. He'd been in the military and had a second career in the bureaucratic DEA. He was trained.

Do as you're told.

Go with the flow.

Don't make waves.

Another part—a new, non-linear part—wanted to smash his fist into the smug expression on the Major's face and break open the wounds on her face.

"I've been though your records front-wise and backwards and I don't see the problem. Can't you take a hint? Are you dense? Losing your mind in your advanced age? Senile? Got first-stage Alzheimer's disease? Do we need more direct communication to get through to you?"

She nodded at the team tearing his car apart. They began hacking up his seats. Soon, mounds of stuffing were scattered around. With a crowbar, one of the thugs broke out the windows and smashed the head and tail lights. The parking lot was not deserted, but the people walking by put their heads down against the sputtering rain and pretended not to notice what was going on.

"Is the situation becoming less ambiguous?"

With a blank look on his face, Steve watched the carnage. The men walked over. Steve noticed how large and muscle-bound they were. Each grabbed an arm. Major Karne got right up into his face.

"I'm very nearly done messing with you, Steve."

She pulled a clasp knife from her jacket pocket and began hacking at his clothes. She sliced off his necktie and left him wearing only ragged strips of cloth. He looked like a scarecrow. She took his wallet and keys.

"Do I have your undivided attention, Steve? Just to be sure, Brady is going to hit you. I don't think he'll do any permanent damage, but I don't know for sure—he hits pretty hard. Any questions first?"

"Do you always travel with prehistoric beasts around to protect you?"

"Mostly," she said. She gestured at the wounds on her face. "It's a lesson I learned a little too late in Irakkistan."

She nodded to Brady who loosened up with a short display of shadow boxing before driving a fist into Steve's midsection. Gasping for air, Steve's legs gave out and he collapsed backward on the pavement.

She leaned over to look into his anguished face.

"Here's the last of my free advice. Take your retirement money, move to Florida and live quietly. Wear beige and keep a low profile. If you keep asking questions, I'm going to cut out your heart and feed it to a junkyard dog. I don't know how I can be any clearer. I don't want to see your face. I don't want to hear your name. If you do pop up again asking inconvenient questions? It won't be a gentle love tap from Brady you have to worry about. You'll be another dead hero. Don't try me, Steve. Because I respect your career and your service to your country, I'm slipping you slack by not offing you here and now. But, from now on, you're living on borrowed time, time borrowed from me. Don't make me regret this kindness, Steve. Don't."

She gestured to Brady. "Work on his face a tad," she said.

When Brady was done, she gestured and her crew walked back to their massive black SUV. Through eyes swelling shut, Steve couldn't make out the plate number, but he recognized the design.

Embassy.

That made them untouchable, or the closest thing to it on earth.

He lay on his back between a Chevy Trailblazer and a Toyota pickup. Rain dripped on his face and cold water soaked into his skin. He turned his head and vomited up his lunch. It was too cold to lay for long—after a few minutes he felt like he might be able to get up.

It was a multi-stage operation. First, rolling over, then getting on his hands and knees, then standing up, hunched over and leaning heavily on the Trailblazer. He hoped Brady didn't rupture his gall bladder or pancreas or something. His belly felt hot and swollen.

What could happen in a busted gut?

What? Peritonitis, hemorrhage?

He staggered toward the mall, noticing how the shoppers gave him wide berth. He didn't blame them; obviously he was a demented rag man living on the street—there were plenty of these hopeless cases around. He hobbled to the private mailbox service.

The clerk, Shirley, looked him over with shock.

"Holy shit, Steve, is that you?"

"Hi, Shirley."

"What happened?"

"No big deal. A hit and run in the parking lot."

"Hit and run? Let me call the police."

"No, please don't. That's not necessary. I don't have my keys, would you clean out my box for me, please?"

"Steve, you're a mess. I can call an ambulance."

"Box, Shirley. Please bring me the contents of my box."

She looked unsure, but disappeared into the back and came back with a bundle of junk mail and the padded envelope he'd mailed himself.

"And, there's a box you're holding for me..."

"A box?"

"Yes, Shirley, a metal box in the storage room on the top shelf by the air conditioner vent."

"I remember. That's been there forever. You want it now after all these years we've been holding it for you?"

"Yes, Shirley," Steve said patiently. "I want it now."

She went to the back room and climbed on a stepladder. The box was covered with dust. She brought it out and placed it on the counter.

"Here you go, Steve. Can I call mall security for you?"

"No, that's okay. Thanks."

He walked toward JC Penneys. After pulling the price tags from a pair of close-enough denim pants and an XXL wool shirt randomly pulled from display racks, he walked to the dressing room, stripped off his wet rags and gingerly pulled on the dry clothes. He admired himself in the floor length mirror. The dark skin of his face looked gray, or as gray as a black man's face could get. He looked bad, but felt worse.

He opened the padded envelope and pulled out his emergency stash of credit cards and fake identification. His new name was Steve Herman. With a thumbnail, he flipped the latch on the metal box and pulled out an old .45 pistol—the twin to the one Major Karne took. After ramming in the clip and checking the safety, he slipped it in his belt and arranged the crisp new wool shirt to cover it.

Leaving the sopping rags in the dressing cubicle, he took the bar coded tags to the register and used the DEA credit card to pay the bill. His guts ached, but he wasn't spitting up blood—a good sign. In minutes, he'd walked across the mall and hailed a taxi. He fished McDonald's business card out of his pocket. It was soggy.

"I'll give you a hundred bucks over the meter if you take me to Baltimore," he said.

"Sure, buddy, no problem," the cabbie replied. "For a hundred bucks over the meter, I'll drive you to Miami. I don't give a shit."

"Baltimore will be fine," Steve replied while sinking back into his seat. Traffic was slow, but soon they were out of the DC area and rolling through heavy rain on B-W Parkway.

Carter Smythe

The pavement was wet, but the rain had stopped pouring down. Blinding shafts of sunlight sliced through scudding clumps of clouds. The motley crowd, perhaps five-hundred strong, milled on the National Mall waving signs. Police in pairs watched casually while pushing their bicycles through the mob. Handheld cameras abounded. Carter locked his van and checked his sign.

Stupidity is the Enemy of Freedom
Disabled Irakkistani Vet Loves Peace

He hadn't nailed his message, but this was the best one he could come up with. Wilson/Brown: Axis of Eagles was too blatantly right-wing; he needed to mix in with the protesters.

Feeling curiously calm and rapturous, he was at one with the cold wind, the stabbing sunlight and the colorful crowd.

He was ready to be delivered from evil.

All of his pain would soon be over. The feeling was liberating, like the opiates the medics injected in him while his shattered legs bled into hot Irakkistani gravel.

It was bliss. The best sexual afterglow multiplied by ten. A sideways glimpse of God's peaceful heaven.

The sweet smell of marijuana wafted in the damp air—a slim dread-locked man wearing a spiffy chocolate brown corduroy suit offered him a toke. Carter shook his head.

"I'm high on life itself," Carter said.

He worked the wheelchair joystick and weaved through the swarm. Under his dress uniform, his body was wrapped tightly with elastic bandages. Under the elastic wrap was an array of RolTom twenty-two millimeter precision ISO grade P6 chromium steel, Russian-made ball bearings liberated from barrels stored in an Adi Dahaar mosque. Carter had picked up the shipment at a bonded Port Jersey warehouse. He remembered the look on the face of the customs inspector after he peeled the top off the heavy crate.

"Strange souvenirs. A hundred pounds of ball bearings?" the inspector had said. "I thought I'd seen everything. We used to play marbles with some just like these. What are you doing with them?"

"Selling them on eBay," Carter had said.

The inspector shook his head and waved him on. "No harm in that. You earned the right. I thank you for your service."

"You're very welcome," Carter had said.

"Can I have a couple for my kids?"

"Sure."

The inspector fished in the crate and pulled out a handful.

"Thanks."

Carter had hired movers from a day-labor company. They wheeled the heavy dolly to his rented truck.

"We're only supposed to lift forty pounds each," one had complained.

"Shut up," Carter said.

Half of the bearings were wrapped around his body and the other half were duct-taped around the wheelchair frame. Sluggish, the wheelchair motor strained to move the heavy load.

Getting MIL-C-45010A C4 explosive was more difficult. To do it legally, he needed a properly filled-out-and-signed explosives authorization form and end use certificate. He created crude forgeries on a laser printer with a Hazardous Work Permit (Form LL-1986) doctored with correction fluid and a FedEx-Kinko's photocopier. The transaction was consummated in a New Jersey parking lot at 9:30 at night. After a cruising through slowly, a white van parked in a far corner. The driver glanced at the paperwork and snorted.

"Yeah, right," he said. "C-4 for stumps. You must have a whole forest to clear out."

"Everything is in order," Carter said.

"Is your cash in order?"

"Yes."

Carter handed over an envelope. The driver quickly thumbed through the bills.

"Alright," he said. He tossed the bundle on Carter's lap. "Don't get any on ya."

The man slipped back into his van and rolled off slowly. The transaction took six minutes.

The plastic explosive was 91% cyclotrimethylene trinitramine mixed with plastic binder and marker chemicals for tracking. He'd packed the bomb himself, improvising his detonator with black powder and gas furnace pilot light igniters. Ten pounds of clay-like explosive in packets were arranged around his broken body—waiting for him to flip a light switch hot-glued to the underside of his wheelchair's arm. He pulled out his bullhorn microphone. He'd composed his song the previous night.

1, 2, 3, 4
We hate this goddamned war

5, 6, 7, 8
It's this goddamned war we hate

It took almost a minute of shouting, but the crowd picked up his spirit. He rolled his wheelchair in tight circles as they roiled about—shaking their fists in the air and dancing.

A rotund mother in a long peasant skirt rhythmically waved her baby in the air—Carter felt a surge of sympathy for the child, but none for the mother.

Innocence.

It's easy to drive a Toyota Prius, recycle aluminum cans, wave signs and feel self-righteous while safely at home in the United States when the blood of patriots spilled on foreign soil.

Well, this is it, hypocrites.

I'm bringing the war home to you.

Almost always, urban terrorism on American soil is done by foreigners, Islamic agents of chaos and left-wingers of all flavors—anarchists, clueless student activists and black militants—never by white ex-military combat veterans.

Until this day.

With a calloused thumb, a soaring heart and a twisted smile, Carter flipped his light switch and performed the tenth-largest mass murder in U.S. history.

Sura 39, Verse 42. It is Allah that takes the souls of men at death; and those that die not, he takes during their sleep. Those on whom he places a decree of death, he holds back from returning to life, but the rest he sends into their bodies for a term appointed. Verily in this are signs for those who reflect.

Book Three—Chapter Seven

Steve Stephens

THE TAXI DRIVER knew a route over side streets that avoided motionless tangles of hopeless traffic, so Steve saw unfamiliar parts of Baltimore. The scenery consisted of block after block of boarded-up and graffiti-adorned storefronts, shit-colored brick row houses and young black men sitting on concrete steps watching the laminar traffic flow by with futile hostility written in their eyes.

A minuscule, one-armed Cambodian sold newspapers to cars stopped at traffic lights. On the streets, relentless fallen heroes decorated sweat-stained t-shirts: Tupac, Che Guevara and Chairman Mao. Fast food wrappers blew through the streets like cowboy movie tumbleweeds. Steve's body was sore and his mood was sour. Lifting an index finger to his mouth, he pressed on a gift from Brady—a wobbly incisor.

It had better hold up—there was no time for a trip to a strip mall dentist.

The driver wanted to talk and ran quickly through a litany of trial topics. How would the Wizards do in the playoffs? Had Steve seen a popular, just-released movie about gay cowgirls? Did he have an opinion about the expensive plans for a new football stadium? Steve did not take the bait.

"Are you a boxer?"

Steve shook his throbbing head to clear away the street images. He chuckled bitterly.

"No."

"Sorry, it's just that…"

"I know," Steve said.

This exchange seemed to exhaust the driver, but he was not done trying.

"Pigtown. They used to release the pigs from railroad boxcars and run them down to the South Baltimore slaughterhouses. That's how the name originated."

"I really don't give a runny shit," Steve said. "Truly."

"Hmmph," the driver grunted.

The rest of the trip passed without any other attempts at conversation.

International Staffing Resources resided in a run-down one-story concrete building surrounded by a huge, empty parking lot. Clumps of weeds grew in pavement seams. Plastic bags, like urban ghosts, fluttered in the tall, chain-link fence. The building looked deserted, though, on the roof, fencing camouflaged a complex and expensive array of satellite dishes. Steve handed the taxi driver an uncounted wad of bills.

"Nice talkin' to you," the driver said dryly before rolling away.

The back gate was locked with rusty chains and a huge, medieval-looking padlock. Steve followed the fence line around the complex and until he found a shiny gate with intercom. High on a pole, the motor of a gimbaled video camera whirred. He pressed the talk button.

"I-S-R," a tinny voice said.

"I'm here to see Will McDonald."

"He goes by William. Do you have an appointment?"

"Yes," Steve lied.

There followed a quiet minute.

Probably laughing themselves to death before they tell me to come back after I really have an appointment.

Steve was a bureaucrat. He knew the bureaucrat way. With slumped shoulders he turned to leave and jumped when the deadbolt on the gate snapped and buzzed.

"Very well, sir. Come in."

Steve felt frozen.

"Sir," she said. "Are you with us? You can come in."

Steve, unfrozen, pushed through the gate.

The lobby was filled with dusty plastic plants. After he filled out the visitor's log (his was the only name on the sheet), the receptionist—with a plump body that abused the restraining buttons on her blouse—pushed a clipboard across her desk.

"Fill this out and someone will be with you shortly."

The form was a job application. He glanced over it and set it aside. The receptionist read from a tattered novel illustrated with black lovers kissing on the cover. A woman wrapped in the arms of a muscular man with whip scars on his back. *Unchained for Love* the title said in swoopy, garish letters.

"I've heard black men like women with a little meat on their bones. You know—full-figured, bosomy women."

"That's a vicious, ugly racial stereotype," Steve said unkindly, "like natural rhythm, low I-Q and an insatiable craving for watermelon and fried chicken."

"Oh," the receptionist said thoughtfully. "I like fried chicken."

"I can see that," Steve said.

The visitor area appeared unused. Steve picked up a Time magazine—it was six years old. The blow-in cards slipped out and he had to stretch his aching back to lean over and pick them up. Oprah, stuffed into a pink gown like a sausage, stood on stage at Oslo accepting her Nobel Peace Prize. He put the magazine back down without opening it.

A young man approached.

"Mr. Herman?" The speaker was young with prematurely-thinning sandy hair. He wore a crisp white shirt and tie. "My name is Mr. Larsen. If you'll follow me please?"

The receptionist flicked her eyes over him as they walked past. Steve crossed his eyes and stuck out his tongue. She pursed her lips with disapproval and returned her attention to her book.

They walked down a long corridor lined with unlabelled doors. None were open. The place was eerily quiet; their footsteps echoed down the hallway. Mr. Larsen opened a door with a key from a huge ring and ushered Steve inside.

"I'm here to see McDonald."

"I know, but I'll do your preprocessing. He'll be available shortly. Might I ask? How did you hear about our openings?"

"From the ad in the newspaper?" Steve suggested.

Mr. Larsen was nonplussed. "We don't use newspaper ads. Almost all of our candidates come from referrals."

"Well then..." Steve couldn't think of anything else to say, so he shut his mouth.

They looked at each other in a long, uncomfortable silence, before Mr. Larsen lost the staring battle. He opened a desk drawer and pulled out a three-ring binder.

"I have to read to you about the working conditions and medical restrictions." He cleared his throat and adjusted his reading glasses. "You will be living and working in a military-style tent city camp and be confined to the base at all times. You will be issued a cot and a sleeping bag. The weather has extreme temperature variations—during the summer it can be as hot as one-hundred-and-fifty degrees and in the winter, as low as zero degrees with ice and snow. It's a dusty and dirty environment, so expect be filthy most of the time. Sandstorms are common and you will get dust and sand in your eyes, mouth and nose. Expect to have a layer of dust on your clothes, food and in your living quarters. There is simply no escape from all the gritty sand and dust.

"In the rare event you get a shower, it will be with cold water and it might come from the water bottle you drink from. The camp will be infested with mice, rats, snakes, scorpions, ticks, sand fleas and camel spiders. The camps are under intermittent attack by random gunfire, rocket propelled grenades and mortar rounds. All job positions are hands-on regardless of your title or position. Every employee must be able and prepared for strenuous physical labor. You will be provided with three meals per day which may consist of hot meals or military Meals Ready to Eat or MREs. The working schedule is seven days a week and eight to twelve hours per day or more.

"If you are a casualty of biological or chemical attack, your body will be cremated before being sent home. Our policy requires all persons working or living in expatriate capacity in regions with limited medical resources to be examined periodically and classified as medically fit.

"All work sites in the Middle East are in remote, hostile environments isolated from medical assistance except for basic first aid. Poor accessibility and limited communication capability may cause long delays in evacuation and convert a minor medical problem into a life-threatening emergency. Evacuation or repatriation of a sick employee may take considerable time and may be a hazardous operation in itself.

"We conduct a thorough pre-employment screening physical examination. Our medical staff perform blood work-ups, EKGs, chest X-rays, pulmonary function testing, audiograms and bring your vaccinations up to date. If you have any of the following medical conditions, you are unqualified for deployment: coronary artery disease with angina or a history of congestive heart failure or hypertrophic cardiomyopathy. If you use anticoagulants or have ever experienced seizures. If you use psychiatric medications. You are unqualified if you have a history of excessive migraine headaches or chronic obstructive pulmonary disease with acute episodes requiring maintenance medications or if you have a history of asthma with acute asthmatic attacks requiring maintenance medications. If you have active cancer or ongoing cancer therapy, or active hepatitis. Insulin dependent diabetics or diabetics requiring oral medications are unqualified. You are unqualified if your blood pressure is in excess of one-sixty over ninety or have coronary artery disease treated by stents, angioplasty or coronary artery bypass, cardiac arrhythmias under treatment, poor oral hygiene or existing dental or periocontal conditions. Obesity. Vision impairments not correctable to 20/40 with glasses. Hearing loss. Skin conditions such as Psoriasis and Eczema or any allergy or other condition which would prevent a smallpox vaccination.[12] Do you understand the restrictions?"

"All that and a paycheck too? You make it sound so appealing."

"If I might be frank, sir, due to your age and obvious physical condition, you are a poor candidate for overseas deployment. Unless you have special logistical skills or experience with pipeline construction, industrial plumbing or high voltage transmission lines, we will not use your services." He stood and extended his hand. "No critical skills? Then I thank you very much for coming by and I hope you have a great day."

"I came here looking for McDonald."

"I don't think he's hiring either."

Steve waved Larsen's hand away. "I can see my own way out."

"This is a secure facility; you must be escorted at all times."

---

[12] This litany is adapted from the Halliburton-KBR careers website. http://www.halliburton.com

"You don't have to patronize me, I know the drill."

Steve opened the door and stepped into the hallway where McDonald walked briskly toward them.

"There you are. What are you doing, Larsen? This one's mine."

"You can't be serious, William. This man is the very definition of an unqualified candidate."

"Go back to work and let me handle it."

"It's your career, sir."

"That's right," McDonald said. "Asshole," he whispered under his breath. To Steve, he said, "I assume he ran you through the wringer."

"Yes,"

"Sorry about that. I was tied up in a conference call. Come along. Cup of coffee? Soda? Bottled water? Uncle Sugar is buying."

"No, I'm fine."

"Okay."

After a few turns in the corridor, McDonald punched the buttons on a pushbutton security lock and they entered a nearly-barren office. He sat and stared at Steve's battered face.

"You got mixed up with Major Karne's private goon squad," William said.

"Up close and personal. Look, I don't expect you spooks to tell me anything, but if I'm going to get the shit beat out of me, can't you give me an overview of the players and the landscape? This isn't a Halliburton contract worker hiring facility. You're a Fed. What flavor?"

McDonald leaned back in his chair and rubbed his head.

"You'll never guess, but take a try at it anyway."

"Homeland security?"

McDonald snorted. "Nope. Treasury."

Steve leaned back in his chair and stared at a corner of the ceiling.

Treasury. The catch-all federal department with a wide assortment of disparate functions. Could be a lot of things. Secret Service. Federal Reserve. IRS. Financial Crimes Enforcement Network.

"And Karne?"

"Army intel, mainly, but she's tied into the State Department and DOD. Consider her independent with inside help and friends in high places. If you know him, her husband is Max Karne."

"No, I don't know that name."

"New York State congressman—an up and comer. You might find this more interesting. She's one of the Bush clan."

"Jesus. What did Curtis get himself mixed up in?"

"I can't tell you, because I simply don't know, but I can get you over there. In return, if you live long enough, let me know what you find out. Deal?"

"All right."

"Fine, you're a petroleum engineer. N-Y-C to Paris to Kuwait City to Khostarak—hop, hop, hop. When you get over there, you might only last five minutes before you're bagged and fragged, but that's not my problem, is it?"

"I guess not. Get me there and that's good enough, I guess."

"For whatever good it might do, I have a suggestion."

"Hit me," Steve said.

"Since you're already headed up to the city to fly out of JFK, why don't you stop in and see Curt's buddies. Jimmy and Shimon."

"Ah, they're not dead either?"

"No, they unplugged and slipped home through a backdoor or something. They're fine. Look for them at a bagel shop in Brooklyn near the pineapple walk. They'd probably appreciate it if you didn't lead Karne to them, but she'll find them easy enough if she hasn't already. Hopefully, they were smart enough to bring back an anti-Karne insurance policy of some kind. On a slightly different subject, Steve, in the spirit of friendly cooperation, do you happen to have any of that funny money on you? I won't ask where you got it."

Steve thought about it for a moment, then pulled the rolled bill from his sock. He spread it on William's desk and patted it flat, but it curled up. They studied it for a moment.

"Thanks. We're trying to take as much of this funny money off the street as possible." He laughed, scooped the bill up and dropped it in his desk drawer. "Now there's only about a million more I need to find."

Sura 23, Verses 55-56. Do they think that because we granted them an abundance of wealth and strong sons, that we would always reward them with more good things? No, they do not understand.

Book Three—Chapter Eight

Steve Stephens

STEVE TOOK THE express train to Central Station and then flagged down a taxi for the remaining part of his trip to Brooklyn. While on the train, he looked through the window at the endless soggy landscape—people huddled under umbrellas as the wind and rain ripped at their jackets and cold-soaked their lonely souls.

The cabby was a shabby-looking man with thinning hair, observant, piercing eyes and an unruly beard. When Steve told him the address, the cabby held up his hands like he was holding a bagel in front of his face.

"I know the place—not bad, not bad at all, but if you want a real New Yawk bagel…"

"Please, Jimmy's Bagels, that's where we're going."

"Fine, pal, no problem, you're lucky you got me, 'cause I'm not taking you the long way around just to make an extra buck. I know a way to get you there pronto-quick. Name's Sy. Maybe youse hoid this a million times and maybe you has not, but I'm going to school and I'm going to make something of myself and I'll be sitting back there someday instead of sitting up here working my ass all day. This is America, pal, and there's opportunities if youse makes a plan and stays focused."

Every cubic millimeter of Steve's body broadcasted pain— every muscle, sinew, organ and cell. He thought about asking the cabby to shut up, but that would be as useful as standing on the street and asking the rain to stop falling. He leaned his head against the cold glass and watched New York City flow by.

Jimmy's Bagels was housed in a rundown building on a corner of a historic brownstone neighborhood. The windows were papered over and every three feet, the notice was printed in bold letters.

Grand Re-Opening Feb 1

Steve gave the cab driver fifty new-dollars and told him to keep the change.

"Thanks, nice talkin' to ya," Sy said before disappearing into the mist and traffic.

Steve peeked through a crack in the paper covering the windows, but the glass had been soaped, all he could see were vague shapes. He rapped on the window, but it took a few times before anyone came.

"We're closed."

It was a woman's husky voice with a thick accent; an Australian accent.

Steve rapped on the window—harder this time.

"All right, don't get your nappies in a bunch." She worked at the front lock and popped the door open an inch. She looked over his overcoat and briefcase, both borrowed from William McDonald. "What?" she said. "We got all our permits and permissions. Health department, building department, structure safety department, department of revenue department, all of you with a form to fill in and a hand out for a fee. What'd we forget? The you-can't-do-that-here department? The that's-impossible department? The it-takes-six-months department? Blood suckers, all of you. What do you want?"

"I'm here to see Jimmy..."

"Why didn't you say so instead of standing in the rain? Jimmy! Company," she bellowed over her shoulder.

She was a large woman. She bellowed loudly.

Jimmy was small like a jockey with close-cropped red hair. He put his arm around the woman. She towered over him like a Sequoia.

"What is it, baby? Is it the man from the you-gotta-get-a-permit-to-get-a-permit department? I swear, you guys act like you don't want a decent bagel in the neighborhood."

"Can I sit down? I have pain coming out of my pain."

The room was small, but there were three tiny tables with wooden stools. Jimmy gestured.

"This is all we got," he said.

Another man came in from the back room. He was a larger man, but still smaller than the woman. He had nappy hair, a crooked nose and a thin mustache that looked as if it had been penciled on his face.

"We don't make money," this man said, "if the customers get too comfortable, see what I mean?"

Steve dropped his briefcase on the small table and eased his aching body onto the stool.

The Jewish man offered a piece of bagel with a thick smear of brown paste on it. "Take a taste," he said, "and see what you think. Be brutally honest, but I think you'll say it's the best bagel you ever had, hands down, like Eve's honey-ambrosia on God's fresh bagel."

"It smells like fish," Steve said. "I don't like fish."

He dropped the bagel fragment on the table.

"Kosher or not, no one is gonna want cold-mackerel cream cheese, Shimon."

"Once they acquire the taste, we'll get rich selling it." To

Steve, he said, "Did you notice the 'apostrophe-s' after Jimmy on the sign outside? That's for me, Jimmy's partner, Shimon."

"No, it isn't," Jimmy said, "and I wish you'd quit saying it."

"See how it is? I put half the money in and I'm supposed to be a silent partner. It's not like I want equal billing, just a hint of a nod, that's all. Who is this man, Jimmy? Did he say what he wants? We got a lot of work before the dough-boiler is ready."

"My name is Robert Stephens, but everyone calls me Steve," he said.

At that instant, there was a rap on the front window made by something hard and metallic.

"Now what?" Jimmy said.

From outside, it was a woman's voice.

"Major Karne. Open up or we'll shoot our way in."

The red-haired woman looked at Jimmy with the question in her eyes.

"We have to let her in, I guess."

Outside, Brady held a huge umbrella so Major Karne was dry when she came in. Charlie walked around the room doing an inspection. Brady furled the umbrella and tap-tapped water on the floor. Steve fought against an instinct to run.

Major Karne seemed surprised to see the red-haired-woman. "I thought you were dead."

"That was my sister, Rocky. I'm Duke Balboa. They've always called me Duke. Why? I don't know. When Jimmy brought Rocky's ashes to Perth, we had a few drinks and he chatted me up. I liked him and was between marriages, so I thought I'd give him a try. It was a little weird, but love can be like that sometimes. So, here I am. We girls were triplets, so there's still a spare, but I'll knock Jimmy into next week if he looks sideways at Minnie." She made the sign of the cross over her chest. "Jimmy? This woman mentioned Rocky."

Jimmy looked up. "Sorry." He made a hasty cross on his chest and shot his eyes upward for a brief instant.

"Before I agreed to have sex with him, I made him promise

to say a prayer every time Rocky's name comes up. Now, who are *you*?"

"Major Karne, Army Intelligence."

"That's like the answer to a Jeopardy question," Jimmy said. "Army intelligence? What's the definition of an oxymoron? How'd you find us?"

"That was real tough. We opened the Yellow Pages website and searched for Jimmy's Bagels," she said. "Is there somewhere we can sit down for a chat?"

"Fuck." Jimmy shrugged with resignation. "The employee breakroom has chairs," he said. "Follow me."

Contrary to expectation, the breakroom was plush. There was a refrigerator, a microwave oven, large lockers for employees' coats and purses and a massive oak table surrounded by eight chairs under a colorful Tiffany-glass light fixture hanging from the ceiling. A museum light spread a soft glow across a painting of a man that looked like a much-older and grayer version of Jimmy.

Our Founder, said the plaque on the frame at the bottom of the painting. *Jimmy O'Connelly*.

"Tell your meat to wait outside," Shimon said.

Karne thought about it, and then nodded. "It's okay, Brady," she said. "You can stay outside with Charlie. I'll be okay with this bunch of mugs."

Brady shot Shimon a look that seemed filled with promise, but he nodded and pulled the door shut behind him.

Once everyone was seated, they looked at each other.

"Who called this meeting?" Shimon said.

Karne ignored the question. "You left without saying goodbye," she said.

"Let's call this a no-bullshit zone and lay our cards on the table, all of us. I'll go first. Major, we have a mutually-assured-destruction scenario going. I have high-def audio and video of our time together in your hotel room. I'm sure your husband would be embarrassed if this got out on the Internet."

"The room was swept daily and I have the best electronic counter-measure toys the government can buy. I don't believe you."

"My toys are better than yours and they always will be. I can show you samples. Jimmy's favorite is a part we call Dick, Arched Back, Moan."

"Fine," Major Karen said. "You have a sex tape. Big deal. I don't think anyone really cares after the Pope and the Cheerleaders video went viral. How can anyone top that? Since we're telling the truth, my husband is gay and I've never slept with him, though I wouldn't object to giving it a try if he passed an HIV test, he's an attractive man. He toys with coming out now and then, and it's no big deal. I don't see it affecting his goal of being Governor of New York. That makes your threat toothless. Want to know something really weird? I liked you, Shimon and I still do. You hurt my feelings when you left so abruptly. What do you say about that?"

"Nothing," Shimon said. "I'm speechless."

"So, you have a gentle, loving side," Steve said. "Great. What about me? Will you apologize for your goons beating the crap out of me and tearing up my car?"

"Steve," Karne said, "that was just to focus your attention. You can go home after this—lick your wounds and get back to drinking yourself to death. No hard feelings."

Non-linear.

Could it be?

She didn't know he was starting the thirty-six-hour trip to Irakkistan in the morning?

"Fuck you, bitch," Steve said.

"Let it all out, you'll feel better."

Steve crossed his arms and looked away. "I'm not talking to you anymore," he said.

Jimmy and Shimon exchanged a look.

"Wow," Jimmy said.

"I know who you are," Shimon said. "Curtis mentioned you a time or two. You're Curtis's uncle Steve. I don't know why I didn't see the resemblance before now."

"Because he doesn't look anything like Curtis?" Jimmy said.

"Yes, but he has some of the same mannerisms."

"Can I get in this conversation? What's with the eye, Major?" Duke said.

"Harlan ratted me out to the Russian who saw a ricochet shot and took it. Do you mind? I prefer not to talk about it."

"Where are we so far?" Shimon said. "You're not going to kill us?"

Karne shrugged. "I worked the idea around in my head. It would be easy to bring down these walls around you, but there's no compelling reason for it. If you guys want to keep a low profile, sell a few bagels and stay out of my hair, then we're cool."

"If you're willing to tell the truth," Jimmy said, "then maybe we feel the same way. Did you have anything to do with Rocky getting shot?"

Duke made a cross over her chest. Jimmy aped the motion.

"I had nothing to do with that," the Major lied. She stared at Jimmy with nothing to be read in her eyes.

"Okay," Jimmy said. "Unless I find out something different, I believe you. Truce."

He reached across the table, he and the Major shook hands.

When this handshake was completed, she extended her hand to Steve.

"Fuck off," he said.

"Okay," she said. "I'll consider you a work in progress," she said. "Shimon?"

Shimon didn't lean forward, but he extended his hand. She leaned forward and stretched further. They shook on the pact.

Truce.

"Now that we're all friends," she flicked a glance at Steve, who still pouted, "and friends-in-progress, let's get down to business. My mission and the only thing I care about is shutting down and destroying the Irakki printing press." To Steve, she said, "They're printing counterfeit money, lots of it." She continued. "If we shut this operation down, then we can declare victory—the troops will start coming home in earnest and everyone can get back to the important things in their American dream—like football, cheating on their spouses, hamburgers and Indian-casino gambling."

She put her hand out to touch Steve's arm. "Get ready for a shock, Agent Stephens. You're part of the inner circle now, so I'm going to tell you, we don't think Curtis is dead. He's missing and on a crazy suicide mission dreamed up by his deranged friend, Harlan Farris."

Steve looked at her.

His mind overboiled with competing thoughts.

Is she serious?

Is this supposed to be breaking news?

How stupid does she think I am?

Is she one of those who think black people are incapable of higher-order thinking?

"Can you help me find him?" she asked while looking at Shimon.

Shimon shook his head. "We hear from him now and then, but we have no idea where he is and we don't want to know. It wouldn't be safe for him and it wouldn't be safe for us."

"So, that's it?" she said.

"Yes," Shimon replied.

She got up. "I'm in town a couple more days if you want to get together for dinner and a show or something."

"Let me think about it," Shimon said.

Karne nodded and waved he hand back and forth.

"Until we meet again," she said before leaving the room.

They sat for a quiet minute, waiting to hear street noise as Karne and her men opened the front door and left the building.

"Would you make sure the front door is locked, baby?"

Jimmy said. Duke leaned over and kissed his head before moving. They heard her arguing with someone.

"We're closed. Come back on February the first."

"Karne…" Steve said.

"Hold on," Shimon interjected. He got up, removed a handheld electronic device from a backpack stored in a locker, and moved it around the room.

"Here's one," he mouthed, pointing. He plucked a small blob of plastic from the floor by the door. He put it on the table. Jimmy removed a .40 caliber Glock from under the table and smashed the bug with the base of the weapon.

Shimon came back in. He placed three more bugs on the table.

One-by-one, Jimmy mashed them, swept them into the palm of his hand and then dropped the pieces in a trash bin.

"Okay," Shimon said. "We can talk now."

"I'm headed to Irakkistan tomorrow," Steve said.

"Why?" Jimmy said.

"His mom wants me to check on him. Because Karne pisses me off. Because…"

"That's enough reasons," Jimmy said. "We'll help you as much as we can. What's your plan when you get over there?"

"I don't know," Steve said. "I thought I'd start with the Commanding Officer…"

"He'll be less than useless, Shimon said. "He doesn't know anything."

"Uh. Okay. I talked to William McDonald, if you know him. Treasury. He suggested I talk to a fellow named Bullyban or something. I have the name in my notes."

"That's a good place to start. Buhlibahn, in Islamidahd. What else?"

"That's all I have," Steve said.

"Okay," Shimon said. "Look up an old tribal leader named Mohammad Zaman Salangi. So you won't be deaf and dumb, I'll give you a communicator so you can reach us while you're

over there."

"If you get a chance," Jimmy said, "and it's safe for you, but don't take any crazy chances—please put a bullet in the Russian's head, Maksim. I'd appreciate it. What else can we do for you?"

"What about Karne? I suspect she'll be pissed when she finds out I went over."

Jimmy and Shimon looked at each other.

"I think she's serious," Shimon said. "All she cares about is the printing press. If you help her with that, she'll leave you alone."

"Maybe," Jimmy said, "but that could be Shimon's dick talking. If you get a chance, you might want to take her down. Fuck her. We owe her no favors. What else can we do for you?"

"This will seem strange," Steve said, "but I could really go for a fresh bagel and a beer."

A big grin spread across Shimon's face.

"Do you want the mackerel spread with it?"

"No," Steve said. "Philly cream cheese will be fine."

Shimon's grin evaporated, but he was a good sport.

"Okay, but we're not licensed for serving beer."

Jimmy stared at Shimon. "The man…"

"Sorry," Shimon said. He held up his hands to stop Jimmy's impending rant. "We have a few cold ones in the back cooler. Of course you can have one."

Sura 24, Verse 57. Never think that the unbelievers will frustrate Allah's plan for the earth. The unbeliever's abode is fire, and it is an evil place.

Book Four—Chapter One

Steve Stephens—Khostarak

HE STUDIED THE barren, sun-baked landscape as the old Airbus jet made tight, stomach-churning spirals prior to landing at the Khostarak International airport. The city itself with tall buildings in the business center, was modern, or at least as modern as the ones he'd flown in to in Quito, Lima, La Paz, Recife and Phoenix, Arizona, for that matter. It was surrounded by wasteland—though pocked here and there with green circles of irrigated farmland and small, blobby clumps of cities, towns and villages all stitched together with straight black arterial highways and wiggly-gray vein-tendrils of gravel and dirt roads.

The only thing he carried on the plane was the briefcase. On the ground, he waited at a customer service counter for an Irakki police officer with an old Chinese bolt-action rifle around his neck to deliver his roller bag—sealed with holographic embassy security tape.

Steve was bleary-eyed and grumpy from the long trip through too many airports. He signed the policeman's paperwork without looking at it and handed it back.

"Can you recommend a good place for dinner?" Steve asked the cop.

"There's a brand new Burger King on Sephashant Street. The desert lizard kabobs are very good there, I hear," the man said.

Steve examined the man's face for mockery.

"Thanks," he said.

The Arfendika rental agency set him up with a spiffy, lime-green Kia Soul. Steve checked the boxes for all the insurance coverages they offered and added GPS, satellite radio and fuel top-off service—all charged to his DEA credit card.

He played with the GPS, programming his destination for the night: the Hilton Hotel. The cop wasn't lying about the Burger King. It wasn't far out off his route, so Steve stopped there for dinner. The cop *was* lying about the lizard kabobs, this Burger King offered kabobs, but the choices were lamb, goat or beef. Steve ordered a Limo Cheeseburger and fries and was pleased to see a refrigerated cooler filled with beer. He bought three beers and soon felt better about life.

In an alcohol-lubricated, beef-sated and jet-lagged haze, he checked into the Hilton and slept for twenty-two hours.

Harlan and Curtis—Khostarak

They moved into a safe-house in a gated community in a wealthy neighborhood in the Sanaa district of the city, a neighborhood shared by oil and mining company executives, NGO officials, bankers, lawyers and mid/upper level politicians. The house was comfortable and was always filled with noisy people coming and going, chattering on cell phones, typing on laptop computers, cooking and cleaning.

A large bedroom with windows that looked out into a courtyard with a burbling water fountain surrounded by miniature palm trees was converted into a meeting room. Curtis, sipping a cup of tea with Aalmah in the kitchen, was summoned to the room.

Inside, the old man, Harlan, Telleh, and several others were seated. One of the others was a young man with a wispy beard that Curtis had often seen around the house. Uhlmarr. There was one chair vacant, the one at the head of the table. The old man gestured. Curtis sat.

"This will seem odd," Harlan said. "I don't want you to freak out."

"Odder than me, Curtis Washington, wearing a bushy chin-beard and a turban and giving ancient-language sermons to tribal elders in mosques and meeting rooms while wearing silk robes and pointy golden shoes? Impossible."

Harlan—not completely convincingly—laughed and was joined by Telleh and Uhlmarr.

"I'm so pleased your sense of humor remains intact," Harlan said. "Before we get to the business of the day, are you comfortable? Hungry? Do you need more tea?"

All eyes at the table were on him. They seemed genuinely concerned for his comfort.

What are these crazy motherfuckers up to now?

Curtis felt a bite in his stomach. Nervous fear. The feeling grew.

"Whatever you're planning, forget it. I'm not doing it."

"You haven't heard the idea yet," Harlan said.

"I don't need to. I don't want to."

Curtis got up. Telleh put her hand on his arm—which was an incredible intimacy coming from her. He looked into her eyes and the battle was lost.

He sat back down.

"I'll listen, but I'm still not doing it, whatever *it* is."

"Maybe I shouldn't have been so melodramatic," Harlan said. "It's not such an odd idea. We're simply respecting history and tradition and working within the parameters of an ancient legend to build a movement that will unite this country, save lives and create a modern, Middle Eastern paradise for the benefit of the children."

"Stop jerking me off and just tell me. I'll say no one final time—then we can get on with our busy day."

"You're going to wield the golden scimitar of Damann and chop off Uhlmarr's left hand."

Uhlmarr nodded his head vigorously. "Yes," he said. "It will be my great honor, sir."

"I'm never speaking to you fools again," Curtis said. "Goodbye."

He got up.

Harlan spoke quickly. "It will be a clean cut and the hand will be sown back on right away with modern microsurgery. He won't play guitar again, but he'll get back most of the useful function of his hand, as much as eighty-percent, we're told, if things go well. And, you can see, he wants this thing to happen; it's important to the storyline and the myth and the mission."

"No," Curtis said. He walked to the door. "No," he repeated. He walked out and closed the door firmly.

Inside, Harlan spoke. "That went better than I expected," he said.

Curtis's room was up two flights of stairs and around a corner on the top floor overlooking the courtyard. He threw himself on his bed and tried to read William Gibson's final novel, but could not concentrate on the slippery words. He laid it aside. There was a gentle knock at the door. Without waiting for his invitation, she slipped in the room.

Telleh.

She sat on the edge of his bed, but did not speak. The silence, decorated only by vigorous fountain-babble from the courtyard, extended and stretched.

"I trust that Aalmah treats you, her master, with honor and respect and she pleases you when she washes your feet."

Curtis could not think of Aalmah—on her knees, washing his feet with warm, scented water from the decorative basin without a stirring in his loins.

Blessed be Allah.

"You are both beautiful glimmers from the eyes of God," he said.

"Each day," she said, "we are reminded that Allah's bounty is truly boundless."

Oh, Lord, here it comes. The irresistible bait hiding the inevitable cruel barbs of God's cosmic fishhook.

There was no escape for Curtis.

In truth, he did not want to escape. Whatever she offered, he wanted. All of it. If it meant his death or everyone's death, it didn't matter. His soul stretched to all corners of the universe. Anything. He would do anything.

"You represent the glory of the emissary—the living body of the prophet's harbinger. As such, there are earthly rewards in addition to the heavenly rewards...."

Whatever it is, you have me. I'm yours. I have no will to resist. Just say it and get it over with.

"As it happens, Aalmah has a friend in a similar situation, her husband was lost in the war. With your permission and approval, if it pleases you, then it would please me, and Aalmah, and Allah if you would allow pretty Jenertseh to join Aalmah in the ritual washing of your feet."

He had a sudden vision of a curved blade slashing through the air. Blood flying and filling the room with a crimson mist. Flash. He was in a field where a hot, brisk wind rippled waves of wheat baking in brutal sunlight. He could feel the strong muscles and the bulk of the black stallion between his legs.

"Yes," he said.

She stood. Her fingernails were painted a rosy, modest pearl-pink.

With heart-rending, spirit-stirring intimacy, she reached out with her index finger and lightly touched the first knuckle of his thumb for one second.

How much can a man be reinvented by others?

And, who was he, the skinny kid playing basketball in a Baltimore suburb or the sword-wielding, arm-chopping angry voice of Allah? Usually, people sell you themselves—peddling images as wholesome preachers, forthright politicians or other stereotypical, smooth-talking pitchman. How much more compelling and irresistible is it when others work hard to sell you a fresh, new, improved version of yourself?

How can a man resist?

It would take a stronger, better man than me.

"Thank you, dear, beloved Curtis," Telleh said. "I will go downstairs and give Uhlmarr the good news."

Sura 24, Verse 63. Do not hold Allah's calling you to be like your calling to one another; Allah knows those who slip away and hide. To those who go against his instructions—beware, a painful punishment will befall them.

Book Four—Chapter Two

Steve Stephens—Khostarak

WITH A FLIMSY disposable razor, Steve shaved. The limp froth he whipped up from the hotel's bar soap was stained pink with blood. At the best of times, his rough beard and the bumpy contours of his face were hard to shave.

Are these the best of times?

Suddenly, it hit him. He felt almost cheerful.

Shit, why not?

To the left of his naval, a dark contusion the size of a large man's fist was barely visible on his very-dark skin. It was sore, but felt much better.

They can knock me down, but they haven't knocked me out...

Yet.

His grin in the mirror was an ugly, fearsome thing. He was almost done shaving when the phone rang; it made him look away from his battered, disturbing, bloody image in the foggy mirror. There was a phone hanging by the toilet. He reached back, grabbed it up and held it up to a soapy ear.

"Stephens," he said.

"Sir, there is a Mr. Buhlibahn requesting a meeting with you in the coffee shop. Can I have the pleasure of telling him you will join him?"

Buhlibahn? Here?

"Yes," Steve said. "I'll be right down."

Taking his time, he finished shaving and then washed the soapy carnage from his face. On impulse, he decided to wear a suit; the whole thing, slacks, dress shirt, necktie, vest and jacket. Then he pulled his .45 from the diplomatic-sealed roller case, checked it to make sure there was no cartridge under the hammer, and slipped it in an unobtrusive side-holster that clipped on his belt.

There was only one man in the coffee shop who looked like a Mr. Buhlibahn—a round man with a round head reading a folded copy of *The Financial Times* and sipping from a tiny espresso cup.

Buhlibahn put aside his newspaper and openly appraised Steve while shaking his hand.

"On reflection, I'm certain my longtime friend Mr. McDonald did not mislead me, though, in the spirit of thoroughness, he might have mentioned your, uh, lack of youth. Perhaps this is an indelicate question, Mr. Stephens, but how old are you?"

"Seventy," Steve said. "No, sorry, seventy-one. I missed a birthday."

"Ah," said Buhlibahn, "then surely there is no time to waste."

Because I might fall over dead at any instant?

"Please forgive my discourteous haste while I quickly come to the point of my visit. I have two gifts for you, Mr. Stephens. One is the name of a club where a certain mad Russian assassin is known to frequent and the other is a location where, for another day or so, a large printing operation might be found."

He slid a manila envelope across the table, stood, and tipped back the last of his espresso.

"And with that, I shall bid you a good day. As you might imagine, I have several things I must do before I go back to Islamidahd."

What? I don't think so.

Steve held out a hand to restrain Mr. Buhlibahn; he squeezed Buhlibahn's arm as hard as he could.

"Many pardons, sir, but I insist on buying you another cup of coffee. Surely you have a few more minutes?"

Steve, perhaps due to his advanced age and failing senses, had not noticed the two large men in a sidewall booth. They started to get up, but Buhlibahn waved them away.

"On reflection, Mr. Stephens, I do have a few minutes and the coffee here is not completely revolting." He sat back down. "American persistence, perhaps that's the secret key to your mysterious leverage on world affairs. Questions, Mr. Stephens? You have questions?"

"I think I get the printing press thing," Steve said, "but tell me more about the Russian."

"The second time the Russian empire imploded, Maksim found himself unemployed, but with an expert skill others found, uh, cost-effective. In respect for your age and accumulated wisdom, I won't try to fool you, Mr. Stephens. There were times when I used the Russian to solve some problems and I always appreciated his giving me the opportunity to outbid the terms of a contract. I was surprised several times by the identities of certain of my desperate enemies, but the end result was a much stronger, more loyal business which I continue to enjoy today. For that, I owe Maksim a great debt of gratitude. However, our mad Russian, as I might redundantly mention, went quite mad. Now he tracks, toys with, and sometimes shoots people without rhyme or reason. So, unfortunately, that makes him an inconvenient wildcard, particularly when our larger scheme is in a delicate state of flux."

"Thanks, that helps a lot. Since we're communicating so effectively, what exactly do you want me to do with the mad Russian assassin?"

Buhlibahn studied Steve's face. "I am an advocate of letting an associate such as yourself, Mr. Stephens, handle the small details as he sees fit. If you can reason with the Russian and convince him to simply leave and cause us no more nuisance, that's a satisfactory outcome. If you feel more certain methods are necessary, then that's your call, I won't second-guess you. You'll see the terms of a suggested agreement in the envelope, but, there's a million new dollars for you if you can resolve the situation."

A million new dollars? That's a lot of cashola.

"What about Major Karne?"

"Ah, Major Karne," Buhlibahn said.

After a minute, Steve grew tired of waiting for a response. "What about her?" he repeated.

Buhlibahn sighed. "Did anyone tell you, Mr. Stephens, that she was the main planner and instigator of the famous nuclear missile and golden Quran episode in the Irakki desert?"

"No, no one mentioned that."

"It might be hard to believe, but I verified this information to my complete personal satisfaction. My first thought was this was an inept symbolic action that would backfire and create more problems with the militants across the Middle East."

"That was my thought too," Steve said.

"However, as time went on and world events played out, it seems the Major's fanatical scheme worked. In certain radical Islamic minds, the fact that Allah did not intervene to protect his holy word gave them a respect for the authority and power of the West and led to new avenues of peaceful cooperation. So, overall, is she a benefit or a detriment? Perhaps Allah knows, but I do not."

"What about my real reason for coming here, Mr.

Buhlibahn? At his mother's request, I am here to find Curtis Washington and ease her mind, to let her know that Curtis is okay."

"I'm not sure the man you call Curtis Washington still exists, Mr. Stephens. However, at the completion of the tasks described in this envelope," he said, tapping, "I will tell you where you can find Mr. Washington."

Harlan and Curtis—Khostarak

As the weeks marched on, the crowds grew larger and the scenes more wild and bizarre. Backstage, Curtis insisted, and no one argued; they poured him one small glass, then another of Arak—the milk of lions.

He felt like a boxer—his shoulders were massaged, aromatic oil was rubbed into his beard, and his clothes (including the gold, pointy-toed shoes) were arranged and adjusted and brushed and touched, over and over, touched, whether it seemed necessary or not.

He tried not to look at the golden scimitar and at Uhlmarr's happy, glowing face, but his eyes were drawn to them. The strong drink did not seem to help, but was worth a try.

Like a famous black president, they brought in teleprompters and Curtis practiced with them until he could read the words without seeming to be reading; he gained expertise and proficiency as time went on.

As the crowd noise reached a crescendo, the old man waved and Curtis, in his resplendent glory, took the stage. It was an inspired performance; he shouted and cajoled and screamed and whispered and cried. Then, at the end, Uhlmarr was led out. Under red-satin ribbons, flexcuffs had been wrapped and tightened around his wrist and forearm to stop the flow of blood. Taking careful aim, Curtis was supposed to raise the gold blade and cleanly chop off the young man's hand between the red ribbons.

Of course, as Curtis stalked the stage, he issued bellows and barks and accusations and implored the heavens for guidance. Then he raised the heavy, curved sword and did the deed. Blood sprayed. The crowd went completely berserk. In a daze, Curtis was led from the stage. Backstage, under bright lights, the surgeon worked on Uhlmarr's arm. The doctor lifted his head and gave Curtis a bloody thumbs-up.

He felt dizzy and sick; he gestured for another glass of Arak, but couldn't stand the smell of it. He held out the glass and someone took it from his hand. There was a small backstage greenroom. Curtis slipped in and locked the door. Almost immediately, people knocked, but he ignored them. There was a toilet. He emptied his stomach into it and then poured an ice-cold bottle of water on his head.

Someone worked at the lock on the door.

"Go away," Curtis shouted.

With a screwdriver, they worked the door open anyway. In stepped Aalmah leading another young woman by the hand.

A younger woman.

Jenertseh?

The new woman was slim with a bobbed-pixie hairstyle and wore western clothes—blue jeans, a form-fitting, white Pacifico beer t-shirt and tiny, white Keds sneakers. Aalmah moved a folding chair by the door and Jenertseh sat in it to prevent anyone else from coming in.

Aalmah tugged his hand and got him standing, then she pulled his robe over his head and removed all of his clothes, which Jenertseh carefully folded and stacked. Finally the gold shoes were neatly placed on the stack and Curtis was naked. Jenertseh openly studied his body—his muscles and the deposits of fat on his upper hips and his scars and his tattoos—her expression was unreadable.

Aalmah opened a canvas bag and handed items of clothing in sequence.

Black jockey shorts.

Black denim jeans.

Black t-shirt…with no logos or captions.

Black socks.

Black high-topped Converse tennis shoes.

A thick gold chain to hang around his neck.

A black stocking cap which she pulled around his ears. She gave him a final inspection—made him turn around—and nodded. There was no remaining sign, other than the chin beard—which was common enough in Irakkistan—of the heroic, wild-eyed Islamic orator. He was ready.

Jenertseh got off the chair and opened the door.

The people milling in the room pretended he was invisible.

Perhaps he *was* invisible.

They walked though the backstage entrance and jumped into a huge, black Chinese-made Hummer H20 and rolled into the night.

In the backseat, Curtis was still invisible. Neither Aalmah or Jenertseh looked at him or talked to him. He watched the city streets flow by outside the deeply-tinted windows. They stopped at an unmarked door. A young man partially hidden in shadows stepped out, opened the backdoor and helped the two women out. Then he extended a hand for Curtis, who followed.

They stepped into a nightclub, the air was filled with hookah smoke. There were fifty or so people, drinking and smoking and dancing to a Bose system pouring out rhythmic disco music. Aalmah gestured for him to climb a narrow, curved stairway. There was no railing and Curtis was afraid of falling, but he didn't.

At the top of the stairs was a small room filled with low couches, beanbag chairs and fifteen people sitting quietly as if waiting for him. Jenertseh led him to an armchair; a young man with wild, bushy hair got up and moved aside. She turned him around and pushed, Curtis fell back into the chair. The room lighted by a wall of at least a hundred candles eased into focus as his eyes adjusted to the light. For a long time, no one spoke.

Curtis did not know what to feel, but he liked the silence.

He craved it.

They didn't look at him.

He was still invisible.

He liked that too.

His mind grew weary of racing in tight little useless circles and slowly calmed. The bright image of spraying blood, as if neutralized by the flat, dull colors of this candlelit room, faded.

There was a voice and it took him a while to realize it was his own. It told a story, adapted from one the old man had told him, about a man on a camel, who rode across the desert with a team of doomed explorers seeking a mysterious woman of the sea[13].

Slowly, Curtis must have become more and more visible, because the young people in the room looked at him. Listened to him. Smiled at him.

Including Jenertseh, who watched him with an expression that hinted she knew something he did not—as if she held some delicious secret in her heart.

After his story was done, a few of the young people told their stories quietly and at unhurried paces.

When the last story was told, the kids patted Curtis's shoulder or leaned over to hug him and left the room one-by-one.

Finally, it was Aalmah, Jenertseh and Curtis—all alone.

"What time is it?" Curtis said.

Aalmah smiled.

"Who cares?" she said.

---

[13] See *Desert Dream* by Adina Pelle in *Ghost Words and other Echoes...*

Sura 25, Verse 1. Blessed is he who sent down the laws of right and wrong to his servants—he is to be a herald to nations.

Book Four—Chapter Three

Steve Stephens—Khostarak

AFTER A LEISURELY breakfast of Kellogg's corn flakes, condensed milk and honey-sweetened yoghurt, he carried the manila envelope to the elevator and then up to his room before opening it.

The contents were simple and undetailed—a picture of the mad Russian printed like a wanted poster with a one-million-new-dollar price tag.

Wanted Dead or Alive

Apparently, Mr. Buhlibahn had a dry sense of humor, or was an inexplicable fan of TV Westerns.

Steve studied the assassin's round face and decided there was something deranged in the man's slitty eyes. Something non-linear, something Steve had recently noticed in his own eyes staring back at him in the mirror. Or, it could simply be Steve's overheated imagination running wild.

The club where the mad Russian was rumored to hang out, sometimes, maybe, was called *The Oriental*—which Steve figured could mean anything from a Chinese take-out joint to a private men's club. It was in the Kardte Parwaan district of the city.

Would there be a men's club in the primarily Islamic city of Khostarak?

Islamic or not, if there are men, there will be a men's club somewhere—and women to service the men and vacuum new-dollars out of their wallets.

It had been a while, but Steve felt a twinge, an itch. He liked the Asian girls in Vietnam, but he was young back then and liked all girls of all nationalities, shapes and sizes. Would the Oriental Club have Oriental girls-for-hire?

Could he achieve any kind of erection or would an attempt just be an embarrassing waste of time and money?

What about the new drugs like Hardon, Wood or Coxparkle, could they be found over here?

It was nine o'clock in the morning. He sipped from a tiny bottle of Canadian Club from the room's minibar. He was thinking about hiring an Asian whore.

More proof, as if any was needed that he was truly losing his mind.

Curtis—Khostarak

They didn't go back to the safe house. Instead, they took a short ride in the Hummer and checked into the penthouse—Presidential—suite at the Safii Landmark Hotel. Curtis sat in the lobby watching the women negotiate with the desk clerk and observed a handful of new dollars get exchanged. They took his hands and led him to the elevator.

Upstairs in the room, there was no basin and no scented water, but the two women thoroughly washed his feet with washcloths soaked in hot water from the bathroom faucet.

That's all they did before undressing him—down to his black underpants—and putting him to bed all by himself.

Curtis was in a physical territory beyond exhaustion. The luxury of peaceful slumber was all he craved. He clutched a satin pillow and drifted into sleep.

In the morning, his feet were still clean, so they dispensed with that part of the service ritual.

But none of the others.

Sura 2, Verse 239. But if you are in danger, then say your prayers on foot or on horseback; and when you are secure, then remember Allah, for he has taught you all you did not know.

Book Four—Chapter Four

Steve Stephens—Khostarak

GETTING DRUNK AT *The Oriental Club* was not part of Steve's plan; it was just something that happened.

The taxi driver was unfamiliar with the place, but after a few wrong turns, they found it in a driveway circle in what looked like an abandoned, single-story, low-budget motel. The street was busy, but the reception driveway was unmarked—covered with trash and with huge speed bumps to discourage random motorists looking for a place to turn around.

There were a few cars in the parking lot, but, from the outside, the place looked closed—garbage-strewn and rundown. There was a sign, a faded arabesque of hand-painted lettering with a few musical notes for ornamentation.

The Oriental Club

Steve paid the driver and walked through the door.

Inside, the place was quiet, cool and dark. It was a bar, but an odd one. Behind the counter, surrounded by a few dusty bottles, sat a large, round man wearing a limp skull cap—sitting on a stool and reading a newspaper. He glanced at Steve, but apparently found him uninteresting compared to the cricket scores in the newspaper.

Steve brushed dust off a barstool and settled on it. He studied the collection of bottles. Most of it was the usual crap: vodka with Russian names and counterfeit high-end brands like Chivas Regal with sloppily applied labels with little regard for the square angle. Steve looked over the selection.

On a corner shelf behind a bottle of Russian Standard vodka, there was a green bottle of Glenlivet that looked unopened and possibly legitimate.

"Give me a shot of the Glenlivet straight up."

The man flicked his eyes at Steve, but pretended not to understand him. Then there was a careful folding ritual while the man prepared the next section of the newspaper for reading.

"Did you hear the joke about the old man with nearly no patience or sense of humor, who flew ten-thousand miles in thirty-six hours just so he could come to world-famous Oriental Club for a much-needed drink? It wasn't what I'd call a very funny story."

The man still ignored him. This irritated Steve, so he got up, walked around the bar, found a shot glass, blew out the dust and put the bottle and the glass on the bar. Then he returned to his seat, unscrewed the crinkly stamped-paper top of the Glenlivet and poured himself a drink.

It tasted good.

The bartender didn't lift a finger to stop him, so Steve took the bottle and his glass and found a spot in a corner booth where he could relax and soak in the scene. The booth was filthy with dust and dead bugs, so he walked back around the bar and found a washcloth. After wetting it from a faucet, he thoroughly cleaned the booth seat and table uncovering a rich, burgundy-leather seat and walnut tabletop gleaming with thick varnish, but scared by many year's worth of cigarette and cigar burns.

He tossed the soiled rag at the bartender—it hit the man's shoulder and dropped to the ground.

The man flicked his eyes at Steve and said, "Bah," but nothing else, before returning to his newspaper.

Steve poured himself another drink and it also tasted good, perhaps better than the first one. He didn't insult the whiskey by drinking it fast, but sat for a long time while the jet lag, his old age and the effect of the whiskey accumulated. Early in the evening, after sitting there all day, the front door opened and two men came in. They walked through the bar and disappeared through a door Steve had not noticed—a hardwood panel door that slid on quiet rollers.

The men were dressed in white slacks and wore loose linen shirts, they were foreigners to this land. Perhaps swarthy French? They didn't speak, so Steve did not know. Twenty minutes later, a man escorted in two middle-aged women. They were thick-waisted women dressed in clunky shoes, old-fashioned skirts and blazers with white pearls around their necks. They disappeared through the door.

As the evening wore on, a stream of people walked by—not large numbers, perhaps five or six per hour. Steve couldn't figure it out, these people did not seem like criminals and they weren't wealthy or poor, just mind-numbingly average.

Then Maksim, the mad Russian, walked in.

It was a stupid and inexplicable impulse, but Steve was far from home and surprised to see a familiar face.

"Maksim, my comrade, sit and have a drink with me," Steve said in a too-loud voice.

Perhaps this is an unfair cliché, but if you offer an older-generation Russian a drink, can they decline?

The Russian stopped and stared at Steve. He glanced at the bottle which was still nearly full. He turned his eyes to the fresh-scrubbed tabletop and Steve's nearly-empty shotglass. He turned to glare at the skull-capped man behind the bar who watched the scene with half an eye's worth of interest.

The Russian spoke in heavily-accented English.

"Give me a glass—a clean one," he ordered.

The bartender put aside his newspaper, slid off his stool and opened a cabinet. He handed a lovely cut-crystal glass to the Russian, who took it.

"One more," he grunted.

The bartended sighed and reached up for another glass, then returned to his paper.

The Russian dropped the diamond-faceted glasses on the table, then picked up Steve's now-empty shotglass and tossed it at the bartender. The bartender flinched, but let the glass hit his arm and fall on the floor. He made no move to pick it up. His eyes returned to his paper.

"Such is the way of the dog-man," the Russian muttered.

Steve splashed an ounce in the glasses and raised his.

"To the good times," he said.

"I don't know you, black man," the Russian said. He tossed the amber fluid back in his throat.

"Please sit and join me," Steve said. "I don't want to finish this bottle by myself."

The taciturn Russian grew more solemn and sad as he drank, but Steve enjoyed the absurdity of the situation. He laughed and told the Russian every joke he could think of, including exceedingly rude, filthy ones about farmer's daughters and randy livestock he vaguely remembered from his tour of military duty.

As evening evolved, the Russian wanted to sing and he did, teaching Steve the words to traditional, mother-country folk songs. Steve fumbled through them the best that he could, singing enthusiastically, though off-key and with a terrible accent.

They drank slowly and deliberately over several hours. At one point, Steve thought it would be funny to show Maksim the wanted poster. The Russian's face and the one-million-new-dollar reward. Dead or alive.

Maksim studied it carefully in the dim light and agreed, it was very funny. For the first time that evening, he laughed.

As the hour neared midnight, the bottle was still half full.

"When I was young," the Russian said, "I would finish a bottle like this by myself, then try to find another one. Now, look." He gestured at the bottle. "I embarrass myself."

He threw the bottle at the bartender, but missed. The bottle did not break and the bartender slipped off his stool to pick it up; he carefully placed it back on the shelf and arranged it so the label faced outward.

The two men leaned over their glasses and their moods grew maudlin and serious. The Russian's age-lined face filled with a deep sorrow and sadness.

"I don't know you, black man, but you might be my one and only friend in the world."

"Yes," Steve said. He tapped his glass against Maksim's and sipped his drink.

"So, I will tell you my problem."

"Yes, please," Steve said. "Tell me, my friend."

"I have the Algenheimer's disease."

"Alzheimer's? The memory disease?"

"Yes, that is the one. An early stage, but the progress is inevitable. I don't want this disease. It's not fair. It makes me angry. It's God's bad joke on me. After the life I've led and the glorious service I provided to the mother country, I want to die, how do you say it? With my shoes on."

"Boots," Steve said. "Die with your boots on."

"Thank you," the Russian said. "So, I shoot at people. Important people? Non-important people? I don't care. Sometimes I hit them and sometimes I don't—with the hope someone will shoot back and I will get the death with dignity I deserve. But, I can't make it easy, that's my habit. Even as my mind flees, no one can catch me. So, I am stuck."

"Stuck," Steve repeated. The word struck Steve as funny. He beat on the table with his fist. "Stuck."

"So, tonight, we will measure you as a friend. We will walk out the back door and there, in a dark, filthy alley, one of us will die. You will release me from this living hell, or I will kill you, and continue to be stuck."

Steve laughed. It took a few seconds for the Russian's thickly-accented words to sink in.

"Oh," he said.

The Russian stuck his finger in his mouth to wet it, and then worked off a heavy gold ring with blazing, blue amethyst. He pushed it across the table. "You can have this ring to prove you killed me and get one-million dollars. If I kill you, then I will take it back." He roared with laughter. "Now, *that* is a funny joke, okay?"

Steve stared into his drink. Suddenly, being *stuck* didn't seem so funny.

Shit.

Curtis—Khostarak

In the back of the black Hummer, they drove for a long time—hours—first on blacktop, then on endless miles of twisty, dusty gravel travelling deep into olive-drab foothills. The girls sat on either side of him, holding his hands and talking to each other as if he couldn't hear them.

He understood nearly nothing of their dialect—just a few scattered words here and there—so he might as well have been deaf. The truck pulled up to an elaborate gate which rotated open with the sound of whining servo motors. Inside was a circle of driveway with several parked cars; expensive, exotic cars—Bentleys, Maybachs and an massive gleaming-silver Jaguar XJ-16 SUV.

They got out of the car. Curtis looked out over the rolling hills and recognized rows of grapevines, raspberries and bulbous cabbage. Farther away, the rows were colorful: red and yellow.

"Poppies," Aalmah said.

Two men surrounded a large, deep-green tree. Curtis walked over to see what they were doing and saw a third man, high up in the branches, shaking the limbs to dislodge the green fruit. One just missed Curtis and rolled on the ground. He picked it up.

Avocado.

Aalmah took the fruit from him and handed it to the worker.

"We can get you a ripe one later," she said, "if that is your desire."

She led him on a cobbled walkway around the huge house where they could see a cavernous stable attached to a large corral of an acre or more. Three men brought out a huge horse. A monstrous black horse with an elaborate gold-and-silver-decorated leather saddle.

Brushed mane and tail.

Gleaming ebony hide.

Muscular and powerful.

Gold-cord bridle.

Silver bit.

Silver stirrups.

I told them a hundred times that I will not ride the damned black stallion. I don't like horses. I don't know anything about them and I have no interest in learning.

Dream up some other dramatic way of entering the historic city.

"I once lived in a house that was smaller than that horse," he said.

Aalmah chuckled politely at his little joke. Then, she and Jenertseh walked to the horse and beckoned for him to follow.

He hesitated. They smiled pretty smiles and gestured.

Come on.

A hundred times he said he wouldn't ride the black horse of tale and legend, but he did.

Sura 25, Verse 49. We give life to a dead land and slake the thirst of all we created—cattle and men in great numbers.

Book Four—Chapter Five

Steve Stephens—Khostarak

OVER SEVERAL HOURS, Steve sipped the remaining whisky in his glass on an empty stomach, and he was high— inebriated and addled. It surprised him how little the level in his glass changed while the word, like a rubber stamp, descended on his thoughts, over and over.

Stuck.

And so it seemed that he was.

Stuck.

"Have you been to The Oriental Club before?" the Russian said.

"Never."

"Ah," the Russian said. "Then you know nothing."

That's right. I know nothing.

Steve was unsure if he said these words out loud.

"Then," the Russian said, "we shall eat to fill our stomach with something more than whiskey, then I will take you on a tour."

He clapped his hands.

"Dog-man! Bring us hot food, and not dog-food. Now."

With sullen, slothy slowness, the bartender folded up his newspaper and left the room.

"The food here is good, but you have to beat the cook once or twice to get his attention and earn his respect. On your behalf, I have already done that and you shall now eat like the ancient King of Irakkistan—did you know he was a black man? The Turbanis hide this, but it's true, you can see the paintings in Athens and in Constantinople, he was as black as the night— as black as my heart. This could be my last night on earth, or yours, so I will not, I cannot, lie to you, my black brother from the United States. Now, let's eat."

The first course included shredded cabbage in yoghurt sauce with crunchy, rice-like grains and flecks of curry-pepper served with scorched flatbread and cubes of lemon-yellow honey-butter. A wine glass was placed on the table and often refilled with a golden-colored mead by the bartender.

Steve did not know he was hungry, but he was. After a few bites, the Russian pulled away the bowl.

"Don't fill up on this," he said, "there is much more coming. Save room."

The next course was rabbit stuffed with tiny, jellied eels. Its head was intact and seemed to stare at Steve with dead, glassy eyes. To be polite, Steve ate a little, but not much. The Russian, with eels crammed in his mouth, roared with laughter and chewed with gusto.

The next course was lamb baked in a huge earthen pot served with multi-colored long-grain rice. The brown sauce was rich and hot—flecked with flakes of red and yellow peppers.

The final course, dessert, was a baklava dripping with honey. The Russian inspected the dish with intense scrutiny.

"I told him exactly how to make this and I will cut off his ears if he fucked it up." He chopped off a large section with a huge knife and tried it cautiously. "It's perfect, or as perfect as it can be coming from anywhere on earth other than Minsk."

He cut and served a huge piece onto Steve's plate. Steve ate it all, then belched and surreptitiously loosened his belt.

"In China, the vigorous belch...."

"I know," Steve said.

The aperitif was a clear, oily liquor smelling vaguely of kerosene which they sipped while their dinner gurgled and settled in their stomachs.

"So," the Russian said, "we sit for a while, and think of the fine, perfect meal we shared, and then enjoy the pleasures of the back room. After that, we step out into the alley and see who walks away and who does not."

The Backroom of the Oriental Club

While they ate, the stream of people passing through was unabated and Steve's curiosity grew. The alcohol inflamed his imagination and he considered many scenarios.

It was a high-end whorehouse? With mates and partners for all tastes and appetites?

Or, perhaps, it was a masochist's playhouse with whips and chains and piercing instruments to fool with?

Was it something more innocent? An exotic massage parlor with tiny Asian women to walk on the customer's backs? A sauna?

Though they never really existed, a Roman-style vomitorium?

Steve's stomach was swollen and tight. He was uncomfortable; a vomitorium didn't seem like such a bizarre idea.

The people who went in never came back out, not this way anyway, so there were no clues from the exiting clients.

"Are you inflamed with curiosity? Shall we resolve this troubling mystery and ease your mind?"

"Okay," Steve said.

Working around his bulging belly, Steve wriggled out of the booth. They walked to the sliding door and stood for a moment.

The Russian looked back at the bartender. "Push the fucking button, Dog-man," he said.

Behind the door was a narrow hallway with another sliding door at its end. As they approached, it opened and they walked into a dark, smoke-filled opium den.

People lounged around on large pillows, sipping tea and toking from hookah nozzles. A white-clad attendant led them to a private corner and arranged two pillows for them. Steve looked around in wonder. The room was quiet and peaceful—any conversations were carried on with hushed voices.

"I've never taken any illegal drugs in my life," Steve said.

The Russian chuckled before speaking softly with his head leaned close to Steve's. "Then this is a night for many firsts, my friend. You will smoke or I will shoot you between the eyes, right here and right now."

The Russian spoke briefly to the attendant who flitted away. The Russian settled on his pillow.

"Make yourself comfortable," he said. He continued speaking after Steve was seated. "There are many flavors and varieties of effects, depending on whether you simply want the troubles of the day to fade away, to sleep peacefully, to stimulate your mind, or fill your body with energy to dance or party or have sex all night long."

"Did you decide to go easy on me?" Steve said. "I hope."

"No." The Russian laughed—his belly heaved and bounced. "I decided your mind is too tightly wound; too western and one-dimensional and you should share a sample of God's colorful imagination."

"Great," Steve said. "I can't wait."

The attendant brought a small, water-filled hookah and fresh, new ivory nozzles wrapped in waxed paper. He screwed the nozzles onto the short, coiled hoses. With a glowing coal, the attendant lighted the grainy paste in the fire-bowl and left.

"Don't try to fool me," the Russian said. "Take the smoke

deep into your lungs and hold it there, then go back for more until I say you're done. I am not joking with you, this thing will be as I say."

Steve smoked.

"I will tell you about the ring," the Russian said. "I was young and impulsive, just released from my military service. I needed a job. A man visited me and told me I could make a lot of money for five minutes of work. What was I to say? I could make a few new-rubles working in a missile manufacturing factory, but those jobs were not easy to get. I could be a waiter or a dishwasher or I could put a bullet in a man's head or gut him like a steer with a knife and make a year's salary, tax-free, in a few minutes. Perhaps I took the wrong road, I don't know.

"My first client was a Vukoil executive and he disagreed on how much taxes the company should pay. On a dark street as he got out of his limousine with his mistress and two bodyguards. I shot the guards in the head with a revolver and stabbed the Vukoil man in his belly with a bayonet I took from the dead hand of an Afghani soldier. I hacked that ring from the dead man's hand; as I understand it, it is worth a lot of money and I could have sold it many times, but I never did. I keep it as a reminder of that night so many years ago. I left the woman alive and I have seen her face in my dreams many times since. A friend waited nearby on a motorbike and in seconds, I was gone. Now you know things about me no one else knows, no one still alive, that is. How do you feel?"

Steve took a toke. His lungs burned and he coughed and felt like vomiting, but otherwise?

"I don't feel any different," Steve said. "Maybe this stuff will not work on me."

The Russian laughed. "Right," he said. "Now you can tell me something about yourself no one knows. It's only proper, since we end this night as the closest, most-intimate comrades. How do the American's say it? You are my very best friend?"

"When I was in Saigon, I could have killed Le Duan, the communist party leader. It would have been as easy as pulling the pin on a pineapple and lobbing it into his helicopter. I was in the diplomatic detail. Flash, bang, that's it. I would have been killed by the troops, but I should have done it—it would have saved the world a lot of pain and suffering."

"That's it? You are a truly boring friend and I am disappointed. Smoke."

Steve smoked. The attendant refreshed the bowl. Steve smoked again.

"Close your eyes," the Russian said.

Steve closed his eyes.

There is a door, painted yellow like gold. It glows. You walk ahead of me and we step into an alley. In the alley, there is a cat, a calico cat, sleeping on a black-plastic water barrel. The alley is narrow and the sky is dark. In front of a tattered and faded political poster with the dear leader's smiling, confident face lays a motorbike, rusty and sitting on flat tires which looks like it has been there forever. You take a few steps, then turn. I want to live, so I reach for my weapon, but I am not ready, I am too slow. You shoot me in the face and I die. Death is black and silent. A painful silence that presses on me. I can't breathe. I don't like death until I get used to it, then things fade away and I am okay.

"Was I speaking?" Steve said.

"No," the Russian replied. "Besides, that can't be a true vision of our future because the alley looks nothing at all like that."

Steve opened his eyes. Around the room, the red glow of hookahs being drawn on sparkled like fireflies. Streams of smoke, like living things, wafted and curled.

I don't see the problem.

What problem *do* you see?

There are no problems.

What *problem* do you see?

Everything is as it is—for the reason that it is. We have a narrow point of view. No narrow point of view is correct, nor can it be made to be correct. Only pictures taken with wide-angle lenses can capture a pinpoint.

"Do you mind, Steve?" the Russian said. "Can we go now?"

"Now would be the perfect time," Steve replied.

The Russian took out his wallet and laid out a few bills on his pillow. After consideration, he took all the bills from his wallet and laid them on the pillow. It made an impressive stack.

Steve's legs had fallen asleep. The Russian extended a hand and helped him up.

"Walk this way," he said. He walked and Steve followed.

The backdoor was yellow. It glowed.

Shit. The Russian is a goddamned liar.

Steve loosened the weapon in its side holster, then pulled it out and held it behind his back.

In the alley, the calico cat, resting on a black-plastic water barrel, raised her head and looked at Steve, then went back to sleep.

Tattered poster.

Motorbike.

The Russian took two steps and started to turn. Steve could see his face, it held a half-twist of a smile. Steve raised his .45 pistol and shot the Russian in the side of the head. The large man sprawled into the dust of the alley with the back of his jacket riding up and exposing the ugly, large-caliber revolver stuffed in his belt at the small of his back. On impulse, Steve grabbed the heavy revolver and dropped his .45 near the Russian's outstretched hand. He then kept walking, unhurried, all the way to the end of the alley. He turned right and walked to the main street, where he easily hailed a cab.

It was a mistake, he knew it, but the ring weighed heavily in his pocket—calling him to look at it.

He pulled it out and examined it in the stroboscopic lighting of overhead streetlights and passing headlights. He could not focus, because he didn't know how big his head was; it seemed to expand and contract like it was breathing in and out.

What was the right focal distance for his eyes?

And, what can you do when you can't trust your brain?

He supposed that was one of the messages the Russian tried to convey: the horror when the mind's machinery rebels or worse, simply fades away and recedes like the tide.

What can you do?

The ring was heavy and dense and there was an alternate universe inside the sapphire with cold, empty space and twisting and turning galaxies and suns forming and exploding. He placed the ring on his finger and it fit perfectly.

Of course it did—because the universe wanted things to fit together this way.

Steve leaned his head back. He didn't sleep, but he drifted.

He'd killed people before, but always in the course of his official duties—and never in such a premeditated, cold-blooded manner. Besides, he liked the Russian and respected his vitality and vigor and humor. He knew the Russian liked him too, but there was no doubt, had Steve not pulled the trigger, it would be Steve's body laying in the dirty alley as the cat watched his spirit sublimate into space.

Steve realized opium still ran rampant in his veins. His brain could not be trusted.

He hoped to return to his more-normal self in the morning.

Hotel. Lobby. Room. His stomach churned and he threw up a hot spew of whiskey and half-digested lamb in the toilet bowl. With a sour taste on his tongue, he fell into bed and the sleep he craved.

He had endless sad dreams about a half-twist smile on the face of a doomed man. So passed the night—his second in Khostarak.

Sura 25, Verse 52. Listen not to the unbelievers—take strength from the Qu'ran and strive against unbelievers with your utmost strength.

Book Four—Chapter Six

Steve Stephens—Khostarak

STEVE ENJOYED STRONG coffee for breakfast. He felt much better than he had any right to expect, though there was still a crisp, unnatural focus to his vision and things in his peripheral vision seemed to twitch and move as if they weren't quite sure where they should be.

Without expecting an answer, he texted McDonald and asked for Karne's flight information. It surprised him when the return ping came a half-hour later. As it turned out, Karne's plane was scheduled to arrive in an hour, though in Khostarak, that could mean three hours or three days late.

Over his coffee, he studied satellite photos of the building where the printing press was supposed to be. From Buhlibahn, he had an address and GPS coordinates and long-distance telephoto-lensed photographs which didn't prove anything, but Steve believed it. The printing press was there.

As he left the restaurant he passed two police officers. Like clones, they were nearly identical—small, wiry men wearing sunglasses and with dark shadows of beard on their cheeks.

They walked in and marched to the front desk, but Steve paid them no attention. He got in his car, programmed the destination into the GPS and pointed the car toward the airport.

Getting to the sun-baked parking lot meant navigating a twisted maze of concrete barriers—then parking a half-mile from the terminal. By the time he walked through the terminal's milling crowds, trinket vendors and machinegun toting soldiers, he was hot, sweaty and grumpy. He bought an icy glass of Ayran[14] and a London Times from a Java Time Oasis kiosk and walked around until he found a place to sit.

On a hard-plastic chair, he read about a fresh set of terrorist bombings in London and studied lurid pictures of double-decker buses on fire in Tavistock Square. Steve looked up from his newspaper and stared through a plate-glass window. Her plane was only an hour late, a minor miracle. He watched the stubby commercial jet corkscrew from the hazy sky and land, then waited for her by the customs kiosks.

From behind him, in a loose lockstep, the two policemen from the hotel approached with a third man dressed in civilian clothes.

Translator?

"Mr. Stephens?" the civilian said. "These two want to take you to headquarters for an interview."

"What?" Steve said. "No. Why?"

"They are investigating a murder of a Russian citizen. You were seen with the man at The Oriental Club. If you won't come voluntarily, you will be arrested for investigation of murder. Please come with us, sir."

"Hold on. I have diplomatic immunity." He sorted through his briefcase and found the paperwork provided by McDonald. The police officers took the stamped, hologrammed papers and walked a few steps away, then, in harsh-staccato voices, vigorously debated the matter with the translator.

---

[14] goat-yoghurt

Steve watched them argue when Major Karne walked up.

"Steve? Is that you? I'm so surprised, you could knock me over with the breeze from a chickadee's tail feather. Are you a more stubborn and resourceful man than I thought? What's going on?"

"The cops want to take me downtown to bust my balls over the murder of the Russian last night. But, I have diplomatic immunity. They'll go away in a few minutes, then we can talk."

"Immunity? Oh, from McDonald. I should have figured he'd poke his nose in when I saw you two talking at Curtis's funeral. Well, I'll show my State Department credentials and revoke your immunity. Then, when you're stuck in an Irakki prison for the rest of your life, maybe you'll be less of a pain in my untouchable ass, Steve."

"Hold on," Steve said. "Before you sell me down the stygian river, I have something for you."

She studied his face.

"What?"

"The location of the printing press."

Karne ran her fingers through her hair and unconsciously touched the wound on her forehead.

"I don't believe you, old man," she said, "any more than I really believe that you, *you* took out the Russian. There's no way. Let's see proof."

"I have a car," Steve said. "I'll be happy to show you once we're out of here."

Karne looked at the arguing men and a resigned smile slowly crawled across her face. "Okay, Steve," she said. "I'll play."

She walked to the arguing men and showed her badge and credentials. Apparently, it did not damage Steve's case, because the police officers seemed mollified, though they did not leave right away. The translator walked over.

"You are free to go, sir, but the officers would find it— *helpful*—to their investigation, if you'd show them whether or not you're carrying the Russian's weapon which would place you at the scene of the crime and implicate you in the man's murder."

Karne walked back. "You don't have to do anything for them," she said.

Steve thought about it. There was a sparkle in the corner of his eye which may or may not have really existed.

"I don't see the harm," he said. He pulled the heavy relic from the back of his belt and handed it over.

"That's quite an ugly blunderbuss," Karne commented.

Chattering rapidly with overheated voices, the officers studied it and noted the notches carved in the engraved walnut of the grip. They handed it back to the translator who handed it back to Steve. It was unnecessary to understand the language, they cursed bitterly and emphatically.

"They want me to wish you a good day and a safe visit in Khostarak, sir," the translator said.

The men turned to go.

"That's not exactly what they said," Karne commented.

"It doesn't matter," Steve said, "it's all good."

With her rollercase trailing behind her, they walked through merciless sunlight to Steve's car. "Do you want to check in at your hotel to freshen up before we eyeball the scene?" he said.

"Your information is probably bullshit, but, let's take a look now and get it over with."

He programmed the coordinates of the printing press location into the GPS and they were off.

They did a slow drive-by and noted the concertina wire on the top of a tall brick wall that surrounded the factory location.

"Looks secure enough," she said. "Let's find a tall place where we can peer in."

They drove through the neighborhood. On a corner of the old city wall, there was a stone lookout tower. For three American new-dollars and a handful of crumpled dinars discreetly passed palm-to-palm, they were allowed through a roped-off area decorated with KEEP OUT signs.

They climbed rough-stone steps and soon had a splendid view of the old city's mudbrick and rammed-earth buildings finished with clay and tile. They were a half-mile from the factory. Karne pulled an electronic telescope from a zipper pocket on her rollerbag. It looked like an old fashioned Admiral Farragut brass nautical telescope. She pulled on it to extend it to its full length.

She noted Steve looking at it. "Binoculars are a waste because my left eye doesn't work so good anymore," she said.

She held the scope to her eye and studied the factory.

"This looks promising," she said. "Again, I'm surprised. Good for you, Steve."

She pulled out a satellite phone and punched in some numbers.

"Shall we gather a team and go take a closer look?" Steve said.

"No. It's always better to ask forgiveness than permission." She handed him a laser pointer. "Paint the water tower in the center—try to hold it steady. Oh, you might put your sunglasses on too."

She issued terse orders into the phone, and then put on her very-dark glasses.

"Three minutes," she said. "Hold the damned beam steady, old man. Stop shaking."

Steve held the green mark on the water tower as steadily as he could. After a minute, there was a bright streak, a roar and steamy contrail from high in the western sky, then a brilliant white blast and a mushroom cloud that climbed in the air. The earth shook and a blast of hot air nearly knocked Steve down.

He peeked. The factory was now burning rubble. The mushroom cloud grew five-hundred feet in the air before the wind began tearing at it.

"Was that what I think it was?"

"It was if you were thinking 'miniaturized tactical nuke'. I always thought—what the hell good does it do if you have the damned things, but don't have the flippin' will to use them? Particularly the new ones, they're small, they're powerful and they drive the worst of the radiation deep into the ground. They are useful tools in our toolbox. Plus, the big bang impresses the hell out of the yokels. Now we can put a team in rad suits, sort through the ruins and see what we have. Molten pieces of a printing press? Everyone's happy except for a few vaporized expendables."

Steve stood with a shocked look on his face.

"Ah, I'm just funning with you, Steve," she said. "that wasn't a nuke, just an electromagnetic gigajoule coilgun round. Not even loaded with explosives, just God's beautiful gift of mass times velocity-squared and fifty pounds of neg-friction shaped-aluminum. People see the mushroom cloud, well, sometimes there's strategic value in letting people believe what they want to."

"The same thing was used on the golden Qu'ran, wasn't it?"

She studied his face.

"Ah, Steve, perhaps I've underestimated you."

She took off her dark glasses and held the telescope up to her eye. She spoke again after inspecting the carnage. "Did you see a devil face in the plume?"

Steve shook his head. He'd seen something just for an instant, but he still didn't trust his opiated mind, particularly when it held an image of the face of God in it bearing a half-twist of a smile.

There was no way he'd mention it to Karne.

"There will be a hundred witnesses," she said, "who swear they did and others who claim to see all sorts of things—the devil, angels, and maybe a football or pop star's smiling face, who knows? Would we doctor up an image or two for printing in the tabloids the unsophisticated people read? Why, yes, perhaps we would, thank you very much."

Steve rubbed his eyes. In spite of the protection of the dark glasses, there was a sunspot—a ghost-black artifact—etched on his retinas. He felt a sudden flash of insight. He no longer felt stuck. In fact, he felt the opposite, free. Liberated. Unleashed. Comfortable and at one with the central nonlinearity of the universe.

"Good job, Steve. You might not be such a bad guy after all. Shall we shake and call everything even?"

Steve studied her outstretched hand, and then—unable to resist the impulse—punched her hard in the belly.

She doubled over and gasped for breath. It took a minute before she was able to speak.

"*Now* we're even," he said.

"Fuck, Steve, was that necessary? I think you busted my ovaries." Holding her abdomen, she leaned back against the stone wall and took deep cleansing breaths. Her face was red, but she slowly regained her proper color and composure. "You hit hard for a broken-down old man."

"Leave me alone or I won't hold back next time," he said. "I'm here for one reason—to find my nephew and let his mother know he's okay. Goodbye. Take it easy, Major."

He turned toward the stairs. She called out to him.

"Steve. Hold on. Let's roll together on that mission." He turned to look at her. She leaned back against the daub and wattle wall. Her face was white beneath rosy makeup. "Like they say—two heads are better than one."

Steve thought about it.

"I guess," he said, "sometimes that's true."

Curtis—Khostarak

They were in the compound's meeting room. Curtis walked in and saw them, Harlan, the old man and the two women sitting around the table. Harlan was dressed all in white. Curtis turned and walked back out of the room.

"Get back here, pussy," Harlan called out after him.

Curtis stopped. He tilted back his head and yawned, and then turned and walked back into the room. He sat in the open chair between the women. They each took a hand and stroked his dark skin.

This is not good.

"Fuck me, what is it this time?" he said.

"Relax, Curtis," Harlan said. "I don't want you to freak out."

"Great," Curtis said. "I'm an expert at riding a big, black stallion. I wear the fancy golden genie slippers with curled-up toes. I wear the gold turban with the peacock feathers and I agree to ride into the city waving a gold scimitar. What additional humiliation can you possibly concoct?"

The two women smiled at him. His heart melted into slag.

"There's little piece of the legend we didn't tell you about. In the original dream of the prophet, a flaming arrow flies through the air and the emissary is killed. This prepares the way for the twelfth Imam and the new caliphate. But, the old man thinks we can spin this and you don't have to die. In fact, you can go away, blow this place with a big pile of cash and live a quiet life somewhere. France? Costa Rica? Back home in the states? Where ever you want, it's not a problem. Anywhere but here."

"Why is it I'm just now I'm hearing about this 'flaming arrow' that kills me?"

"We were still working it all out and we didn't want to trouble you with all the small details."

"Wait, how can I unite the tribes and save the country if their glorious new Moorish leader is dead."

Harlan scratched his head.

"There may be a bit of a misunderstanding. There's no way these people will unite under a black leader. You are the golden-tongued Shaitan[15] prince and in a beautiful bit of religious theater, you will be felled by the flaming arrow of the twelfth Imam."

Curtis looked into Harlan's eyes for a minute before speaking.

"You're a bastard. A fucking bastard."

He got up and walked to a cabinet where he picked up a blue-patterned vase and held it up. He stared at the elaborate pattern—snowberries and green leaves. It was old and probably worth a fortune. He held it out and prepared to release it onto the hardwood floor. Aalmah, after magically appearing at his side, gently removed it from his grasp and put it back. She tugged his hand and led him back to the table.

Curtis pointed his finger at Harlan.

"You lied to me," he said.

Harlan shook his head. "Never. I never have and I never will. Perhaps we let you believe a thing or two that was not completely true, but that's not lying."

"Yes it is," Curtis said.

"You have a part to play in ending this war and uniting these people. That part is 100% true."

"You're not my friend. I don't want to you speak to me ever again. I should smash your face."

Jenertseh got up and left the room.

"Forget it," Curtis continued, "I'm done. Whatever your plans are, I'm out. Fuck you."

With a satisfied smile on his face, the old man leaned back and groomed his long beard with his fingers.

"What's he grinning about," Curtis said.

Harlan shrugged. "You're still sitting with us. If you were serious about abandoning our plan, you would have got up and walked out."

"Shit," Curtis said.

---

[15] Satan

Jenertseh came back with a steaming basin and placed it at Curtis's feet. She kneeled. Aalmah joined her. They pulled off his sandals.

"Will these women come with me when I go?" Curtis said.

"They are free to if they wish."

Curtis lifted Aalmah's chin. "Do you love me?"

"Love is not a thing that is or isn't," she said. "The oak tree does not fall wholly-formed from heaven. It starts with a particle of Allah's love in the center of an acorn-seed and grows. I don't know if love will grow between us, but I will travel with you until we find out."

"And Jenertseh?"

"Her husband is dead. She's a widow—she's alone. She will come with us."

Curtis took a deep breath. "I want to make sure I'm absolutely clear on this. A flaming arrow shoots down from heaven—and I live. Unscathed. In one piece. Unharmed."

"There's commotion and hysteria and a big show—and you disappear, but yes, that's the plan. You live. In the end, you're well."

"Wait a minute, I know how this works. You have a volunteer don't you? A black guy who takes the arrow for me."

"Actually, we have eight volunteers to choose from, but we don't think it will be necessary. Eyewitnesses will see you rise into heaven on a silver flame. There's a bit of a show captured by Imax cameras. Fanfare. Spectacle. The Imam is revealed. Women swoon. The Gods smile on a united people. No one needs to die."

"If it's not me, then who is this unveiled messiah?"

Harlan shrugged. "It turns out that Buhlibahn's son-in-law is a handsome and charismatic young man."

"Buhlibahn? Why am I unsurprised."

"We're handling everything. All you have to do is go along for the ride. The henna party is tomorrow, I get married the next day and the world changes for the better the following day, and you retire to Cadaqués or Monaco or Flatbush with your women."

Curtis placed his hands on the tops of the two women's heads as they worked soap and hot water between his toes.

"Okay," he said. "You guys scare me to death, but I'll do this one final thing."

The women dried his feet and worked the golden slippers on him. They took his hand and guided him to his feet. Aalmah draped a gold cloth across his shoulders.

"Now what?" Curtis said.

"Now," Harlan said, "if you're done bitching, I would like you to bless my marriage."

Telleh entered the room wearing a long, white dress with a lacy white veil over her head. Harlan stood and picked up a golden bowl; he took off the satin cloth that covered it. An egg—brilliant white as if polished—lay in the bowl. Harlan picked it up and placed it in Telleh's outstretched palm. She lifted the veil and Harlan joined her underneath.

The old man handed Curtis a scroll and gestured for him to unroll it.

From under the veil, Harlan spoke. "I paid her father the mehar[16] already, almost ten-thousand new dollars worth of gold coins. We've already been to the judge's office to sign the contract—all that's done. All that's left is you reciting the poem."

Curtis looked over the calligraphy.

"Fine," Curtis said, "but mark my words, one day I will claim back my life if there's anything left of it. Here we go. *He sends blessings on you, as do his angels—that he might bring you from the depths of darkness into light. He is full of mercy for the believers. If Telleh is a believing woman and gives herself to Harlan with the true desire for marriage—and offers privileges for Harlan only, and not for any others, we enjoin*

---

[16] Dowry

wives and those whom our right hands possess—that they may be free from blame forever, for Allah is ever-forgiving and merciful." Curtis re-rolled the scroll and dropped it on the table. "Is that it?"

"Almost," Harlan said.

With a flourish, Aalmah pulled the cloth off their heads. "Now we do the wedding vows," she said.

Telleh looked at the floor as she spoke. "I, Telleh, offer myself in marriage in accordance with the instructions of the Holy Qu'ran and the Holy Prophet, peace and blessing be upon him. I pledge, in honesty and with sincerity, to be an obedient and faithful wife for you."

"I pledge," Harlan said, "in honesty and sincerity, to be your faithful and loyal husband."

"So?" Curtis said. "That's finally all? I can get drunk now?"

"No," Jenertseh said. "We already told you there's a henna party, then the official wedding ceremony the next day."

"This takes forever." Telleh stepped forward and pressed something into Curtis's mouth. "What now?"

"An almond for health," Telleh said. She pressed in another. "Happiness."

"I don't really care for almonds," Curtis said while chewing.

She pressed three more into his mouth. "And wealth, fertility and longevity."

Sura 25, verse 54. Allah created man from water, then established the relationships of lineage and marriage: for thy Lord has power over all things.

Book Four—Chapter Seven

Steve Stephens—Khostarak

STEVE WAITED IN the bar sipping a Red Star while Major Karne checked in. A bellman dressed in a linen suit dropped an envelope on the table and waited while Steve fished around his pockets for a few coins to offer as a tip. The envelope was sealed with blood-red wax imprinted with a rearing stallion. After breaking the seal, Steve studied the flowery silver calligraphy on thick, embossed paper.

"What is it?" Major Karne said.

"It looks like an invitation."

"For what? When?"

"I don't know what it's for, but it's for now. It says a limousine is waiting out front. We need to roll out of here."

"There's no time for a beer?"

"No."

She picked up Steve's bottle and drained it.

"Fine," she said.

The limo was an old Lincoln Continental which looked like a

monster compared to the tiny Vietnamese cars on the street. The driver held open the rear door.

"Ladies first," Karne said.

"Fuck you." Steve pulled her back by her arm and slipped in ahead of her. "You're not even invited."

"Try leaving me here—that's not happening."

"Then shut your yap and get in," Steve said.

The streets were packed with pedestrians, but most moved aside when the driver shouted and honked. The ones that did not listen were nudged aside by the heavy car. The ensuing hand and arm gestures were unfamiliar to Steve, but the messages were clear. Slowly the car made progress.

"I think we're going to the old presidential palace," Karne said.

"No shit," Steve replied.

They turned into a narrow alley; the walkers had to dash into doorways to avoid being crushed by the car. They stopped by a battered metal door covered with graffiti. The driver gestured.

Out, then up.

The car's door would not open much, but they were able to squeeze out. The metal door was locked, but Steve banged on it with the heels of his fists and it opened. Inside, the stairs were concrete and gray-painted metal. The man who opened the door pointed upwards, then showed them seven fingers.

"They count thumbs, so that means floor nine," Karne said.

"Shut up," Steve replied.

They trudged upward. The air in the stairway was hot and thick. At every floor after four, Steve had to stop and rest.

She waited for the first two rest stops, then climbed on.

"Meet you up there," she said over her shoulder.

"Bitch," Steve said while panting.

He bypassed floor nine. The next floor was the roof. Floor ten. Though exhausted, Steve grinned when he saw a table with one chair. She was not there.

They don't count the ground floor, Karne.

On the table, protected by a Pellegrino umbrella, rested a champagne glass and a vase with a yellow primrose. Steve leaned over the granite railing. The square was jam-packed with people.

What the hell is happening?

Steve pulled the chair closer to the rail and sat. The door behind him opened and a waiter carrying a silver chalice and bottle of Dom Perignon walked out. Major Karne peeked through the door.

"Oh, there you are," she said. "I need a chair too."

The waiter looked at Steve with the question in his eyes. Steve shrugged, then nodded. She leaned out over the railing and Steve stifled an impulse to push her over. After a few minutes the waiter returned with an additional chair and champagne glass.

"I've never seen such a crowd. What is Harlan thinking?"

Steve gestured to the waiter and the bottle. The waiter waved his hand.

Wait.

For what?

Loudspeakers blatted, but Steve could not understand what was said. The crowd roared. Karne pulled out her telescope.

"Shit," she said. "I think that's Curtis."

Curtis and Harlan—Khostarak

Jenertseh handed Curtis an ice-cold bottle of water. He guzzled it.

"Are you calm?" Harlan asked.

"What do you think? It's hotter than a pizza oven back here and I'm wrapped up in robes like a mummy. Let's get this fucking thing over with already."

"It will be over soon enough," Harlan said.

259

The black stallion looked very out of place in the marble entry. It wore blinders, but still snorted and waved its head around—expressing extreme dissatisfaction. As a further message, it produced an aromatic heap of manure, but the mess was quickly cleaned up. The mane and tail were brushed and rebrushed to perfection. The bridle and stirrups were brightly gleaming gold.

"Put on the slippers," Harlan said. "It's time."

Steve Stephens and Major Karne—Khostarak

It was hard to tell; the stallion was unhappy and would not stop moving, but Steve was sure the man wearing the black turban and black robes was his nephew, Curtis. The crowd roared and threw things—rotten fruit—on the main palace entrance while the horse marched back and forth. Curtis cursed the heavens and waved the curved blade of the giant gleaming sword.

Behind barricades, men in military uniforms screamed at the crowd and pushed the people back.

They want to kill him.

On the far left, a figure appeared. This man was dressed in a golden robe and turban. He wore a black mustache like the dear, departed leader; he strode back and forth and gave a fiery speech. The crowd surged and howled.

"I'm not sure Curtis is the hero of this passion play," Karne commented.

"Shut the hell up," Steve said.

The golden man held up his hand and giant golden bow was placed in it. An arrow was notched, drawn back, lit aflame and released. The arrow disappeared behind a ripply banner. From their high angle they could see beyond smoke that poured out, the golden bolt flew toward the earth while the stallion and Curtis toppled into a pool. The crowd could not see this, but Curtis and the horse were quickly hustled back into the building. While the golden man waved the bow and shouted at the mad crowd, the waiter opened the champagne and poured two glasses. Steve and the Major tapped their glasses in toast and drank. They were not allowed to finish—the waiter motioned for them to come.

"Hurry," he said.

Steve Stephens, Major Karne, Harlan and Curtis—Khostarak

The passageway was narrow, it twisted and turned. Soon, Steve had no idea which direction they were going. They emerged on a balcony over a glittering blue pool where a welcome breeze cooled them. Curtis was dressed in black jeans, sneakers and a t-shirt. He was sitting at a table drinking a tall beer from a frosty mug. The two beautiful women stood behind him.

"Uncle Steve," Curtis said.

"Curtis," Steve replied. He leaned over for a hug.

After Steve stepped aside and accepted a mug from one of the women, Karne held out a hand for a shake, but Curtis waved it away.

"I'm not going to pretend to be glad to see you," he said. He turned to Steve. "Did you enjoy the show?"

"I can safely say I've never seen anything like it," Steve said.

From the other side of the palace, the new prince still shouted—the crowd erupted in a deafening roar.

"Wait until you see the next part. If it's half what Harlan planned, well, you'll see."

A row of howling helicopters hovered three hundred yards out. They trailed cables which appeared to be connected to huge canvas tents.

Curtis continued. "Harlan will be along any minute. Ah, here comes the master of ceremonies now."

Harlan carried a heavy, ruggedized tablet computer. With his free hand he shook with Steve.

261

"It's a pleasure to meet you, sir."

Steve studied Harlan—he was tall and lanky with a big nose and a mouthful of crooked teeth.

Dogpatch hick, Steve thought uncharitably. *This guy is supposed to be smart?*

Two more men walked from a walkway covered by an ornate arch. One was tiny like a scrawny monkey and the other had olive skin and thick, nappy hair. Steve knew them. The bagel guys, Jimmy and Shimon.

Major Karne and Shimon exchanged a long, complicated look. They did not speak.

"Oh, good," Harlan said. "We're all here. Are you ready? This next part is spectacular."

Harlan put the terminal on the table and pressed a code into the touchpad. A red square—flashing—appeared on the display.

"When the helicopters take off we press the button. We can do it all together if you like."

Major Karne pushed past Harlan.

"Don't even think about pressing the button without me," she said.

Harlan stared at her coolly.

"You can press it all by yourself, if you like," he said. "Wait for the helicopters."

"I know what you're doing," Karne said. "All the drones are programmed with the new micro-warheads. How many? Thousands? Do you think you can win this war with one massive kill of the insurgents?"

She raised her index finger.

"You heard the man. Hold on and wait for the helicopters," Steve said.

"Fuck off, Stephens," she said. She gave Steve a willful, stubborn look then pressed her finger on the screen.

"Patience is not one of her strengths," Harlan said, "but that's okay, its close enough."

The helicopters growled and the lines grew taut. In an instant the canvas covers were lifted and a golden dome was uncovered; it gleamed in the late afternoon sun like a beacon. Steve, who expected something like this, was still impressed— it was as if God unveiled heaven. The crowd on the other side of the palace screamed in wonder and erupted into bellowed song.

From behind, uncountable streaks of smoke rained from the sky. Around them, the city erupted into bedlam. Fires flared and there were distant wails of despair and pain.

"You misunderstand me, Major," Harlan said. "I don't really give a shit about these obsolete Islamists, I just wanted to kill a bunch of them. Though, technically, *you're* the mass murderer, aren't you? We loaded the gun and pointed it, but you pulled the trigger."

Karne turned white and looked at her index finger.

"Shit," she said.

Harlan patted Steve on the shoulder. There's no room on the chopper, but don't worry. We'll send for you."

Steve watched as Harlan, Curtis, Jimmy, Shimon and the women sprinted toward a chopper that sat down fifty meters away on the tiled terrace. In an instant the helicopter lifted off and disappeared into the clear, blue sky.

Sura 18, Verse 26. To Allah are known the unseen things of the heavens and the earth; how clear is His sight and how clear is His hearing. None shall be a guardian beside Him—He does not delegate to anyone in dispensing Judgment.

Book Four—Epilogue

Steve Stephens—Sorrento

STEVE STUDIED THE itinerary. It still did not make sense. After a long flight from Washington, DC, there were short hops from Frankfurt, München and then to Napoli. He was supposed to take a taxi from the Napoli airport to the marina and then a hydrofoil boat across the harbor to Sorrento. The water was choppy and the boat rocked from side to side—he felt queasy. The view of the forbidding volcano in the background did not improve his mood.

Volcanoes are dangerous. Didn't we learn anything from Pompeii?

Around him, the tourists spoke many languages. French, Spanish, German and some guttural Slavic language he did not recognize.

Romanian?

Overhead, the clouds were low and he could see lightning pinning the mainland with vivid bolts. The close air was hot and humid. His clothes stuck to his skin as if glued.

The boat retracted the anchor and slewed around quickly.

The crew sailed like the taxi driver—there was no wasted time and the trip was over quickly. Once across the bay, the anchor was dropped and the boat whipped around and backed up to the dock. In a minute, the gangplank was lowered and tourists streamed off—hurrying around his roller bag. It was an unusual scene: most of the buildings were high above on top of a cliff— a cliff Steve hoped he would not have to climb. He looked at his printed instructions; he was supposed to wait by a brown door on the far left as he faced the mainland.

Good, no climbing at all.

He waved away menus offered by restaurant waiters on the dock and towed his bag past a gelati kiosk and a repair shop where motorbikes were strewn around in pieces. He found the brown door. It was securely locked.

Marina Piccola.

This can't be right. It looks like an abandoned ruin, not a hotel.

After waiting a few minutes, he shouted.

"Hey, I'm here."

He didn't see anyone, but the lock buzzed and he pushed through.

A cat slept on a small couch. Next to it, a dog slept too. They did not look up as he pulled his rumbling bag up the rough walkway. He passed three other napping cats. Before wide-open red doors was a table holding three bottles of white wine.

"Uncle." Steve looked up. Curtis grinned down on him like a black sun. "Leave your bag, grab the wine and come up."

At the top of the walkway, Steve walked down a short hallway and emerged on a wide balcony. To the side, a brazier was filled with red-hot coals. Curtis's mother, Natalie, wearing a long flowing dress, wrapped her arms around Steve and kissed his cheeks.

"You're here too," Steve said.

"Everyone is here," she replied.

Curtis shook his hand and patted him on the shoulder.

A small man wearing a floppy hat read *The Economist*. In the lounge chair next to him was a large woman with red frizzy hair. She wore a pink, one-piece bathing suit.

"That's Jimmy and his girlfriend. Duke." They nodded in greeting. "Shimon and Karne are in town shopping."

"Shimon and Karne are a couple?"

"On again, off again."

Duke spoke with a thick Australian accent. "Judging from the noises through the walls last night, they are very *on* for the moment."

"And these are my wives, Aalmah and Jenertseh. And Telleh, Harlan's wife."

"He only gets the one?"

Curtis shrugged. "Just the way it worked out," he said. "Look, here comes Harlan now."

Steve looked out into the small harbor. A brown-skinned man wearing only ragged cutoffs drove a small boat onto the gravel beach, then tied it off. He waved a net bag full of fish.

"He caught them?"

Curtis laughed. "No, he buys them from a boat coming in. If we had to live off what he catches, we'd starve."

Harlan jogged up the walkway and dropped the fish at Telleh's feet. She brandished a thin, very-sharp knife. Within seconds, the fish were gutted and smoking on the grill. She tossed the guts over the side of the balcony for the cats. Harlan grabbed Steve's shoulders and gave him air kisses on both sides.

"Bongiorno," Harlan said. "Welcome to our humble casa. Make yourself useful and open the wine. I'm sure you have questions. Have a seat and take a load off. Make yourself at home."

Steve took a glass of wine and stared at the harbor and across the Mediterranean. A storm moved quickly toward them with lightning bolts every ten or fifteen seconds.

"Things are still a mess in Irakkistan."

Harlan shrugged. "That's okay, it's not our war anymore."

"They almost killed the new Premier twice."

"Three times," Harlan said. "There's one you didn't hear about, one that almost got him. His bodyguard shot him three times in the chest, but Premier Buhlibahn was wearing a Kevlar vest under the robes and just got a couple of broken ribs. If the assassin had taken a head shot, it would have been all over. But, that's someone else's problem. We're retired."

"Back in Iraakistan? What was the deal with the drones? Almost ten thousand Talibani militants were killed."

Harlan grinned. "I handed out spray cans to the women's groups. They tagged the hajjis with UV-active paint and when the drone found an isolated target, the programming was automatic. Hajji turns to hamburger. Things got better for a while, but those people don't really want peace badly enough to fight for it. Islamic militants slipped through the city walls like rats and the women put their veils back on."

Curtis spoke. "Harlan tagged a waiter who cheated him on a bill."

"The waiter is safe, right? There's not much chance of a Predator Xn loaded with mini-Hellfires all the way out here."

"We might get a stray if things heat up in Libya again. Then what? The kill order can't be overridden."

Harlan shrugged. "Missile go boom, waiter cheats no more."

Steve looked around the rooftop patio and shook his head. "I don't believe in happy endings."

Telleh placed a plate of steaming fish in front of him, then topped off his glass of Pinot Bianco.

"No more talk," she said. "The sad winds of tomorrow will swirl around us soon enough. For now? Shut up and enjoy your dinner."

An hour later, Steve's eyes had drifted shut, but he was roused by a vigorous pinching of his cheek. He sat up and saw a woman's face through his blurry eyes.

"Karne," he said.

"Hello, Steve," she said. There was a wild look in her eyes—she'd been drinking grappa, a lot of it. She stood and gestured. "Look who followed you home."

He peered around her.

McDonald.

"You led the spooks to us," Harlan said.

Steve shook his head. He wasn't thinking clearly. He addressed McDonald. "You followed me?"

McDonald shrugged. "You were our only hope. These guys covered their tracks good."

"What are you doing here?" Harlan said. "We fucked things up good in Irakkistan. Leave us alone."

McDonald grinned. "You gave them a chance—that's all anyone can do unless we create a new epoch of colonialism. For a small group, what you did was amazing. The classified reports caught the attention of the new president—he likes bold gestures."

"Bold, but ultimately futile," Curtis said.

"Wait," Harlan said. "What did you say? A new epoch of colonialism? Is that what this is about?"

"Let's throw this motherfucker over the side," Jimmy said.

Duke nodded and patted his hand.

"Wait," Shimon said. "Where?"

McDonald smiled. "The suits in Foggy Bottom think Egypt is ripe and ready."

Steve spoke. "You have no right to ask anything more of these people."

"It's okay, Steve," Harlan said with a mad, crooked grin on his face. He stood and raised his glass. "We'll think this through tomorrow. Tonight we drink."

The wine flowed freely deep into the night.

Sura 55, Verse 42-43. Which of your Lord's favors do you deny? *This* is the hell the guilty believe.

www.ingramcontent.com/pod-product-compliance
Lightning Source LLC
Chambersburg PA
CBHW022151170626
46807CB00005B/2161

* 9 7 8 1 9 4 1 0 7 1 0 5 2 *